Frank Derrick's Holiday
of a Lifetime

Frank Derrick's Holiday of a Lifetime

J. B. Morrison

W F HOWES LTD

This large print edition published in 2016 by
W F Howes Ltd
Unit 5, St George's House, Rearsby Business Park,
Gaddesby Lane, Rearsby, Leicester LE7 4YH

1 3 5 7 9 10 8 6 4 2

First published in the United Kingdom in 2015
by Macmillan

ISBN 978 1 51002 376 5

Typeset by Palimpsest Book Production Limited,
Falkirk, Stirlingshire

Printforce

Printed and bound by
Nederland bv Alphen aan den Rijn,
The Netherlands

For Holly

PROLOGUE

An eighty-two-year-old man wearing a pair of Desert Storm camouflage cargo pants, with long white hair that ended halfway down the back of what was – even at an airport where all day flights arrived bringing passengers back from holidays in Hawaii and Acapulco – an incredibly loud shirt, was walking towards the check-in desks. He was carrying a large suitcase in one hand and an overnight bag in the other, both with a pattern like that of a stair carpet in a country hotel. Despite the abundance of pockets available in his trousers his passport and plane tickets were clenched between his teeth, like a dog with a newspaper.

Frank Derrick's suitcase was the only one in the airport that wasn't on wheels and he kept tripping over all the other wheelie cases, like a pedestrian who'd accidentally wandered onto the M1. In the queue for the check-in desk Frank caught his breath, got the feeling back in his arm and wiped the dribble from his passport.

'Good morning, sir.' The woman behind the check-in desk smiled. 'Los Angeles?'

1

'Yes,' Frank said. He gave her his passport and ticket and she entered some information into a computer.

'I'm going to visit my daughter,' Frank said, 'and my granddaughter, to help her with her reunion project.'

'That sounds like fun,' the woman said and she asked Frank to put his suitcase onto the conveyor belt by the side of the desk.

'Did you pack the bag yourself?'

Too exhausted from carrying the case to think of an entertaining and witty answer, Frank simply said, 'Yes.'

The woman strapped a paper label around the handle, the conveyor belt started moving and the suitcase disappeared through a set of rubber curtains like a coffin in a crematorium. For the moment at least Frank hoped that it would be mistakenly loaded onto a flight to New Zealand or blown up by the police in a controlled explosion.

It felt good to be free of the heavy baggage, and not just the suitcase but everything that he was leaving behind at home in Fullwind-on-Sea, including his actual home and the village itself. Frank said goodbye to the woman, picked up his hand luggage and started walking towards passport control, the departure lounge and America.

CHAPTER 1

HALLOWEEN

F rank's daughter, Beth, had once told him that she always dreaded receiving an unexpected phone call that began with, 'Is that the daughter of Francis Derrick speaking?', and although it was less likely to happen the other way around, there was a serious tone in Beth's voice that told Frank that it was going to be one of those phone calls.

'Now, Dad,' she said, 'I don't want you to worry,' which naturally made him immediately worried. 'It sounds more dramatic than it necessarily is. Maybe you want to sit down, though. Are you sitting down?' The longer Beth took to reach her point the more worried Frank became.

'I'm sitting,' Frank said. 'What is it?' He sat down.

Beth paused, preparing herself to say something that, clearly, she found difficult.

'There are two things I need to tell you. I wish I could give you the option of choosing which you want first, the good news or the bad news. But I'm afraid they're both fairly bad. Oh God,'

3

Beth took a deep breath, 'I've made myself too nervous to tell you either of them now.'

'Beth,' Frank said, trying to appear calm and in control and not sound as desperate as he was to find out what was troubling his only child so far away from him on the other side of the world, 'what is it?'

'Jimmy has left me and they've found a lump.'

It was such a lot of information delivered in such a short and almost poetic sentence that Frank wasn't sure that he'd heard what Beth had actually said correctly and yet he didn't want to ask her to repeat it. He was sitting down but he felt as though he was standing. He had the sensation that the room was moving and he thought that he might throw up. He needed to say something. He should at least ask what kind of lump and where it was. When Frank's wife Sheila was alive she always dealt with Beth's medical emergencies, the grazed knees and the calamine lotion, thermometers and plasters. Sheila knew where the dock leaves grew when Beth had fallen into a field of stinging nettles and how to remove a splinter without Beth even noticing. What would Sheila say now?

While Frank searched for the right words, Beth inundated him with technical details, symptoms, prognoses and Latin terminology. She talked about the wonders of modern medicine and some of the best doctors on the planet, about early diagnosis, expected full recovery and how different things were nowadays and thank God that she had medical insurance. Beth told Frank that a month or so after the lump from her breast was removed she'd have a few weeks of radiation therapy to eliminate any remaining cancer cells.

'Radiation therapy?' Frank said. It sounded so violent.

'It's just an X-ray, Dad,' Beth said. She continued to play down the severity of the disease, as though Frank was the one who needed comforting. She told him about increasing survival rates rather than decreasing death rates and least-invasive surgeries and how the tumour was smaller than a nickel.

'How big is a nickel?' Frank said.

'Around the same size as a ten-pence piece. I think.' The conversation took a bizarre but welcome turn as they tried to determine the comparative size of different British and American coins. 'They're operating on Monday,' Beth said.

Frank couldn't work out when that was. He had forgotten what day it was. He tried to factor in the time difference in his calculations.

'The day after tomorrow,' Beth said, picking up on Frank's loss of bearings. 'I've been scared to tell you.' She paused. 'Are you okay?'

'Me? You shouldn't be worrying about me,' Frank said. 'I mean, how are you? Are you okay?'

'Apart from the break-up of my marriage and the cancer?' Beth said and then she apologized for being flippant and blamed that on her daughter Laura. 'She's been keeping my spirits up by making tasteless jokes about it all. They do say that laughter is the best medicine.'

They're wrong, Frank wanted to say. It isn't the best medicine. A year and a half ago on his eighty-first birthday, he'd been run over by a milk float. It was travelling at five miles an hour and he'd ended up beneath it covered in milk and eggs. It should have been hilarious. But it didn't help with the pain. All the other things that Beth had just explained to him and that he had already forgotten or not understood because they were in Latin or American or medicinese: he hoped that those things were the best medicine. Medicine was the best medicine.

'How is Laura?' he said.

'She's fine, Dad. Actually, she genuinely has been great. With both things.'

'Both things?'

Frank had forgotten about Jimmy. They weren't equally bad pieces of news. Not to him at least. Neither was good but one of them was clearly far worse than the other.

Frank had always liked Jimmy. He was the first of his daughter's boyfriends that he had liked. Up until she'd met Jimmy, Beth appeared to be attempting to break some kind of bad boyfriend record. Frank had wondered whether she was doing it as an act of rebellion against something that he or Sheila had done. Had they been too strict with her? Was it their fault that in her teens Beth dated so many self-centered, boorish, rude, slovenly and thoughtless boys? She went out with petty thieves, racists and two drug pushers in the same way that other girls were attracted to blond boys or nerds. Jimmy was a whole different set of Seven Dwarfs by comparison. He was charming, helpful, humble and polite, conscientious, affable and kind. He was more faithful than Lassie. Jimmy had been a better father to Laura than her actual father, who hadn't stayed around long enough to witness Laura's first picture being taken in the hospital. Laura's father had left before the first ultrasound scan. Frank had agreed never to speak his name, but David might have been Beth's worst bad boyfriend. He was at least her last.

Five years after David's departure, Beth had brought Jimmy home to meet her parents and he'd seemed so perfect. It was impossible for Frank not to feel relieved. Jimmy brought flowers for Sheila and he gave Frank a bottle of what looked to him like very expensive wine (the bottle was dusty). Almost a year after Sheila had died, Jimmy asked to speak to Frank in private. He addressed him as 'sir' as though they were in a movie and he asked for Frank's permission to marry his daughter. Frank was overjoyed and he'd said yes of course and Beth and Laura, who had been eavesdropping in the hall, came rushing into the living room. Jimmy, who bought and sold wine for a living but rarely swallowed any of it himself, opened a different equally expensive-looking bottle and they raised a toast to the future Mr and Mrs Brooks.

Beth said that Frank wasn't losing a daughter but was instead gaining a son. The thought hadn't crossed Frank's mind until then but once it was there he couldn't get rid of it. Soon after the wedding, tired of the constant travelling back and forth to America to get his US passport and visa stamped, Jimmy moved permanently to Los Angeles, taking Beth and Laura with him and Frank lost his daughter all over again. Ten years later, it appeared as though he might lose her forever. And he'd lost his son too.

It was because Frank liked him so much that Beth had waited until two months after Jimmy had left to tell Frank how they'd been gradually drifting apart for the past year. Sometimes, if she didn't feel that there was any benefit to Frank knowing it, Beth would keep bad news from him. She hadn't told him when Jimmy's mother had died, for instance, or when Laura had been arrested for underage drinking. She wanted to protect him from things that wouldn't affect him directly and that he would otherwise never have any way of finding out. She had even battled with her conscience before telling Frank about the cancer. Could she go through surgery and a month of radiation without telling her father? Would she be able to carry that secret around with her, if not for the rest of her life, for the rest of his?

Beth had planned on eventually telling him about Jimmy but the more time that went by the harder it would have become. If she hadn't found the lump it was possible that she would never have told Frank about Jimmy leaving and Frank could have lived the rest of his life blissfully ignorant of the fact that charming, helpful, humble and polite, conscientious, affable and kind Jimmy, whom he liked so much, didn't live there any more. But two pieces of bad news delivered together seemed somehow to lessen the blow of them arriving individually.

'Does Jimmy know? About the . . .' Frank was afraid to say the word out loud. He'd been just as reticent in naming Sheila's Alzheimer's; even now he talked about how she wasn't herself and he referred to her forgetfulness, as though she just needed to go back into the room where she'd forgotten everything and she would instantly remember it all.

'No,' Beth said. 'He doesn't know.' Frank thought it was likely that she was never going to tell Jimmy.

'Where is he now?' Frank asked.

'He's staying at his brother's in Pasadena.'

'Is that far?'

'About an hour's drive.'

'Right.'

Frank was no wiser. Beth had often talked about the terrible traffic in Los Angeles. How far was an hour's drive? Five minutes' walk? He felt that he should be contributing something to the conversation, at least asking questions, but once again he felt lost.

'Is Laura okay?' he said, his default question.

'She's fine.' Beth's default answer.

On any other day, Frank would have been devastated at the news of Jimmy's departure from the family but for now he could only focus on his daughter. She told him to promise not to worry and she wouldn't hang up the phone until he did. Frank promised, however meaningless that promise was. Because he *would* worry. Beth told him that she loved him and they said goodbye. When she hung up, Frank listened to the phone line. There was a second or two of nothing and then the short loud boop of disconnection, followed by silence and the crackle of the static and dust in the wires of Frank's ancient phone that he'd had for so long that he didn't realize he was still renting it from British Telecom. The basic £30 plastic phone had so far cost him over £750. Almost a minute passed and then he put the phone down.

CHAPTER 2

THANKSGIVING

Halloween seemed to go on for days. Frank sat in the dark watching television with the sound down, ignoring his doorbell ringing from dawn till dusk with people trying to trick him out of his treats. It carried on right the way through November.

Dong-ding – 'Do you need a gardener?'

Dong-ding – 'Did you know you've got a few loose slates on your roof, mate?'

Dong-ding – 'Can I interest you in boiler cover?'

Dong-ding – 'Have you considered an emergency twenty-four-hour call-line neck pendant?'

Dong-ding – 'Are you happy with your mobile provider?'

Dong-ding – 'Have you thought about Jesus today?'

Frank Derrick's doorbell was the talk of Fullwind. The paperboys passed the news to the postmen, who sent a letter up to the roofers, who shouted it from the rooftops to the window cleaners below. Jehovah's Witnesses spread the word to the charity collectors, to the political canvassers and the gardeners touting for business who, in turn, told all the trick-or-treaters and knock-down-gingerers. It seemed like everybody wanted to have a go on Frank's doorbell.

It was, to be fair, an unusual doorbell. The two notes of Frank's doorbell were the same as those of the world's most recognizable and popular door-bell – the 'ding-dong' of sitcoms and Avon ladies – but when everyone pressed Frank's doorbell, the two notes ascended; they went up instead of down – 'dong-ding' – as though the bell was asking a question or as if it had an Australian accent.

When the doorbell rang one morning at the end of November, Frank decided to ignore it. It would only be more door-to-door spam. He wasn't expecting anyone. He doubted that all his neighbours would be waiting on the doorstep to sing him an early Christmas carol before presenting him with a huge hamper and an enormous card too big to fit through the letter box, signed by them and everyone else in Fullwind-on-Sea. And if it was carol singers, they'd be tone-deaf carol singers or local children who didn't know the words. The same lazy local children who dong-dinged Frank's doorbell at Halloween with the hoods of their sweatshirts pulled over their heads or stood outside the library on 5 November with a balloon in a pushchair.

The doorbell rang again.

'Perhaps it's for you, Bill,' Frank said. He looked

down at his cat and the cat looked back with the same impossible-to-read expression as always. It never changed, whether he was happy or sad, indifferent, hungry, thirsty, full, bored, excited, angry, scared of a dog, chasing a mouse, coughing up a fur-ball; the same blank expression of Botoxed irascibility that, today, seemed to be saying:

Whatever, Frank. Just answer the door and let me out. Going to the toilet indoors is so bloody uncivilized.

Frank sighed. 'Dong-ding merrily on high, Bill.' He walked across the living room, stepping over DVD cases that he was in the middle of putting into alphabetical order. Frank had a lot of DVDs and he'd made it as far as 'I' before he'd stalled for almost an hour to perfect his impression of Michael Caine in *The Italian Job*. With Frank's impressions it could sometimes be as star studded as the red carpet on Oscar night in the living room. Michael Caine, Humphrey Bogart, James Stewart, Sean Connery and Roger Moore could all be there. Most of the time, though, the carpet wasn't red; it was cream-coloured, more freshly so underneath the armchair and sideboard. And it was just Frank and his poker-winning-faced cat Bill – which hadn't seemed such a daft name for a cat when Ben was still alive – eating their individual dinners for one in front of the TV.

Frank stepped over the DVDs and walked into the hall and down the stairs, with Bill following behind, weaving between Frank's legs to undertake and overtake and almost trip him up.

13

At the bottom of the stairs Frank picked up the day's post. The junk mail was plentiful at this time of year and it all had a seasonal theme. Thermal underwear catalogues, warm cardigans and fleece pyjamas, Christmas stocking-filler gift ideas, bed-socks, anti-slip over-shoes and SAD lights. At some point in his life Frank had neglected to tick a box on an order form and now everybody had his address. There was another free pack of charity Christmas cards that he had no one to send to and a leaflet from the Government containing helpful but often contradictory tips for surviving the winter. 'Keep moving', 'stay in one room', 'wear a hat in bed', 'eat a hot meal', 'keep your spirits up', etc. He put the leaflet and the Christmas cards on the bottom stair and picked up an envelope. It had a US stamp and was addressed to Frank in Laura's handwriting. He opened the envelope and took out a greetings card. 'Happy Thanksgiving', the card said above a cartoon picture of a smiling turkey with surely little to be smiling about or giving thanks to at this time of year. The card was signed 'Beth and Laura', both names in Laura's handwriting.

When Beth had announced that she was moving to Los Angeles ten years ago, she had reassured Frank that it was only twelve hours away. She would be back to see him soon and often. She would telephone at least once a week, write regular letters and, when Frank had set up his computer account at the library, they could exchange emails and eventually they would even be able to talk face to face over the Internet via webcams. Beth had joked that Frank would probably see more of her than he had when she was living just fifty miles away and he would soon be sick of the sight of her. She'd said that it took longer to travel to Scotland or Cornwall than to Los Angeles and Frank had joined in by making his own joke about how it would probably be cheaper too, because he didn't want his daughter to feel guilty about going to live so far away.

Frank knew that the flight to England might only take twelve hours but there would be a two-hour journey through heavy LA traffic to the airport and another few hours for check-in and security, a couple more hours in customs, passport control and waiting by the baggage carousel at Heathrow, plus three or four hours in a taxi or on delayed, overcrowded and dirty trains and rail-replacement buses from Heathrow to Fullwind to take into account. By the time they arrived they'd be exhausted and jetlagged and it would be almost time to leave again. And Frank knew that the plane ticket wasn't really cheaper than a train to Scotland or Cornwall. He knew all of this but he didn't want to hold Beth back. He didn't want to be her anchor.

For her first six months in America Beth was a tourist. She sent Frank postcards and letters folded around photographs of her, Laura and Jimmy at Disneyland and Universal Studios, window shopping on Rodeo Drive or posing with their hands and feet in the cement prints of the stars outside the Chinese Theatre. She sent Frank a picture of them cycling along the beach at Santa Monica, with the sun glistening on the Pacific behind them, the water the same vivid blue as the sky so that it was difficult to be sure where one ended and the other began. Frank knew that the charity shop, the mini supermarket, the poorly stocked library and the brown tide bringing seaweed, carrier bags, nappies and tin cans onto the hard stones of rainy Fullwind-on-Sea would be almost impossible for Beth ever to think of as a holiday destination again.

Every year she sent Frank a new photograph of Laura, taken on or around her birthday and Frank put them all in a photo album that his wife Sheila had started when Laura was born. Frank had taken over the job when Sheila's illness meant that she couldn't remember how to perform the simple task and also because her not knowing who these strange people in the photographs were upset Frank. There were times though, right up until just before Sheila's death, when Frank would sit with her and they'd look at their photo albums together. Sheila would place her fingers on the unfamiliar faces behind the protective plastic and Frank would detect the tiniest spark of recognition. It was as though her fading memory was stronger in her fingers, in the same way that they were more susceptible to the cold on a winter's day.

In the album's first photograph of Laura she was only a day or two old. She was perched awkwardly on Frank's lap in the hospital with her tiny hand wrapped around his finger, and Frank had watched his granddaughter growing up in the birthday photographs. At first she was desperate to have her picture taken, excited and showing off in her ballerina dress or fairy princess costume or cuddling her latest favourite doll or soft toy. In her early teens she became more camera shy and reluctant to smile and then in her mid-teens she was determined not to smile at all, not wanting anyone to see the braces on her teeth and hiding her face with her fringe, or 'Laura's bangs', as Beth had written on the back of the picture taken on her fifteenth birthday. After her sixteenth birthday, the photographs had stopped. Frank presumed that Laura was now too cool, too self-conscious or too busy with boys to have her photograph taken by her mother any more. Or perhaps there was no-where left in Santa Monica that still printed photographs. Next year Laura would be twenty-one and Frank wondered whether the birthday photographs would resume again now that she was officially an adult and in charge of her own photographic destiny.

In the ten years that Beth had been away she'd visited England twice. The second time was five years ago when she, Laura and Jimmy had stayed not far from Frank, in a guesthouse that made Fawlty Towers seem welcoming. After a week and a half of drizzle, jigsaw puzzles and only three television channels, they went back to America. Beth said that the next time they would have to stay for longer to make the exhausting journey more worthwhile.

At the end of their stay in Fawlty Towers, Beth had repeated the same promises to Frank that she'd made when she'd first left for America. She said that she would be back soon and she would write and she would phone. Frank asked her to at least make sure that she rang him as soon as they were safely home, no matter what the time of day or night, as he would worry otherwise. He'd presume the plane had crashed or that they'd been mistakenly arrested for drug smuggling. Beth forgot to ring. Just as she had always forgotten to phone when she returned home after visiting Frank when she still lived in England. Frank would watch the phone, waiting for it to ring until eventually he wouldn't be able to wait any longer and he would call Beth, who would apologize for having not rung, saying she was exhausted from the fifty-mile drive back to Croydon. So Frank knew that it was unlikely that she would ring him after a five and a half thousand-mile journey home to LA and it would be he who would have to ring her.

When Frank had been run over by a milk float on his eighty-first birthday, he'd spent three days in hospital before returning home with a broken toe and his arm set in plaster at an angle like a boomerang. Frank knew that Beth felt awful for not flying back across the Atlantic to look after him so soon after her last visit but he didn't want to be her anchor again – or, in this case, her boomerang – and as a compromise Beth arranged and paid for a care worker to visit Frank once a week for three months to tidy his flat and do the washing-up and to scratch the itch inside his plaster cast and keep him amused until he was fit and well again. During that time Beth had phoned more frequently, perhaps out of guilt as much as concern, but by the time the plaster cast was off she was phoning less and less often and soon it would be Frank who would have to phone her.

When Beth had first moved to America, Frank had phoned Beth all the time, often getting the time difference wrong and waking everyone up or interrupting their dinner or breakfast or catching them all as they were just going out the door to work or school or a mall. Sometimes Beth's husband, Jimmy, would answer the phone and even though in person they got on so well, somehow over the phone neither man would really know what to say beyond things like 'How are you?' and either 'Is Beth there?' or 'I'll get Beth.' If Laura picked up the phone, when they first moved to America she would answer with an excited *'Helloo, Gaga'* – her name for Frank, from when she had been too young to pronounce 'Granddad' – followed by a breathless commentary of all the things that she'd been doing at school and the names of her new friends and so on. After she'd turned thirteen Laura was less verbose, her mind elsewhere, and then in her mid-teens she would simply say hello and then call out, 'Mom!' Frank would sometimes mistake her voice for Beth's, even though Laura was already more American-sounding than her mother and he listened to her growing up on the telephone in the same way that he'd watched her do in her birthday photographs.

Since Halloween, Laura had kept Frank updated on Beth's progress via email. She would assess her mother's mood, her sleep patterns, appetite, frame of mind, energy and outlook. She'd told Frank of the success of the lumpectomy and how Beth was coping with the prospect of weeks of radiation therapy. The emails hadn't stopped Frank worrying but they had helped him worry a little less.

In her emails Laura always referred to her mother's cancer as 'Lump'. Even after surgery when the lump had been removed, dissected, pathologized and incinerated as medical waste, Laura continued to refer to her mother's cancer by the nickname that she'd given it. She said that it was important to give your enemies a name and that somebody famous – 'Jesus or some other guy' – had said something clever about it. Later on she'd emailed Frank again to say that she'd got the quote wrong but it was from JFK: 'Forgive your enemies, but never forget their names.'

Frank put the Thanksgiving card back in the envelope, He was eighty-two years old. He had to scroll down to the very bottom of the drop-down menus on the auction websites that he'd registered on to find his year of birth. He was almost too old to be considered alive or at least to be using the Internet. Even the private health and insurance companies had stopped sending him special offers for free health checks or 'full body MOTs'. Medically he was a write-off. He was uninsurable. An accident waiting to happen, whether it was falling down the stairs or being run over by another milk float. The Grim Reaper had more than just a scythe. He had an armoury larger than North Korea's. Alzheimer's, Parkinson's, pneumonia or a stroke, so many natural causes; Frank was probably carrying something around with him already. Diabetes or heart failure, osteoporosis, or perhaps he'd die from something mundane such as the flu or a septic finger. Maybe he'd choke on a peanut because there was nobody there to stand behind him, wrap their arms around his waist and squeeze. Frank wasn't one of those people who, when nearer to the end of their lives, cheerfully accepted their fate. Frank wasn't unafraid of dying: it terrified him. He wasn't ready for it and he doubted that he ever would be. He wasn't prepared to meet his maker. He didn't even believe that one existed. But he would have dropped down dead right now if it meant that Beth would never be ill ever again.

Even though she had assured and reassured him that everything would be fine, and in spite of how well the surgery had gone and how rose-tinted she made the prognosis sound, ever since Halloween, his daughter's illness had never been far from Frank's mind. And when he managed to forget about it for a while, there it was in the plot line of every soap opera and in news stories on the television and in the papers. It haunted his dreams, both at night and during the day. In spite of everything he'd been told to the contrary and regardless of all the medical opinion and secondary medical opinion from doctors, surgeons and oncologists, he couldn't stop himself from thinking that his daughter was going to die before him.

He looked at the silhouetted figure through the frosted glass of the front door. He didn't hurry to open it. Whoever was on the other side of the glass would have seen him too and they wouldn't be going anywhere until they'd at least tried to sell him something: a stair lift or a burglar alarm, or until they'd had the opportunity to offer to landscape his garden, repoint his chimney or steal his pension. He unhooked the chain and opened the front door.

It was Frank's landlord. Frank had only met him twice. Once when he'd moved in twenty-four years ago and this was the second time. When the landlord spoke he mumbled. It was difficult to understand what he was saying. He sounded like he had too many teeth or had been stung on the tongue by a wasp. The landlord shook his hand and, in a voice that was similar to Frank's impression of Marlon Brando in *The Godfather*

– an impression that he'd dropped from his repertoire after almost choking to death on a small ball of cotton wool – he made Frank an offer he couldn't refuse.

CHAPTER 3

Frank lay in bed wondering what the time was. He looked over at the alarm clock and tried to bring its numbers into focus. He thought if he could tilt his head to just the right angle he would be able to see the numbers through his glasses on the bedside table next to it, but he couldn't. The first movement of the day to reach either his glasses or the clock was always the most difficult. It was worse than getting out of a deckchair opened out to the last notch. The first move of Frank's day was an activity that would be better suited to the afternoon when his joints were fully warmed up. He looked at the clock again. If he got out of bed too early, the day just seemed to go on forever. The last thing he wanted to do was to get up too early. Usually Frank would wait until he heard the first plane from Gatwick flying over above his flat. It would then be around 5 a.m. and he'd get up.

He rubbed his eyes and one more time tried to bring the alarm clock into focus. The cheque that his landlord had given him was on the bedside table next to the clock. Frank had put it there the night before in case he was burgled, even though he knew that to anyone without a bank account in the name of Frank Derrick the cheque was just as worthless as everything else in the flat.

On the doorstep yesterday morning, when Frank had first looked at the cheque – which the landlord hadn't let go of, as though he was Chris Tarrant on *Who Wants to Be a Millionaire?* – he'd looked at the pound sign, the number five and the five zeros that followed and he'd wondered how his vacating his dull two-bedroom flat could possibly be worth half a million pounds to anyone. He understood that house prices had rocketed and that he was living on one of the most sought-after roads in one of West Sussex's retirement hotspots. With the flat empty the landlord, who already owned the flat downstairs, would be able to knock the whole building down and build ten bungalows in its place, but half a million pounds?

It hadn't been the first time that Frank's landlord had suggested that he should move out. His rent arrears reminders often came attached to details of more affordable, smaller flats nearer the town centre that Frank might be interested in: something on the ground floor or with a lift and without a garden, as it was obvious to anyone who'd seen the long grass and the weeds that Frank had no interest in gardening.

When Frank's eyes had eventually focussed on the comma after the five and the full stop after the first three zeros, he saw that the cheque was for five thousand pounds and not five hundred thousand, hardly a life-changing amount. Unless the timing was right of course; if it came at the right time in your life, like now, *now* was the time that five thousand pounds could really change Frank's life. He was overdrawn at the bank, he had unpaid phone, gas and electricity bills: the next cold winter could finish him off. With five thousand pounds he could have paid off all his outstanding bills, he could have had the heating on in more than one room in the winter. He lay in bed looking up at the ceiling. It needed painting. So did the walls. He could have decorated the whole flat with five thousand pounds. He could have got the hot water boiler fixed or have bought a wider-screen television – he'd had to move his armchair closer to the screen to be able to read the subtitles of all the Scandinavian crime shows that he'd been watching lately. He could have had laser eye surgery with five thousand pounds and the TV could have stayed where it was. With five thousand pounds he could have built the home cinema in his garden shed that he'd always dreamed of. The next time a roofer or landscape gardener rang his novelty doorbell to offer their services Frank could have given them a heart attack by saying yes.

Of course, if he had accepted the five thousand pounds he was being offered to move out of the flat, then he would have had to move out of the flat. Catch twenty-two. There would be no point fixing the roof or landscaping the garden, no use turning up the heating or widening the television if he wasn't there to appreciate it. And besides, weren't all these repairs and renovations the landlord's responsibility anyway?

There was a distant rumble and as it grew louder and closer Frank started to get out of bed. Whether he took the sound of the aeroplane passing over his flat as a sign or simply felt that it was time to get up didn't really matter. He'd already decided what he was going to do long before it had even been cleared for take-off.

It was ten o'clock at night in Santa Monica when Frank took his address book out of the desk drawer to look up Beth's telephone number. It was the only number that he ever actually dialled. The majority of Frank's phone calls were incoming and cold. Calls that came from withheld numbers in warehouses on industrial estates. And yet still he could never remember Beth's number. He found it in the book and dialled.

'Hello.'

'Elizabeth,' Frank said.

'Hi, Dad.' She sounded tired and a bit irritable.

'I hope I didn't wake you.'

'Just snoozing.'

'Now,' Frank said. 'I'm not expecting you to pay. I should probably get that out of the way first. But I've been thinking . . .'

Frank rattled through a series of advance codicils

and preliminaries on the way to making his point, just as Beth had done when she'd called him at Halloween. But she'd been preparing Frank for bad news; her preamble was a warning of scenes that some viewers might find upsetting. Frank's preludes were a jovial 'fasten your seat belts, it's going to be a bumpy ride' warning before a funfair thrill.

'I can get a taxi from the airport and stay in a hotel, obviously,' he continued. 'I wouldn't get in the way and you could carry on as normal. Just for a couple of weeks and obviously not until after your treatment is finished. What do you think?'

Beth didn't answer for such a long time that Frank wondered if they'd been cut off.

'If you want me to, of course,' Frank said.

'Dad,' Beth said, 'I'm not really sure what it is you're talking about.'

'I was thinking that I could come over. To see you.'

'Right,' Beth said. Frank had hoped that she would have sounded more excited.

'I'm going to organize it all myself. You won't need to do anything.'

'Right,' Beth said. 'You're coming here?'

He could feel rainclouds gathering above his parade. He put up his umbrella and continued.

'I thought that I could be there for Laura's birthday.'

There was another really long pause before Beth answered.

'Wouldn't you prefer it if I looked into it for you first?' she said. 'The flight isn't cheap.' She sounded so weary and for once Frank selfishly hoped that it was because of Lump.

'I want to do it myself,' he said. 'Of course, I know you'll probably want to speak to Laura about it first.'

There was another long pause before Beth answered. It was like a satellite interview on the news.

'Laura will be thrilled, Dad. But do you even have a passport?'

'Yes.'

'A valid one?'

'I'll renew it.'

'Travelling all that way, though? On your own?'

'It will be an adventure. I'll be like Michael Palin.'

'Michael Palin always has a huge film crew with him,' Beth said. Frank detected the hint of a light, if somewhat resigned, humour in her argument. 'Aren't you afraid of flying?'

'I don't think so,' Frank said.

'The seats are very close together on planes now, you know; you're not young any more, Dad.'

'I know that. But I'm shorter than I once was.'

There was another long pause and then Beth asked the five-thousand-dollar question that Frank had been dreading.

'How are you going to pay for it?'

He had hoped that he could email her later about his surprise lottery win or the old bank account

that he'd thought he'd closed down years ago that
had built up thirty years' worth of interest. It was
so much easier to lie electronically. If he told Beth
the truth, she would only make him tear up the
landlord's cheque after pointing out the elephant
in the room – the homelessness elephant.

'Premium Bonds,' Frank said.

'What?'

'I won some money on the Premium Bonds. Not
a huge amount but just enough for a holiday.'

'Do they still have those?' Beth said.

'Yes, of course.'

'And you won?'

'Yes. I forgot that I still had them, to be honest.'

'How much did you win?'

'Five thousand pounds.'

'Really?'

'It isn't all that much.'

Unless the timing is right.

'I really didn't think they existed any more,' Beth
said.

'They do. It took me ages to find them after
the letter arrived. I had to turn the whole flat upside
down.' The more detail Frank added to the lie the
more he began to believe it himself; he just needed
to make sure that he stopped before he went too
far and introduced an alien invasion, a romance or
he broke into song. 'They'd fallen down the back
of the drawer in the kitchen,' he said. 'There was
a coffee stain on the envelope but the Premium
Bonds are all right. I cheered when I found them.

I frightened the life out of Bill.' Involve Bill, Frank thought. His star witness. All three wise monkeys in the form of the world's most inscrutable cat. Try cross-examining that, Perry Mason.

Beth was so used to Frank's get-rich-quick schemes that it was difficult for her to see this as anything different. He was always sending emails or leaving excited messages on Beth's answering machine about a horse running with the name 'Beth's Chance' or a jockey named Derek who was riding a sixty-six-to-one outsider called Lucky Francis.

Last year he'd bought a digital camera and every day for a month he'd taken pictures of charity shop bric-a-brac, ornamental wildlife, decorative plates and metal serving trays and eggcups that he insisted were silver rather than simply silver-coloured. He'd attached the photographs to emails and sent them to Beth, freezing her Internet connection for hours because the files were so large.

'Well,' Beth said. 'I suppose. I mean, I'm going to need to look at my planner.' She translated for him, 'My calendar.'

'Of course.'

'I can't just drop everything.'

'I wouldn't want you to.'

'It is a very long way, Dad.'

'It's only twelve hours,' Frank said, unknowingly using one of Beth's own arguments from ten years ago.

Before she could change her mind or ask him to fax the Premium Bonds letter to her, Frank talked her into getting her planner now and deciding on suitable dates. He knew that he would still need to show her proof that he was serious, either a copy of his plane tickets or him standing on her doorstep in Santa Monica, before she fully believed that he was really coming. He hoped that she wouldn't remember that he'd cashed his Premium Bonds in years ago to pay the rent that was long overdue on the flat that he was about to give away and also that he didn't drink coffee.

He said goodbye and opened his address book again and for the first time in a long time he dialled a different number to Beth's.

It was very early in the morning but the landlord answered, his mumbled voice seeming easier to understand over the phone, as though he was talking through a kidnapper's voice disguiser on its reverse setting.

Frank told him that he wanted to accept his offer. The landlord asked Frank to sign the letter of agreement that he'd given to him with the cheque and to post it in the stamped, addressed envelope that he'd provided. In the letter Frank agreed that he would vacate the flat within three months. The landlord said that he would transfer the money into Frank's bank account straight away and he told him to tear the cheque up. It was just for show. It was like a huge stunt cheque presented to a charity by a supermarket on a telethon. If

Hilary, the head of Fullwind's Neighbourhood Watch, had been at her window opposite Frank's flat yesterday, she might have taken a photograph of Frank and the landlord, each of them with a hand on the cheque. She could have given the photograph to the local newspaper to go under the headline 'Local Man Makes Huge Mistake'.

CHAPTER 4

Frank wrote a list:

Book flights.
Get passport form.
Passport photos.
Post form.
Buy suitcase.
Dollars.

He added a separate list of 'essentials' to the main list. On this sub-list he included any toiletries, sun creams, holiday clothes, sunglasses, maps and so on that he needed to buy. He put the items on the list in order of importance, and the most urgent items, or those that might take longer to get, like his passport, he underlined in red felt-tip pen. He wrote 'AMERICA' in capital letters at the top of the list and folded it in half. When he was on the free bus to the big Sainsbury's the next day, he realized that he'd left the list behind. He should have written 'Take list' on the list.

Invariably, Frank would be the only man on the bus to the big Sainsbury's. All the other passengers were female and over seventy and they would giggle and whoop with laughter and generally react to any man who got on the bus as though he were Colin Firth in a wet shirt. Today was no different. Frank made his way through the sea of sniggering bus women and sat down at the back where it was empty and he tried to make himself invisible. He stared out of the window and thought about America and how different it must be to Fullwind. He imagined neon signs and skyscrapers, long cars on long streets with no bends or turns for hundreds of miles. He thought about policemen with guns, swivelling their nightsticks, and of kids on street corners shooting basketball hoops and knocking the tops off fire hydrants. He thought about Beth and Laura sitting next to him in a yellow taxi, his daydream only slightly marred by the thought that it might be too cramped for the three of them in the back of the taxi and he would have to sit on the jump seat facing in the wrong direction, which always made him feel car sick. He looked out of the bus window at the passing West Sussex streets and imagined that the free bus was a yellow taxi and he was with his family as they made their way along Mulholland Drive and Melrose Avenue, streets that he wasn't entirely sure actually existed outside of the many films and television shows that he'd seen them in or in the lyrics of songs that he'd heard on the radio. He wasn't even sure that the taxis in Los Angeles were yellow or if they had jump seats.

When the bus reached the big Sainsbury's, Frank waited for all the mad women to get off, which seemed to take forever. He walked to the front of the bus, exchanged a *cor-blimey-women-eh?* eyebrow raise and nod with the driver and then got off.

At the cashpoint machines outside the big Sainsbury's he checked his bank balance. The £5,000 was already in his account and the bank had immediately reduced it to £4,963.67 in overdraft fees. He needed to move fast before the bank took it all. He walked into the supermarket and through to the in-store travel agents at the far end of the vast shopping space. Fifteen minutes later he'd booked his flights – thirteen days in Los Angeles. Not a week or two weeks or the more traditional ten days, but thirteen days in Los Angeles because the flights were slightly cheaper that way – and he was walking triumphantly to the photo booth at the front of the superstore. There was a man inside the booth cleaning the glass.

'Won't be a second, mate,' he said to Frank.

'There's no hurry,' Frank said, although he hoped the man wouldn't be too long. He was currently the only person waiting to have his picture taken and he didn't want to have to rush his passport photographs because there was a queue of people behind him tut-tutting and looking at their watches. If he posed for his pictures under any kind of pressure he'd end up with a passport photograph of somebody who looked like they were under some kind of pressure: such as a drug smuggler or a terrorist.

'Passport?' the man said.

'Yes.'

'Holiday?'

'America.'

'Nice,' the man said.

'I'm going to see my daughter.' He wanted to tell somebody, anybody, everybody. 'And my granddaughter.'

'Nice. All done,' the man said. 'You can see your face in that.' He picked up his cleaning equipment and held the tiny curtain open for Frank. 'Don't forget to say cheese.'

'Thank you,' Frank said. 'The last time I used a photo booth the pictures were sepia.'

He was exaggerating but photo booths had definitely changed in the past fifteen years or so. No wonder some people his age didn't renew their passports. Getting passport photos used to just involve sitting down, selecting grubby curtain or white wall, inserting your fifty pence and hoping for the best. These days it was like being in the cockpit of the Space Shuttle.

Frank sat on the round stool and looked at his reflection in the glass. He wondered whether he should have tied his long white hair behind his head in a ponytail. He brushed it away from his eyes and tucked it behind his ears. He needed to raise the stool. He stood up and spun the stool and sat back down. He needed to lower the stool. He stood up again and spun the stool in the opposite direction. He was too low now. He decided to hover above the stool slightly. Like he would have done if it was a public toilet. He took his glasses off. Now he couldn't read the instructions. He put them back on.

There were a number of buttons, onscreen options and various diagrams. Next to the screen there were four pictures of a woman's face, three of them with a red cross in the corner and the word 'WRONG' above them and one picture with a green tick and 'CORRECT' above it. Frank thought the woman looked miserable in the picture with the green tick. Cheer up, he thought, you're going on holiday. He knew that he was going to find it hard not to smile if he thought about why he was having his picture taken. He would have to try and think of something else when he posed for the photographs.

At the bottom of the photo booth's glass screen it said: 'Please ensure this glass is clean before taking your photograph.' As a man had just done that for him Frank put coins into the slot and posed. Trying not to smile but also not frown. Face forward, neutral expression, no smiling, no raised eyebrows, face and ears uncovered, no comedy moustaches. Frank tried to emulate 'Laura age fourteen', or 'Bill whenever'. The machine beeped, counting down – three, two, he wondered whether the man cleaning the machine had been joking about saying cheese, one.

'Cheese,' Frank said. The flash surprised him and resulted in a startled Charles Manson photograph. And he'd forgotten to remove his glasses. The machine asked him whether he wanted to accept or decline the picture. He declined. He had three chances.

He posed again. He sensed a change in the light somewhere in his peripheral vision to his left. He turned his head and saw a small child holding back the curtain and peeking inside. Underneath the four pictures of the woman it said, 'No other people in the photograph. No head covering unless worn for religious beliefs or medical reasons.' The small child was almost in shot and she was wearing a woollen hat, although it was unclear whether her reason for wearing it was religious or medical.

The child stared at Frank. This happened a lot. Usually on buses or in shopping queues. It made Frank uncomfortable and he always felt under pressure to entertain. The urge was often intensified when the staring children would point at him and say, 'Look, it's Father Christmas', or Gandalf or Dumbledore. More than once an entranced child had embarrassed its parent by asking, 'Why has the man got lady's hair?' Frank envied them their licence to say whatever they wanted to say.

'Hello,' Frank said. 'Are you looking for the Wizard of Oz?' The child stared. Frank smiled. 'I'm getting some photographs done for my passport. I'm going to visit my daughter and my granddaughter.'

A woman's voice called out, 'Samantha, come on.'

The girl let go of the curtain leaving Frank alone.

When Beth was a child, Frank would often go into Woolworth's with her to have their photos taken. Just for fun. They would smile and frown, have their hair in their eyes, cover their ears, stick their tongues out or pull their jumpers up over their heads. He imagined that people didn't do that any more. Because of the Internet and mobile phones. He didn't want to be one of those old people who believed that sort of thing. But he knew that it was probably true.

He rejected his first photo, almost shocked at how non-photogenic he was, and posed for another. His second photograph was better – not perfect by a long way, he still looked like an old man sitting on a telescopic stool in a supermarket – but he didn't want to risk taking a third and final photograph in case he ended up back as startled serial killer in a suicide vest again.

He selected 'accept' on the screen in front of him and the machine offered him the option of postcard versions of his face or a sheet of stickers, which he contemplated for a moment; he thought it would be good to cover Fullwind in Frank Derrick stickers, but he declined and selected 'passport photographs'. Seconds later his digital prints were waiting for him. He didn't have to stand by the booth while his pictures developed, struggling to get them out from behind the small metal bars before all the people queuing up to collect their own pictures saw his photographs and laughed at them. He didn't have to waft the soaking wet strip of photos all the way home until they were dry. His five identical photographs were printed and bone dry almost before he could open the tiny curtain.

Frank took the bus back to Fullwind. He went into the library and logged on to his email account to send his flight details to Beth. Now it was real. He was going to America. There were seventeen emails in his inbox. Fifteen of them were spam and the other two were from Laura. The subject title of the first one was 'Lump'.

Hey, Frank,
  Mom says you're coming over.
I can't wait to see you.
Mom's mood today 8/10.
I think that's because you're coming.
I'm looking at tourist attractions now.
    Peace out.
    L

The subject title of the second email was 'Reunion Project'. Frank opened it and read the three short enigmatic sentences.

I don't think Mom's sadder moods are all
  Lump's fault.
I've had an idea.
  More soon.
  L x

41

On the way out of the library Frank asked the librarian whether they had any books on Los Angeles.

'I'm going to America to see my daughter and granddaughter,' he said. 'That was my granddaughter just now.' The librarian looked around. There was nobody else in the library other than herself and Frank. 'On the computer,' Frank said. 'She sends me emails.'

The librarian looked on her computer for LA books. Five minutes later, Frank left the library with a book on San Francisco and crossed the road to the post office where he asked for a passport renewal form.

'Holiday?' the woman behind the counter said with her back to Frank as she looked for the form.

'I'm going to California,' Frank said.

'Lucky you,' the woman said.

'To visit my family.'

The woman in the post office would tell the postman, who would tell the paperboys, who would pass it on to the roofers and the window cleaners, the Jehovah's Witnesses, charity collectors and political canvassers, who would tell the librarian, who already knew, and the librarian would tell the gardeners, who would send the news along the grapevine to the trick-or-treaters and the knock-down-gingerers. Eventually Frank's backwards doorbell would ring and he'd answer the door to somebody telling him how Frank Derrick was going to America to see his daughter and granddaughter and he'd say, 'Yes, I know. Isn't it wonderful?'

CHAPTER 5

CHRISTMAS

There were no aeroplanes on Christmas morning. The skies were deserted. No birds sang a dawn chorus outside his window and there were no traffic sounds from Sea Lane below. No postmen or milkmen whistled. There were no paperboys. No hopeful roofers. Everyone was taking the day off. Even Bill, who was on top of Frank's trousers, which were draped over a chair next to the wardrobe at the end of the bed, was having his Christmas lie-in.

For Frank, Christmas Day was very much a busman's holiday. If it wasn't for the thicker television guide and the tree in his living room he could have mistaken it for just another ordinary day.

He climbed out of bed. His first step was like the first step of an astronaut back on earth after a three-month space mission in zero gravity, and he felt dizzy and fell sideways, only stopping himself from falling over completely by putting an outstretched hand on the wardrobe. The permanently ajar door temporarily closed and in the

43

kitchen the door of the oven opened. It was the flat's butterfly effect. He pulled open the curtains, the left one snagged and another plastic curtain hook fell from the rail and onto the floor.

'I must fix that,' he said to Bill, who wasn't listening. He picked up the curtain hook and put it on the window sill with the others. He wiped the window with his hand to see outside. It was raining. 'Bing Crosby is going to be disappointed again,' Frank said.

He took off his pyjamas. He was already shivering from the cold but if he didn't get dressed now he might end up staying in his bed clothes the whole day. He put on a shirt and, just to prove how like any other day it really was for him, he pulled on a plain blue V-neck jumper. There was no reindeer or Santa Claus in the knitting pattern, and if he'd pressed the jumper with his thumb, 'Jingle Bells' would not have played. He gently began to pull his trousers out from under the sleeping cat like a tablecloth on a laid table, but Bill woke up immediately and trotted off into the hall with what might or might not have been a grumpy look on his face. There was no way of knowing.

Frank picked up his glasses and looked at the clock: it was almost 6 a.m. He followed Bill to the kitchen, fed him and went downstairs to collect the newspaper, forgetting that today there wasn't one. He picked up a pizza menu with the words 'Turkey pizza!!' in green letters across the top and he opened the front door to let Bill out. He picked up an animal charity Advent calendar that had been on the bottom step since November and he went back upstairs.

Frank made a cup of tea and turned on the gas fire – it took twenty turns of the knob before there was a flame. A new record. When eventually it caught light, the flame almost took his face off. He sat down in the armchair in the living room and opened all of the windows on the Advent calendar. Behind each window there was a different sad-faced puppy, neglected cat or mistreated donkey. There were two flaps on today's window. The perforations on the right flap weren't cut properly and only one side opened. When he tore the sealed flap so that he could see the rest of the maltreated Labrador's face behind it, a Christmas card from the local church fell off the mantelpiece. The flat's butterfly effect again.

Frank picked up the fallen card and put it back on the mantelpiece between a brass elephant and a china giraffe. When Frank had bought the giraffe the woman in the charity shop had said, 'I was going to put this aside for you before you came in today. You must have quite a few giraffes now.'

Frank had never been happy with the idea that he might be that predictable. He'd once gone into the local pub and the barman had asked him if he wanted 'the usual' and as it was the only pub in the village, he felt that he had no choice other than to stop going to the pub. He hated the fact that he was thought of as a regular in the charity shop. Somebody that all the old ladies who worked there talked about and put giraffes aside for. Probably referring to him as 'Giraffe Man', in a similar way that Frank had given some of his neighbours Native American names to match their personalities or their activities – 'Trims His Lawn With Nail Scissors' and 'Washes His Car Too Much'. He was glad when the woman stopped working there. Although he hoped she hadn't died, as was often the case when there was a change in staff at the charity shop.

She was right, though. Frank's collection of ornamental animals – which were all priceless but not in the way that he believed – was substantial. He himself had joked to his cat that he had the fourth-largest mantelpiece zoo in the country. It was lucky that he had so few Christmas cards.

There was the Christmas card from the local church on the mantelpiece, advertising the previous night's midnight Mass, one from a local roofer called Dennis who was keen to begin his new year on Frank's roof as it was the only roof on Sea Lane that wasn't a bungalow and required the use of his ladder. There were two cards from Beth and Laura: the Thanksgiving card and a card with 'Happy Holidays' on the front in lettering the same as that of the famous Hollywood sign. Frank was pleased that Beth had been well enough to sign her own name this time. There were two other cards on the mantelpiece, one from either Stephen or Stephanie that came every year, with Frank never having worked out who either Stephen or Stephanie was, and there was a card from Christmas herself – Kelly.

Kelly Christmas was the name of the care worker who'd looked after Frank following his accident with the milk float. Once a week for three months Kelly had brought light into Frank's flat. It was like having an extra window or as though somebody had moved Fullwind closer to the sun. Kelly's home visits had given Frank a reason to put his teeth in in the morning. When her Christmas card had arrived he'd been reminded how much he missed not just her company, but company in general.

There was no stamp on the envelope and Frank had wondered whether Kelly had hand-delivered it herself. He wondered if she'd rung his doorbell at a time when he wasn't in or one of the many times that he'd chosen to ignore it. He thought that perhaps she had posted the card and snuck away and that he was just another name on her list of former clients, in the same way that he was on the lists of all the charities and catalogue companies who sent him packets of Christmas cards and Advent calendars every year.

He heard a car outside. He thought for a moment that it might have been Kelly Christmas. Badly parking her little blue company car, driving onto the grass verge that ran along the side of the road and knocking over the white concrete bollards as she'd so often managed to do.

He looked out of the living-room window at a white car that had just been parked on the other side of the road. A young family got out of the car and walked up the path of a bungalow opposite. Frank watched the front door of the bungalow open and an elderly couple welcomed the family inside with hugs and kisses.

Frank sat down and switched on the television. Double murder, street market suicide bomb, flood . . . the news wasn't taking the day off. He changed the channel and watched *Herbie Goes Bananas* while he waited for his Christmas phone call from his daughter.

Christmas Day was one of the three days in the year that Frank was guaranteed a phone call from Beth. She also rang him on his birthday and on Father's Day, even if sometimes that call was a week too late or early, depending on whether the UK and US Father's Days coincided or not. But Frank looked forward to his three annual phone calls from his daughter more than the holidays they arrived on.

At 2.30 p.m. Beth still hadn't rung. Bill was back in the living room with Frank and they were both eating turkey dinners. Bill's dinner looked disgusting but no less appetizing than Frank's, which had come frozen and complete with vegetables and gravy from a cardboard box. He ate it from a plate on his lap.

Battle of Britain was on television and during the scene where Christopher Plummer has an argument in a pub with Susannah York Frank fell asleep. When a telephone rang Frank didn't know if it was in the film or part of a dream. The shrill tone sounded more recent than 1940. His paper hat had fallen over his eyes and he thought he was dead. On the third or fourth ring he realized that it was his telephone and he wasn't dead. He rearranged the hat and stood up, sending the plate from his lap onto the carpet. He picked up the phone.

'Hello,' he said.

'Happy Christmas!' It was Beth.

Frank was confused. Even though there was a tree in the room he'd momentarily forgotten what day it was. 'What's the time?' he said.

'Here?' Beth said. 'Just after eight.'

'In the morning?'

'Yes. Is everything all right?'

'Just a moment.' Frank put the phone on the desk. He picked up his plate from the floor and took a sip from the glass of wine that he'd poured five hours ago and had hardly touched. The wine had first been opened three months ago and when he couldn't get the cork back into the bottle he'd covered the opening with Sellotape. It tasted sour and he pulled a face like a baby sucking a lemon.

'Sorry,' he said. 'I must have dozed off. Happy Christmas. After Eights? Do you have those there?'

'The chocolates? I think so. Yes. I always preferred Matchmakers. I've never seen those here. Anyway, Dad, enough about chocolate, Laura wants to speak to you first. Let me put her on.'

Frank took another sip of wine. It was slightly less tart on the second sip.

'Merry Christmas, Frank,' Laura said.

'Happy Christmas. I fell asleep. What are you up to today?'

'I'm helping Mom cook and then we might drive to the beach for a bit.'

'The beach? I presume that it's nice weather there, then?'

Laura didn't answer straight away, as though she was checking the window or Googling the weather forecast.

'It's pretty sunny,' she said eventually.

'Thank you for the card.'

'Thanks for yours,' Laura said.

'I'm sorry if it was a bit boring. The choice of greetings cards available here hasn't really changed since the nineteen fifties.'

'I liked it,' Laura said. 'Retro.'

'Retro,' Frank repeated. 'A bit like me.'

'You're super modern, Frank,' Laura said. 'Everybody says so.'

'Thank you.' Frank hoped that she wasn't being sarcastic; it was difficult to pick up subtle nuances in her speech pattern – which was more of a straight line than a pattern – and he wondered who 'everybody' might be. 'I hope Beth didn't wake you up just to talk to me,' Frank said. 'I expect you were out last night.'

'Just a few friends. Nothing major.'

'I remember when I had a few friends,' Frank said. He meant it as a joke but it was true – a few friends and then a couple of friends and then just one friend and finally no friends. 'How is your mum?' he said, unnecessarily lowering his voice in case Beth could hear him.

'Good.' Frank read from Laura's one-word answer that Beth was still in the room and Laura didn't want to talk about her but the short, positive adjective was enough to settle him in the same way that her emails could.

In Frank's inbox on the library computer he had more than twenty emails with the subject title 'Lump'. They were all short, often just a list of markings out of ten for Beth's physical state or the weight of her world in pounds that day or the height or depth of her spirits at the time of writing. Laura sent Frank an email update at least once a week and sometimes as many as three times. For a man who very rarely opened a book any more, Frank was spending a lot of time in the library. A week before Christmas Frank opened Laura's longest ever email. It had the subject title 'The Reunion Project'.

Hi, Frank,
Feliz navidad.
Don't laugh.

I was thinking about Mom and how she's been so miserable lately. I thought it was Lump and the radiation and the back and forth to the hospital, but guess what, Frank? I don't think Lump is completely to blame. I think the melancholy started pre-Lump. I think she misses Jimmy. I also think both Mom and Jimmy really want to be together again. They just don't know that yet.

I said not to laugh.

In the email Laura explained how she was going to attempt to manipulate her mother's emotions. She would play music in her room and leave her door open so that Beth could hear the song that she'd first danced to with Jimmy at their wedding. She'd put music on in the kitchen, too, and in the living room, songs by the bands and the singers that Beth and Jimmy had been to see in clubs and concert halls in their first years in America. Every film that Laura selected on the TV movie channel would be about rekindled love and old flames reigniting. The food that Laura would cook would be the same as the food that Jimmy used to cook. Every sight, sound and smell that Beth experienced would be controlled by her daughter. When Laura had said on the phone just now that she was helping Beth cook, Frank wondered if it would be another forgery of one of Jimmy's signature dishes.

Frank was distracted by a car's headlights flashing on and off outside his living-room window. He watched a middle-aged couple and their dog, all three of them wearing tinsel scarves, walk through a front gate a few buildings along the road.

Laura seemed to sense his distraction.

'Shall I hand you back to Mom?' she said.

'Thank you,' Frank said. 'Have a nice day.' He realized how unintentionally American he sounded. He was going to fit right in over there.

He listened to the activity thousands of miles away at the other end of the line. There was music playing and he wondered if Laura had chosen it. He heard her say something to Beth that he couldn't make out but it made Beth laugh. She was still laughing when she picked up the phone. Frank was pleased that she seemed to be having the happy Christmas that he more than ever before wished for her.

'Father,' she said in a mock-posh English voice and then in comic American, 'Whassup?'

'I don't think I'll ever get used to my grand-daughter calling me Frank.'

'It is your name,' Beth said.

'She says that you're going to the beach. On Christmas Day?'

'We always go to the beach at Christmas,' Beth said. 'I'm sure I have to tell you every year.'

'I hope you're taking things easy,' Frank said.

'I'm fine, Dad. A little tired. They gave me the day off.' Frank guessed that 'they' were the hospital and the day off would have been from radiation therapy, but he never pressed Beth for any medical information unless she herself offered it. If he needed to know anything he could send an email to Laura. 'How about you?' Beth said. 'What do you have planned for today?'

'Planned?' Frank said. 'Watching television. Eating some cold turkey. Falling asleep in an armchair.'

'A traditional English Christmas. Is it snowing there?'

'Only on the television.'

'What's on?'

'At the moment it's an advertisement for settees. Hang on.' He picked up the *Radio Times* and read out the programmes and the films that he'd marked with a red pen in the magazine and they talked about old TV shows and the things Beth missed most from England, and Frank wanted to tell her that the things that he missed were all in America but he knew that such schmaltz would upset her.

They talked for another ten minutes and then they said goodbye, wishing each other a happy Christmas again and a happy new year in case they didn't speak before then. After the phone call Frank twisted a few of the bulbs of his Christmas tree fairy lights until the lights all came on again and he closed the living-room curtains even though it wasn't yet dark. There were a lot of unfamiliar cars parked along the road now. Somebody had put a red Father Christmas hat on one of the white stone bollards on the grass verge. When a car drove by Frank thought that he could hear the bell at the end of the hat ringing.

He sat down in his armchair and changed TV channels and watched the end of *It's a Wonderful Life*. He thought about going to America at the beginning of February and he didn't know if he could possibly wait that long. Sometimes the thought of going to see his family made him want to run through the centre of the village shouting at the top of his voice, like Jimmy Stewart was doing on the television now – *Merry Christmas, library! Merry Christmas, charity shop! Merry Christmas, you wonderful old Fullwind Food & Wine!*

After a turkey sandwich Frank watched *The Two Ronnies*. The same episode that he'd first watched forty Christmases ago with Sheila when they were both younger than Beth was now and the same show that he'd later watched with Beth there too. And, when Laura was born, they would have watched the TV show again. If it wasn't on television, Frank would put his video copy on. After the turkey and the Queen. Frank and Sheila and Beth and Laura, who didn't understand why it was funny but she laughed because the rest of her family were laughing and the sight of her grandfather laughing was a thing that she found particularly amusing.

Not long after Frank had first met Jimmy, he'd

come down to Fullwind for Christmas with Beth and Laura. Jimmy had brought a turkey too large for the oven and had cooked the best Christmas dinner that Frank had ever eaten. He brought his own homemade cranberry sauce with him and he mashed potatoes and roasted vegetables. For dessert Jimmy made a plum pudding which he set alight and ceremoniously carried into the living room. After dinner they'd all watched *The Two Ronnies*.

The following year Sheila's Alzheimer's was noticeably advanced and Beth was worried that Laura would find her grandmother's confusion, unpredictability and outbursts of anger too upsetting, and so they didn't drive down to the flat and Frank watched *The Two Ronnies* on his own with Sheila once more. He hoped that the familiarity of the jokes and the sketches would be powerful enough to coax Sheila's lost sense of humour out of hiding but they'd both watched the show in silence, Frank not laughing either as a show of solidarity to his wife.

Twenty million other people had watched *The Two Ronnies* with Frank and Sheila when it was first broadcast in the late 1970s. He doubted the audience was anywhere near that figure now. Perhaps the families that he'd seen arriving in their cars on Sea Lane earlier would all be sitting down together in front of the television to watch it. Or maybe it was just him and his poker-faced cat, who hadn't even noticed the programme was on until he'd been woken by the sound of Frank's laughter and had looked over at the television and then up at the old man in the green paper crown laughing hysterically in the armchair next to him:

Yes Frank, I get it, very clever, four candles.

CHAPTER 6

In the twilight days between Christmas and New Year, a period of time that Beth called the holiday taint, Frank started packing. First, he bought a new suitcase from the charity shop. The case was the largest part of a three-piece matching luggage set – large suitcase, a smaller suitcase and an overnight bag – all covered in fabric that had a pattern like the stair carpet of a country hotel. Frank only really wanted the large suitcase but he told the woman who served him in the charity shop that he didn't like to break up a family.

'What's that, love?' the woman said. She had a lazy eye, maybe two – Frank wasn't sure, as he found it as difficult to look at her as she did to look at him. When she spoke to Frank she appeared to be looking down and to her left, like one of the broken dolls in the 'everything 20p' basket at the back of the shop.

'I'll take all three cases, thank you,' Frank said, and then, referring to the blank address label attached to the suitcase, he said, 'A suitcase that has never been on holiday. It's like the toys in *Toy Story*.'

'Toys?' the woman said.

'Toys really want to be played with. Perhaps it's the same for suitcases.'

The woman didn't answer. Frank gestured towards the shop's DVD shelf where both his copies of *Toy Story* had originally come from. The woman looked in the shelf's general direction.

'It was on one of the DVD extras,' Frank said. 'It might have been on the director's commentary. Suitcases *want* to go on holiday. It didn't actually say that. It was about toys, but maybe it's the same sort of thing for suitcases.'

Frank realized that the woman didn't know what he was talking about. She probably didn't even know what a DVD extra was, or that there was anything other than the actual film itself on a DVD. Or she knew that it was in there somewhere but she couldn't navigate her way through the DVD menu.

Frank presumed that he would one day live up to this stereotype. He was eighty-two. He was probably ten years older than the woman behind the counter. He was bound to start forgetting things soon, or at least stop learning anything new. But, so far, technology wasn't his nemesis. He could operate all the remote controls in his flat, the buttons were normal-sized and when the batteries ran out he could replace them the right way up. He had an email account at the library and often used the Internet there. Typing the pin number into a debit card machine didn't terrify him so much that he couldn't remember what the number was. He still paid all his bills by cheque but that was more to do with his financial ineptitude and lack of thrift, which was a gift that he'd had since he was old enough to be given pocket money. But he could easily find his way through a DVD menu or around the worldwide web like a teenager. Sometimes Frank felt like he was a method actor preparing for his role as an eighty-two-year-old man. A much younger man dressed in an old-man suit and prosthetic make-up so he could walk around town to see how differently people reacted to him. Like Dustin Hoffman in a dress and wig researching for the part of *Tootsie*.

He paid the woman with the 20p eyes and she put the luggage together, fitting the overnight bag into the smaller case and the smaller case inside the large one, like they were Russian dolls.

'Are you going anywhere nice?' she said and Frank wasn't sure whether she was talking to him or the matching set of luggage.

Frank had thought that because the large suitcase was empty he'd be swinging it about like Rita Tushingham's handbag, windmilling it along Sea Lane like a clown's prop or a gymnast's ribbon. But it was surprisingly heavy with the other bags inside and by the time he'd reached the library, less than fifty yards away from the charity shop, he'd already changed hands three times. His mind may have been rehearsing for the role of a man in his eighties but his body didn't need the practice. Frank felt like he was carrying two corpses: him and the one in the suitcase.

Outside the library, Fullwind's nativity scene was set up in a glass-fronted box on a wooden plinth. Last year somebody had stolen the baby Jesus and there was a new Messiah in the manger this year and a new padlock on the box's glass door. Mary and Joseph and the three wise men were still the same wooden figures that had been used in the Fullwind nativity scene for as long as Frank could remember. They were of a similar age and condition to the angel that sat on the top of his Christmas tree every year. Frank's angel had a leg missing and the wings had been replaced with two triangles cut out of a cereal box. The angel was as much a traditional part of Christmas as gluttony, sloth and the Queen's Speech.

Getting the plastic tree and the box of decorations down from the loft was one of Frank's least favourite annual chores. In the winter the loft would be the coldest place on earth and in the summer it was the hottest; it was like a thermos flask. The cardboard box containing the decorations would be covered in a thick layer of dust and even though its contents were always exactly the same, every year the box felt a bit heavier. Last year Frank was halfway down the ladder with the dusty box above his head when it upended and dropped tinsel and glitter onto his head and a glass bauble onto the carpet below, where it broke into a thousand pieces. Frank was vacuuming up wafer-thin slithers of bauble for ages and there was still glitter and tinsel in his hair and on his cheeks over a week later. The sarcastic man who worked behind the counter of Fullwind Food & Wine had asked him if he was in a glam rock band.

Putting the decorations back in the loft after Christmas was an equally joyless task, and the box and the dismantled tree would often sit in the hall way beyond the twelfth day of Christmas, sometimes until after Easter. Frank had only bothered getting the tree and the decorations out of the loft this year because the fairy lights that he draped around the tree on a table by the living-room window would keep the neighbours from calling the police to kick his front door down because they thought that he might have died.

Frank walked along Sea Lane with his suitcase. He was now holding it in front of his chest in both hands like a squirrel holding an acorn on the front of a birthday card. He could see his flat as soon as he turned the corner, towering above the bungalows that led up to it and continued after it. At this end of Sea Lane Frank's first-floor flat was the closest thing to a skyscraper. Most of the other multi-storey buildings on Sea Lane had long ago been demolished and replaced with two, three or more bungalows. Once he was out of it, Frank's flat would probably suffer the same fate.

Sea Lane's Christmas decorations were subtle – a wreath on the front door or a sprig of holly on the gate. There were no flashing lights or inflatable snowmen, no novelty Father Christmases tied to the chimneys, not a single singing Rudolph or dancing Santa in any of the immaculately kept gardens.

Frank wondered what the decorations were like in America. He imagined teams of reindeer pulling sleighs, driven by life-size and lifelike Santa Clauses along fake snow-covered streets and a brightly lit Christmas tree standing tall in the centre of town, tall enough to make the one in Trafalgar Square look like a Bonsai. The Santa Monica nativity scene probably consisted of a full-sized stable with actors and a real donkey.

Frank tried to remember the names of Father Christmas's reindeer: Dasher, Dancer, Prancer, Donner and Blitzen – what were the others? How many reindeer were there? He knew Rudolph wasn't actually one of the original reindeer. He thought of turning back and going into the library to look it up on the Internet. He thought how the Internet had not only ruined the simple pleasure of a family passport photo but it had also spoiled the fun of trying to remember the names of Christmas reindeer.

Frank made it home and through his gate and safely into his flat without meeting any of his neighbours. He was happy to tell the travel agent, the man cleaning the photo booth and the woman working in the post office that he was going on holiday but he didn't want to have to explain to any of his neighbours why he was carrying a suit-case. Had he been on holiday? Why wasn't he tanned? Was it cold where he'd been? Hadn't he been yet? Where was he going? Why was he carrying a corpse?

Luckily, most of Frank's neighbours were indoors. It was too cold for 'Washes His Car Too Much' to wash his car or for his next-door neighbour 'Picks Up Litter' to use her spiked stick to pick up litter, and the grass didn't grow in the winter so there was no need for Trims His Lawn With Nail Scissors to live up to his Sioux name.

Frank opened the suitcase on his bed. He took the two smaller bags out and started looking in the wardrobe for holiday clothes. Laura had said that it was sunny on Christmas Day. Frank needed some more suitable clothes. The last time he'd been on holiday it had rained sideways for a week and he'd worn the same thick jumper and raincoat for the whole holiday. He took his least warm-looking clothes out of the wardrobe and put them in the suitcase. He had no idea what he would be doing when he got to America. He didn't know if he'd be going out to restaurants with his family or whether they'd spend the whole time on the beach. He put a couple of plain white shirts and a few ties in the case and he took his two flowery shirts out of the wardrobe.

The shirts were so loud and brightly coloured – a mess of flowers, fruit and shapes, like the combined designs of an art class of primary school-children – that without them his wardrobe was like a party after all the fun people had left. It was the wardrobe of a man Frank didn't want to go on holiday with. He took everything back out of the suitcase except for the two flowery shirts, closed the case and made a mental note to add 'clothes' to his holiday list. He would also add 'travel pillow', 'travel plug', 'Matchmakers' and 'Bill?'

On New Year's Eve, Frank stayed awake until midnight. He watched Big Ben chiming on television, the crowds counting down in Trafalgar Square and Edinburgh – 'five, four, three, two, one' – and then the firework display, and he took the Sellotape off the top of the wine again while everybody on television sang 'Auld Lang Syne' and then he went to bed because, as he discovered, no matter how hard you try, you can't link arms with a cat.

When the first plane of the year flew overhead he got out of bed. Once the giddiness had passed and he didn't think he was about to fall into the wardrobe again, the stiffness took over. Sometimes he felt so comfortable in bed that he wondered why he ever got up. It was always bound to be a disappointment. The stiffness was in his hips and his knees, and in his shoulders and at the base of his spine. His first steps of the day were like walking with somebody else's legs. And not new legs. Charity-shop legs from the 'everything 20p' basket at the back of the shop.

Frank was envious of Bill. He'd got up at the same time as Frank but he was already on his way down the hall to the kitchen as though he'd been doing warm-ups in his sleep. Though, of course, Bill might have been hiding his pain or discomfort behind his unfathomable cryptic clue of a face.

Frank went to the toilet, then he fed Bill and let him out into the garden. His joints were gradually warming up and his bones creaked less on the way back up the stairs than they had on the way down. By midday, he would have built up enough kinetic energy to get him through the day. By two o'clock, he'd be bored. All charged up with nowhere to go.

He rang Beth to wish her a happy new year. Even though it was still last year in America and the holiday taint wasn't quite over.

'Hello?'

Frank had realized in recent years that Beth was more amused and even flattered when Frank mistook her for Laura than Laura ever seemed to be when she was mistaken for her mother, so when he wasn't sure which one of them had answered the phone he always asked the same question.

'Is that Laura?'

'Hi, Frank.'

'Happy New Year.'

'Is it? Thanks.' He could hear the television. There was laughter and applause, singing and gunfire, a heated argument in Spanish and a fitness instructor counting loudly between intakes of breath. He presumed she was switching channels.

'I thought you'd be out tonight celebrating,' Frank said.

'It's my least favourite night of the year, to be

frank. Frank.' With the pause between frank and Frank, she obviously knew that she was making a joke, but with her polygraph-baffling voice it was hard to be sure. 'I don't like being dictated to when I should be having fun,' she said.

'Oh, neither do I,' Frank said. 'What are you doing instead?'

'Just watching TV.'

'What's on?'

'Nothing.'

'I watched that last night.'

'Disappointing, isn't it? I won't watch it again.'

'Neither will I. Not till next New Year's Eve at least.'

'Exactly.'

'Is your mother there?'

'She's asleep. Do you want me to wake her?'

'Oh no. That's all right. It isn't midnight yet there, is it?'

'Not yet.'

Even when she was a child Beth would always insist on staying up until midnight on New Year's Eve. When she was yawning and nodding off she would force herself to stay awake until the twelve chimes and then she'd be fast asleep in seconds and Frank would carry her up to bed; so now Frank was worried.

'Lump has worn her out,' Laura said. She switched off the television or muted the volume and the gunfire and the singing, the laughter and applause stopped abruptly. 'I just sent you an update.'

'The library's closed,' Frank said. 'I'll have to read it in a couple of days. What did it say?'

'Brief synopsis?' Laura said. 'Have you seen *Roman Holiday*?'

'The film? Yes.'

'You know how Audrey Hepburn is in love with Gregory Peck even though she's a princess and he's a journalist and at the end she's smiling at that press conference but she just seems so sad?'

'I'm not sure. Yes. I think so.'

'Mom's a bit like that at the moment. There's an undercurrent of Audrey melancholy to her.'

'I see. At least I think I do. You mean she's unhappy?'

'And happy at the same time. You won't need to read the email now.'

'And how are you?' Frank said. He thought that he might have already asked but he worried that Laura might begin to resent her mother for having the monopoly on everyone's sympathy. There was little chance of that, though, as Laura shrugged Frank's enquiry off with her usual nonchalance.

'I'm about to miss this movie, that's how I am,' she said.

Frank asked her to wish Beth a happy new year and they said goodbye. Before Laura put the phone down Frank heard the volume of the television go back up and what sounded like the crackling and warped opening music of an old black-and-white movie.

He went into the kitchen and made a cup of tea. While he waited for the kettle to boil he looked out of the kitchen window. The rain was overflowing from the guttering that ran along the underside of the roof. It needed fixing but that wasn't his problem any more. Homelessness, or at least the notion of it, was surprisingly liberating.

For the next two days Frank packed and repacked his suitcase, laying his clothes flat in the case and then taking them out and replacing them rolled up. He tried a combination of shirts and trousers laid flat at the centre of the case and pants and socks rolled up and inserted around the edges. He wanted to fill the suitcase enough for him to have to sit on it to shut it, but he didn't have enough clothes that he wanted to take. He hadn't realized how many woollen products he owned. Would he need a jacket or a coat? Was it going to be too hot for socks?

He filled in the suitcase address label and wondered what would happen if his suitcase was lost and eventually returned; would he still be here to accept it? Would the address on the label even exist? He probably should have been packing the flat up to move rather than for a holiday but he carried on packing and repacking. He bought a pair of Desert Storm chocolate-chip and cookie dough camouflage cargo pants from the charity shop that many people would have said he was too old to wear, which was exactly why he bought them, that and the six pockets: side, back and halfway down the legs of the trousers. Frank thought that he would need extra pockets in America, for his passport and his money. He bought some flip-flops with soles like Liquorice Allsorts and some new socks and underpants in the big Sainsbury's and, just in case six pockets weren't enough, he bought a zip-up travel document pouch. It was difficult to choose the right clothes for a Californian summer holiday in the midst of an English winter. Like shopping for food just after a big meal, and Frank wasn't sure if anything he bought was suitable.

While he was in the supermarket he went back to the travel agents and picked up some more Californian holiday brochures. He sat at home and stared at pictures of Disneyland and Universal Studios, the Hollywood sign, Griffith Observatory and the billboards on Sunset Strip. He looked at photographs of the Chinese Theatre and the Egyptian theatre and at the beaches of Venice and Santa Monica, where Beth and Laura had cycled. Where better to go to escape reality than Hollywood? When he'd turned the knob on the gas fire so many times to unsuccessfully get it to light that he felt blisters forming on his thumb and his forefinger, he gave up and went to the library instead because it was warm there and he could look at the seating plan for his flight on the Internet one more time. He worked out where the emergency exits and the toilets were and he imagined who he might be seated next to and what the food would be like and what inflight movies would be showing.

Frank had seen a lot of movies but he'd never seen an in-flight movie. At least there wouldn't be any films about air disasters. Ever since he'd booked his flights, every film he watched seemed to have a plane crash or hijacking in it. They'd taken the place of the cancer stories on his TV. There were bombs on planes, snakes on planes, engine fires and failures, planes crashing into mountains and the passengers eating each other. And then there were the air-crash documentaries, the planes landing on rivers and on busy freeways on the news and the drunk-pilots and lost-luggage stories. Last night Frank had watched a report on the news about deep-vein thrombosis on long-haul flights. Like a lot of other things – the flu, cold weather, hot weather – as an eighty-two-year-old, Frank was in the at-risk group. He typed 'DVT' in to Google images on the library computer and almost fainted onto the keyboard. After adding 'flight compression socks' to his holiday shopping list he read the latest email from Laura.

Subject: 'Lump'.
What's up, Frank,
   Lump has had a particularly spiteful couple of days. Mom says she's tired but she's too tired to sleep and she's been moping about the house like a grounded teenager.

Sleep patterns 6.5/10 (erratic).
Appetite 7/10.
Energy 6/10.
Mood – Audrey Hepburn with traces of Princess Diana.
Happy whatever year it is now where you are.
L

Frank didn't know if the traces of Princess Diana were positive or not. He sent a short reply to ask her and left the library and went over the road to the chemist and then to Fullwind Food & Wine, but neither shop sold flight compression socks. In the charity shop the angle-eyed woman, whom Frank had given the Sioux name of Eyes Facing South-West, suggested that he might try wearing a pair of pop socks instead. She went over to one of the shelves and brought back a packet.

'They're new,' she said and she put the pop socks on the counter. 'They haven't been worn.' On the front of the packet it said *5 Pairs 15 Denier Knee-Highs – colour nude* above a picture of a woman's crossed legs. 'Would you like to take them?'

Frank nodded and Eyes Facing South-West picked up a pile of brown paper bags.

'They're made for women,' she said – she had such a loud voice, though Frank hadn't noticed it before – 'but I'm sure that doesn't matter.' She rubbed the paper bags together to free one of the bags. 'My husband worked on the oil rigs and he used to wear my tights to keep himself warm.'

Frank just wished she would stop talking or at least turn the volume down and put the women's socks in the bag so that he could leave. He felt like he was buying a dirty magazine. After he'd paid and left the shop, just as the door was closing, he was convinced that he heard high-pitched laughter just like on the bus to the big Sainsbury's.

In the second week of January, a man arrived in a van and hammered a FOR SALE sign into the grass verge outside Frank's flat. The sign was twice the height of most of the other FOR SALE signs outside the bungalows on Sea Lane even though it advertised a property that was at least half the price. Frank had presumed that the landlord would be selling his flat to be demolished to make way for more bungalows or developing the property himself and he was surprised to see the sign. It would also mean that he would now have to answer a lot of annoying questions every time he saw one of his neighbours.

'Are you moving?'

'Where are you moving to?'

'What's the asking price?'

And so on.

The first people to view the flat were a young couple. Frank's neighbours came out and pretended to wash their cars, trim their lawns and pick up litter so that they could see who their new neighbours might be. Hilary, the head of the Neighbourhood Watch, would have created a spreadsheet and a wall chart.

The estate agent showed the young couple around while Frank sat in the living room watching television. When they came out of his bedroom Frank heard the man say to the estate agent that it would be a nice flat once all the clutter was cleared and Frank knew that he wasn't talking about the dismantled Christmas tree and the box of decorations in the hall; he wasn't referring to the DVDs and charity-shop ornaments on every available surface in the living room; he didn't mean the giraffes and elephants or any of the ornamental animals in the oversubscribed ark on the mantelpiece; he wasn't even referring to the mess in the garden, the cat litter tray in the kitchen or the junk mail at the bottom of the stairs. The man was talking about him. Frank. He was the clutter.

After that first viewing, whenever people came to look at the flat, Frank tried to make sure that he was out. He felt as though many of the people who came to look around were just being nosy and had no real interest in buying the flat. He thought that he recognized some of them from the village and they were only there to snoop around and to have a go on his unusual doorbell. So whenever a viewing was arranged he'd go to the shops or to the library to look at America online and read the latest email from Laura.

Hi, Frank,

Today Mom's mood was Sandra Bullock. I think it's because you're coming over soon. And just one more week of X-ray zaps left for Lump.

PS: Reunion Project is progressing well.

L

Frank was pleased that Beth was in a better mood. He was sure that was what 'Sandra Bullock' represented. He sent a reply to say how much he was looking forward to coming even though he was a little apprehensive about the flight. He joked about the last plane that he had been on, saying that the pilot wore goggles and the propeller had to be started by hand.

When Frank's passport arrived the photograph was terrible. Worse than he remembered on the screen when he'd chosen to accept it. The man in the photograph didn't even look that much like him. His skin was a greyish-green colour and it hung from his cheeks like the jowls of a drooling dog. He looked as though he was in some form of discomfort. Frank had been trying so hard not to show any emotion in his photo-booth pose that he looked like he had piles – and was he really that old? He held the passport open to show Bill.

'Do I look like that, Bill?' he said.

Bill seemed to be considering his answer, looking at the passport and then at Frank, the inanimate object that was always his face seeming to be asking the question:

Why have you got a passport? Where the hell do you think you're going?

Frank picked up a silver-coloured serving tray and compared his reflection with the picture on the passport.

'It's like the passport of Dorian Gray,' he said, and felt a little too pleased with himself for his pun and made a mental note to repeat the joke for Beth or Laura as he put the passport away in the desk drawer. On the calendar in the kitchen he wrote, 'passport in desk drawer'.

As January headed towards February and Frank's holiday, he became more and more paranoid; he was convinced that something would prevent him from going. He took more care walking down the stairs in case he should fall and he avoided eating anything that he might choke on. When he heard the sound of the first aeroplane above his flat in the mornings it had taken on a new meaning. It wasn't simply a way of telling the time any more, it was also a sign that there were no Icelandic volcanic eruptions or baggage handler strikes today and his holiday was still on. Whenever the phone rang, he was afraid to answer it in case it was Beth with more bad news or the landlord asking for his money back because nobody had viewed the flat for almost a week. But it would just be more silent phonebots, telesales reps and market researchers wanting just a few minutes of his time.

There was one last email from Laura, reminding Frank not to mention the Reunion Project to Beth. She also asked if he could pack any old photos of the family and requested that he 'bring memories'. She ended the email by telling Frank that she was excited about seeing him and that he was her 'secret weapon'.

The night before he left for America Frank was unable to sleep. He still didn't really believe that he was going. If he did manage to fall asleep, he half expected to wake up to find that he'd been having a dream more complex than Judy Garland's in the *Wizard of Oz*. And he'd still be stuck in boring old monochrome Fullwind-on-Sea, looking up at the bedroom ceiling that needed painting, in his bed surrounded by Beth and Laura, Jimmy, the funny-eyed woman from the charity shop and his landlord, all looking at him with the identical freeze-framed features of his cat.

He closed his eyes and tried to picture Beth and Laura at the airport in Los Angeles, their faces wet with tears of joy and happiness. They were holding a sign with his name on. He thought about hamburgers and about popcorn, drive-in movies and cycling along the beach beside the blue sea with the equally blue sky above. He could almost feel the sun on his face just thinking about it, even though his flat was freezing and the bedroom window was etched with frost. He opened his eyes and looked over at the clock on the bedside table; it was the one and only time that he'd ever set the alarm and he'd tested it about ten times, terrified that it wouldn't go off. He thought about checking it once more to be sure. He turned over in bed and closed his eyes again, and even though it wasn't due for hours yet, he listened out for the first aeroplane of the day and thought that tomorrow it could be him up there.

CHAPTER 7

4 80,000 flights on 84 airlines, serving 184 destinations, take off from and land at Heathrow Airport every year. Seventy million passengers pass through the airport, an average of 191,200 a day, all watched from hundreds of different angles by over ten thousand CCTV cameras, relayed to a vast wall of monitors in a security-camera control room, where, finally, there was something worth watching.

An eighty-two-year-old man wearing a pair of Desert Storm camouflage cargo pants, with long white hair that ended halfway down the back of what was – even at an airport where all day flights arrived bringing passengers back from holidays in Hawaii and Acapulco – an incredibly loud shirt, was walking towards the check-in desks.

As he walked through the airport, sidestepping and tripping over wheelie suitcases, a text message would be circulating around Heathrow's other security staff telling them to come quickly to the control room and have a look. Someone would suggest ordering a pizza or some popcorn. It would have been a good time to steal a plane or smuggle a few hundred cigarettes through customs.

When Frank had almost reached the safety of his check-in desk, a small child riding a tiger-skin suitcase with a face and ears for handlebars ran over his foot, and other passengers in the queue stifled their laughter in various different dialects. An Albanian woman laughed out loud. Frank would probably now be as popular a comedian in Albania as Norman Wisdom.

The woman behind the desk checked Frank and his heavy suitcase in. She strapped a paper label around the handle and sent it on its journey through the rubber curtains. Frank was seriously considering not collecting it when he arrived in LA and leaving it to circle round and round on the baggage carousel indefinitely.

He walked towards security. Without the cumbersome baggage he could now afford a swagger more suited to his shirt, swinging his overnight bag by his side like John Travolta with his paint pot during the opening credits of *Saturday Night Fever*.

In the security area Frank took off his shoes and removed his belt. The 15 denier nude women's knee-highs that he'd been so desperate for Eyes Facing South-West to put in a brown paper bag could now be seen by the passengers and staff at the world's third-busiest airport. Ten thousand CCTV cameras filmed him from hundreds of different angles as he edged towards the hand luggage X-ray machine in his ladies' tights, trying not to slip on the polished airport floor.

He put his shoes and his belt into a grey plastic tray with his overnight bag and placed the tray at the entrance to the X-ray machine; it reminded him of when Laura had described Beth's radiation therapy as 'like being passed through an airport bag scanner five times a week'. He tried to get the image out of his mind in case it made him laugh or burst into tears in this high-security no man's land between ground and airside where laughter or tears might be enough to get him barred from ever getting on a plane.

The grey tray disappeared inside the X-ray machine and while he waited to be ushered through the metal detector arch to retrieve his hand luggage he checked all six of his trouser pockets for coins. He wondered whether the small gold studs on the belt loops of the trousers would set the alarm off. A member of the security staff waved him through the metal detector arch and he was relieved that it didn't make a sound. His trousers were a couple of sizes too big and he was worried about what might happen if he let go of the waistband to be searched.

On the other side of the arch the conveyor belt conveyed his belt, shoes and bag through the X-ray machine. For a moment it stopped and the security staff studied the monitor. Then it started moving again, a uniformed woman following the plastic tray along the conveyor belt. She picked the tray up and asked Frank to come with her to a table, where she unzipped Frank's bag.

'Is this your bag, sir?' she said, putting on a pair of white latex gloves.

'Yes,' Frank said.

'Could you tell me what's in the bag, sir?'

'Um,' Frank said, 'toiletries, um . . . a comb . . . oh yes, a sandwich. I wasn't sure what the food would be like. On the plane, I mean. Not in America. Er—' he scratched his head – 'this is a bit like The Generation Game.'

'I'm sorry, sir?'

Frank wanted to do his Bruce Forsyth impression to illustrate: *'Good game, good game. Cuddly toy.'* But he knew airport security was a serious business. Everyone knew that airport staff didn't appreciate jokes about bombs and even though there was no red-circled picture of Bruce Forsyth on the forbidden-items chart behind the woman (there was a firework, a gas canister, a Stanley knife, lighter fuel, matches and a bottle of acid but no Brucie), it was possible that any joking, however light, was best avoided.

'I'm sorry. Nothing,' he said.

'Where are you travelling to, sir?' the woman said. She took his folded jacket out of the bag and put it on the table.

'America.'

The security woman took a small alarm clock out of Frank's bag.

'A clock,' Frank said, suddenly remembering that he'd packed it.

'Business or pleasure?' the woman said. 'Your trip today?'

'Holiday,' he said. 'I'm going to visit my daughter and my granddaughter.'

The woman took another clock out from the bag.

'Oh yes,' Frank said. '*Clocks.*'

'Can you tell me why you have so many clocks, sir?' the woman said as she removed a third clock from Frank's bag. It was the clock from his bedside table. The lid of the battery compartment on the back of the clock had snapped off and the batteries had fallen out into Frank's bag. The woman took the batteries out of the bag and put them next to the three clocks.

Frank explained about a leaflet that his daughter had sent him once and how the leaflet had suggested ways to prevent dementia.

'Being aware of the time is important,' Frank said.

The security woman took a small A5 children's charity calendar out of the bag.

'And the date,' Frank said.

He explained to the woman how his daughter was always asking him whether he was looking after himself and if he was eating properly. He didn't tell her that they had recently reversed those roles and it was now he who was constantly concerned about his daughter's health. He said that he'd packed the clocks and the calendar so that Beth would see that he was taking his health as seriously as she did.

'It's a sort of joke,' he said.

'A sort of joke?' the woman said.

'She sends me emails with titles like "Are you eating well?"' Frank said. 'Or "Ten great memory tips". Sometimes I put them straight in the trash, thinking they're spam.'

'Spam?' the woman said. Frank had the distinct feeling that she was one of the few people left in the world without a computer and she might have thought that Frank was talking about processed cold meat. He looked for a picture of Spam on the prohibited items board behind the woman.

'Can you tell me why today's date is circled, sir?' she said, looking at the open calendar.

It seemed such a ludicrous question to Frank, with such an obvious answer, that he had to try really quite hard not to say something hugely sarcastic. He wondered if the airport security was always this thorough. It seemed a bit over the top right now but their diligence actually made him feel more comfortable about stepping onto an enormous aeroplane with four hundred complete strangers.

As he explained that the date was circled because it was the day he was flying to America to see his daughter, the security woman took a fourth clock out of Frank's bag. Even Frank now accepted that carrying four clocks in your hand luggage was a bit unusual.

'That one is set to Los Angeles time,' he said.

The woman looked at Frank and decided that he wasn't a terrorist but just a bit of an idiot. She wished him a nice trip and waved him on with a gloved hand and a look of bewilderment.

Frank put everything back in his bag, letting go of the waistband of his trousers so that they slipped down his hips revealing his underpants like he was a rapper. He dropped the belt into the bag and put his shoes back on. The laces of the right shoe were still tied in a knot and he couldn't get his heel in and he had to hold the shoe on by clenching his toes and dragging his foot along the ground. With his passport between his teeth, his bag unzipped, his jacket slung over one arm and the other hand holding his trousers up by the waistband, he walked into the departure lounge. The older members of staff in the airport's security-camera control room sighed as they were reminded of 1970s sex comedies and the hero escaping through the window of his lover's house after her husband had come home early from work unexpectedly. The same woman who'd laughed at Frank earlier walked past smiling at Frank: Albania's Robin Askwith.

He sat down in the departure lounge and rethreaded his belt. He took off his right shoe and untied the knot in his shoelace. He rolled the pop socks down almost to his ankles and scratched his legs. He put his jacket on, careful not to rush things and crick his neck. And then he relaxed as best he could. He had quite a while to wait before his flight but he was so paranoid that he would be late and miss it that he'd turned up far too early. He squinted at the departures board but the words were too small. He would have to walk over and take a closer look.

There were more shops in the departure lounge than Frank had ever seen before in one place, and certainly in an airport. The last time he'd flown anywhere was to Portugal in the 1980s. He couldn't remember which airport he'd flown from but he was fairly sure there weren't this many shops and restaurants: just a duty free shop selling booze and fags and somewhere to buy a drink and a sandwich. At Heathrow now there were chemists and jewellers, bookshops and toyshops. There was a mini Harrods and a tiny Tiffany's, a caviar house, a Sunglasses Hut, a perfume gallery and a World of Whiskies. People were sitting on stools at a circular bar eating sushi and oysters and washing Beluga roe down with pink champagne. There was even a posh luggage shop for anyone who hadn't had time to pack properly and had turned up at the airport with everything in carrier bags.

Frank thought that he should buy something for Beth and Laura. He went into the main duty free shop. He looked at all the different alcohol on sale but he had no idea what they liked and certainly didn't want to buy cigarettes. Perfume was out of the question. How could he possibly hope to choose the right one? And even free from duty it all seemed too expensive to make a guess on.

Frank looked at the chocolates. There really was such a thing as too much choice. He'd already packed two boxes of Matchmakers in both orange and mint flavours in his suitcase. He paused by a shelf of chocolate oranges and recalled how he'd once attempted to demonstrate to Beth how to 'tap and unwrap' one. His plan to tap the ball of chocolate lightly on the table so that Beth would see the segments break away like a magic trick failed and the chocolate stayed in one piece. Frank had to hit it with a hammer instead, which, it turned out, was a feat that Beth was more impressed with.

Frank gave up on the duty free shop; he walked past a luggage shop and considered buying a folding trolley for his suitcase but it might not fit and it would be just one more thing to carry. He went into a shop called Glorious Britain selling souvenirs. He doubted that either Beth or Laura would be interested in Manchester United, the Royal Family or flags. There was a lot of Beatles merchandise. Everybody in America loved The Beatles, didn't they? Unless they hated them, of course. Frank thought they were one of those 'Marmite' things. *Marmite*. He should have bought Beth some Marmite.

He stopped by the postcards. They were mostly of London landmarks. He looked for a postcard with a picture of his friend Smelly John, taken back in his punk rock days. John had been dead for over a year and a half now and Frank missed him. If he'd still been alive, perhaps Frank wouldn't have accepted the landlord's offer so readily, fearing that once he was homeless he might be rehoused too far from John to ever see him again. Unless he'd bought them both tickets to America. After seeing Beth in LA they could have driven across the desert to Las Vegas in a hired convertible wearing the cowboy hats that they'd bought from a truck stop. They would have sat for days and days in front of the slots with a jug of frozen margarita and a bucket of loose change until they'd lost everything or had won enough to buy guns to shoot rattlesnakes on their way back to LA and the flight home. Frank suddenly felt very lonely. As romantic as the notion of the lonely traveller was, like Beth had said, even Michael Palin had a huge film crew with him. If nothing else, as John had been in a wheelchair they could have jumped all the airport queues and been given better seats on the plane. Frank gave up on the postcards. There were none with Smelly John on, just palaces, royalty and clock towers.

With John gone it occurred to Frank that while he was on holiday he wouldn't have anyone to send a postcard to. He could post one to the library, or to Fullwind Food & Wine, or Eyes Facing South-West in the charity shop. But they wouldn't know who he was – unless, perhaps, he signed it from 'Giraffe Man'.

Postcards were another extinct tradition, killed off by technology and laziness, along with remembering the names of reindeers and dwarfs and pulling faces in a photo booth. Most of the postcards bought at Glorious Britain were probably being bought as souvenirs, never to be written on or sent. They were like the toys in *Toy Story* or Frank's suitcase. An unwritten, unsent postcard was surely an unhappy postcard.

Frank followed a circular path around the departure lounge, browsing in shops and not buying anything and dodging everyone's hand luggage, which also seemed to be on wheels. He walked past a tie shop and thought about going inside to ask if they could recommend something to go with the shirt he was wearing. Just to give them a challenge.

Finally, he sat down next to the departures screen and ate the sandwich that he'd brought with him while he waited for his gate number to come up.

CHAPTER 8

Twenty minutes into the 'fifteen-minute walk' to the departure gate, Frank saw the plane that he'd be flying on. Through the window of the terminal it was obviously huge but it looked like an Airfix model or one of the toys they sold in the duty free shop. He sat down in the waiting area and tried to guess who would be in the seat next to him on the flight. He gave them Native American names – Voice So Loud on Mobile Phone, Boy Child That Cries, Carlos the Jackal, and so on.

When he watched a war film or disaster movie Frank would often play 'background actor roulette': he would choose an extra in the middle of a battle scene, flood or earthquake and imagine that he was that character. He'd watch the film, waiting to see if he survived or not. Frank had died in *Zulu* and *The Last of the Mohicans*, he'd been shot down from a crumbling wall of *The Alamo*, been blown up at *Pearl Harbor* and eaten by dinosaurs at the centre of the earth. He'd died under the sword at the Battle of Falkirk in *Braveheart* and didn't make it up Omaha Beach at the start of

Saving Private Ryan. He'd twice survived *Apocalypse Now* and, although he hadn't seen it to the end, at the point that Frank had stopped watching *Independence Day*, he was still alive.

In the departure gate waiting area, he played a similar game with the other passengers, practically willing himself to be seated next to someone unbearable or stinky for twelve hours. He was psychologically profiling the other passengers. Working out who the heroin smugglers and the shoe bombers were. He wondered what they thought of him. Widower? Lost grandfather? Competition winner?

An announcement that the plane would soon be ready for boarding was made and passengers rushed to get to the front of the queue for the gate as though the plane might take off without them. Others stayed seated and carried on reading their newspapers, not even looking up, demonstrating how experienced and frequent they were as fliers.

Frank joined the back of the queue. A stewardess – whom Beth had told him to remember to call a flight attendant – invited him to come to the front of the queue with the adults accompanying small children, the physically disabled and the pregnant women flying for two. Frank didn't like being pigeonholed as 'elderly', but he was willing to accept the few perks that it offered him and he walked past visibly perturbed younger, childless and better-abled passengers towards the front of the queue.

His ticket was checked and he followed the other passengers along the walkway to the plane, the walls and ceiling denying him a sense of the full scale of the aircraft. And unless there were steps leading down to the tarmac at the other end, he would also miss out on his 'Beatles moment' – waving from the top step – which he'd been looking forward to.

In the doorway of the plane he showed his ticket again and was pointed in the direction of the passenger seats (rather than in the opposite direction to the cockpit of the plane). He walked through Upper Class, which was more spacious and better furnished than his flat, and where there was a smell of leather and disposable income, and he went on through Premium, where passengers would have two more inches of legroom than he would and crockery made of real china, until he found his seat in the DVT and plastic cutlery section of the aircraft. He put his bag in the overhead locker and looked at his ticket and the number above the seat. He sat down and checked his ticket a few times until he was sure that he was in the right seat and then he fastened his seat belt. The plane was hotter than a maternity ward. His trousers felt cumbersome and overcomplicated with too many pockets. He unfastened his seat belt and stood up and took his jacket off. He took his bag out of the overhead locker, stuffed his jacket into the bag, put it back in the locker and sat down. He fastened his seat belt and looked down the plane at the other boarding passengers, resuming his game of 'adjacent passenger roulette'.

There was music playing. It was a pop song that Frank didn't know, possibly a song that was exclusive to the airline. From the moment that he'd climbed into the taxi that morning, his journey had been soundtracked with a musical bed of incidental music. In the taxi it had been homogeneous pop and dance music interspersed with shouted adverts and excitable early morning DJs laughing at their own jokes. At the airport there was a gentler stream of unrecognizable music, too quiet or distant to be heard properly in the vast space. Just quiet noise. It was interrupted every so often for an announcement, just as the music had been in the taxi and as it was now in the plane.

The longer the seat next to him remained empty the more Frank wanted it to stay that way. He wished traffic jams and broken-down trains on whoever's seat it was. Mini cab no-shows and alarm clock flat batteries. As the plane was almost full and the seat still empty Frank was really hoping for something bad to happen to whoever had the corresponding ticket. Just as he opened the bomb doors over the missing passenger's house, a man walked towards him. Frank willed him to sit down in one of the other few remaining empty seats before he reached the one next to him. The man was one of the blasé frequent flyers who hadn't moved when boarding had been announced, casually waiting until the very last moment before getting on the plane. He stopped in the aisle next to Frank and put his bag in the overhead locker. He took his suit jacket off and put it in with the bag and sat down next to Frank, who did his best not to sigh openly.

They exchanged nods and, to avoid the nods turning into words, Frank stared out of the window. He watched the airport ground crew in their high-visibility safety vests and huge ear-defender headphones, waving brightly coloured marshalling wands and throwing suitcases around.

'Could all ground staff please leave the aircraft, all ground staff please leave the aircraft. Ladies and gentlemen, as we are about to close the aircraft doors in preparation for our flight to Los Angeles, phones and portable electronic devices must now be in flight safe mode, Wi-Fi disabled and switched off and headsets stowed.'

The plane started to move and a video showing safety instructions appeared on all of the aircraft's TV screens. Frank listened closely while the passengers around him carried on chatting and laughing. The man next to him was changing the time on his wristwatch. Frank felt like he was the only person on the plane interested in surviving a crash, even though he doubted that he would be able to manage the brace position without permanently putting his neck out.

'Are you a nervous flyer?' the man next to him asked.

'I don't know yet,' Frank said, barely turning to face him.

'It's pretty safe these days,' the man said. 'And it's getting safer all the time.'

Frank nodded and looked out of the window again. His body language said go away, shut up, stop talking to me.

When the plane reached the runway it picked up speed and suddenly seemed to be a few hundred feet off the ground. Frank gripped the armrest and took a deep breath. After a few bumps and shakes, and the opening and closing of the wing flaps – which Frank had to turn away from watching because it looked as though the plane was falling apart – they were in the air, the ground below looking like the map that was now showing on Frank's seat-back TV screen, with its tiny aeroplane that was actually bigger than London showing the flight's progress along a dotted line from Heathrow to LAX almost twelve inches away.

Frank wondered whether they would fly over his flat and if a late Fullwind-on-Sea riser would use the sound of the aircraft to tell them that it was time to get out of bed. He wondered if his flat had been sold yet, with the locks already changed and his furniture dumped outside in the garden. He pictured the flat's new owner sweeping an open palm from one end of the living-room mantelpiece to the other, sending his collection of decorative fireplace animals into an open rubbish sack below like ceramic lemmings. He thought that squatters

95

might have moved in already, cuckooing his home as soon as he was out of sight in the taxi. It didn't matter now. Apart from faking a heart attack or writing 'there's a bomb on the plane' in lipstick on the toilet mirror, there was nothing he could do about it now.

The pilot welcomed everybody on board and read the weather forecast for Los Angeles, giving an estimated arrival time. He apologized for the short delay and wished everyone a pleasant flight. The pilot sounded like Roger Moore, which was one of Frank's impressions too, and he wondered if the pilot was raising a single eyebrow for his impersonation. Frank had never quite mastered it. Perhaps the pilot had.

'You seem more relaxed now we're up,' the man sitting next to him said.

'Yes, it's just that first bit I suppose.'

'It is an incredibly safe way to travel. There's always the risk of debris on the runway, naturally. Hitting something that's fallen from another aircraft – and the weather, of course. Ice and snow can make planes slide off the end of the runway and enough ice on the wings can affect the lift of the plane.'

Frank hoped that this wasn't going to go on for the eleven hours and thirty-two minutes that Roger Moore had just mentioned.

'Engine failure, of course,' the man said. 'This one has four engines, so it can still fly – or rather, emergency land – if one of the engines goes, say there's a bird strike, for example. But most of these big jets can survive a few birds in the engine. And they have people on the ground with shotguns and falcons to deal with the birds before they become a problem. Once we're up high it isn't an issue anyway.'

'Right,' Frank said and looked out of the window, hoping the man would finally take the hint and stop talking to him.

The fasten seat belts sign pinged off and the woman in front immediately reclined her seat, reducing Frank's legroom by an inch. He reached down and pulled his pop socks up.

'People. That's what you can't legislate entirely for.' The man next to him hadn't quite finished. 'One drunk demanding more booze, or a religious nut – sorry,' he said, stopping himself mid-flow. 'You're, er, not one of those, are you?'

Frank shook his head no, now concerned that he might be spending the next twelve hours with a man who had the Sioux name Racist Taxi Driver.

'Anyway,' the man said, 'it is an incredibly safe way to travel.'

He then started listing the safety records of different airlines. Frank decided he would instead give him the Native American name: Dustin Hoffman in *Rain Man*.

CHAPTER 9

Dustin Hoffman in *Rain Man* had finally bored himself to sleep with airline safety statistics and Frank was relaxed and watching his first ever inflight movie. At some point he was going to have to ask Dustin to get up so that he could go to the toilet. He was also worried that he might get deep-vein thrombosis if he didn't move from his seat soon. But at the moment Dustin Hoffman in *Rain Man* was sleeping and not talking and Frank didn't want to change that.

Before Frank had started watching the inflight movie, Dustin had offered to show him how to use the seat-back TV and Frank had politely declined. Technology was not yet his nemesis. He tapped at the glass of the screen and pressed the up and down buttons, learning how it all worked, trial and error, like a mouse discovering how to reach the cheese at the centre of a maze in a science experiment. All the time Dustin watched – out of the corner of his eye, via Frank's faint reflection on the screen's glass, and sometimes openly staring right at him like a curious child on a bus. Dustin was longing to share or rather show off his experience and knowledge with the old man and teach him how to operate this space-age machinery.

Without Dustin's help, Frank navigated his way through the options: Movies, TV, Audio and games, Drama, Comedy, Documentaries, Kids and Radio. He browsed the Nordic Noir selection. He'd seen it all.

Frank had hoped that he might have subconsciously learned a new language by recently watching so much Swedish and Danish TV. But so far all he'd picked up were a few words that were either the same or similar in English, such as *okej*, meaning okay, and *komma in*, which he thought was come in, and a phrase that he was unlikely ever to use in English, let alone Swedish. Unless a member of Abba turned up at his front door, of course. Frank was quite fond of the music of Abba. It was one of the many surprising things about him. An eighty-two-year-old man who liked Abba would probably blow Dustin Hoffman in *Rain Man*'s mind.

A flight attendant leaned across the sleeping Dustin to clear away the empty teacup from in front of Frank, and Dustin woke up. He yawned and shook his head like a wet dog.

'Where are we?' he said to Frank or himself. He tried to see past Frank through the window as though he was such an experienced flyer that he could tell their whereabouts by the cloud formation or the colour of the sky. He pressed the flight attendant call button above his head. There was a single ping and a light came on. An attendant walked along the aisle to him and Dustin asked for a drink.

'Anything?' he said to Frank, making it appear like the aeroplane was his house and the flight attendant was one of his staff. Frank took his headphones off. 'I was having a drink,' Dustin said. 'Did you want one?'

'Oh. No thank you,' Frank said. He put his headphones back on.

'Holiday?' Dustin said and Frank took the headphones off again.

'Yes.'

Dustin nodded. He was waiting for Frank to return the enquiry but Frank sensed that would lead to a long conversation and he'd miss the end of the film. Dustin Hoffman in *Rain Man* was bound to have some out-of-the-ordinary reason for being on the flight. He was probably a bounty hunter or a private detective. He'd be on a case now. Shadowing a perp across the ocean, Voice So Loud on Mobile Phone or Carlos the Jackal perhaps. Frank would then have to tell him about what it was he did. And he really had no great anecdotes about being a pensioner.

'Do you fly often?' Dustin said.

'Not really,' Frank said. 'This is my first time in years.'

'I love flying,' Dustin said.

Frank couldn't believe that anybody actually

loved flying. He wanted to ask what it was that he enjoyed the most about it. Was it the queuing or the waiting?

The flight attendant arrived with Dustin's drink. She placed it on a small paper napkin on the tray in front of him.

'Are you going to see someone? In the States?' Dustin said. He stirred the ice around his drink with a short plastic straw. 'Family?'

'My daughter,' Frank said. 'And my grand-daughter.'

Dustin waited for Frank to ask him what it was that caused him to be travelling alone so that he could tell him about his life as a spy or an assassin. Frank would then have to return with something about arthritis or being cold. He watched the flight attendant walking down the aisle of the plane and remembered something.

'She wanted to be an air hostess, stewardess, flight attendant,' Frank said, correcting himself twice. 'My daughter, that is. She used to put her school blazer on and do her tie up like a . . .' he mimed something that was similar to Oliver Hardy playing with his tie. 'Like one of those silk scarves they wear. She'd serve me and my wife tea from a wheelie trolley and show us where the exits were and how to put on a life jacket.'

Frank had forgotten about Beth wanting to be an air hostess. When she left school she was going to study modern languages and geography at college and apply for a job with one of the big airlines.

'And what did she do? When she left school? Your daughter?' Dustin said. 'British Airways or Pan Am?'

Frank thought for a moment.

'She worked in an office for the London Underground,' he said, only now realizing the irony.

'They grow up fast, don't they?' Dustin said. 'I've got four. Girl twenty-two, boy nineteen, twin girls sixteen,' he said as if he was reciting the deaths of the six wives of Henry VIII.

'They do,' Frank said, and, because they now had something in common as two family men travelling a long distance alone, he told Dustin about the first time that Beth had put on her school uniform and about how he was proud and also amused, because his tiny daughter looked so funny, but also how he'd had such a deep feeling of sadness.

'I quite literally didn't know whether to laugh or cry,' Frank said.

Seeing his daughter standing in the kitchen in her brand new school uniform was a marker of the beginning of the end of their father-and-daughter trips to the zoo and the cinema for Frank. She would be too cool soon or too heavy to stand on his feet and hold on to his hands while he walked her around the room. He wouldn't be able to follow Beth up the stairs any more, pretending to break into a run to chase her, making her scream and laugh in the same breath as she tried to escape. Because it would seem weird for both of them.

Frank looked at the TV screen to see the film

credits scrolling down. He'd missed the ending. Somebody behind him was kicking his seat. He navigated back to the map to see how the tiny aeroplane was progressing. It had moved about an inch along the dotted line and was somewhere over the Atlantic Ocean heading towards Greenland. Although ordinarily being able to go for hours without needing to use the toilet was right up there with his appreciation of Abba, his long hair and grasp of new technology in making him the enigmatic eighty-two-year-old that he was, Frank really needed to go to the toilet.

CHAPTER 10

The scale of the seat-back map was too large to show any further movement as the plane began its final descent into Los Angeles. Frank watched the lights from the cars on the highway far down below. He could see nondescript buildings, nothing that he recognized from any film or travel brochure, and what he presumed was the outskirts of Los Angeles – LAX's Hounslow and Hillingdon, Uxbridge and Staines.

He appeared relaxed. He didn't grip the armrest when the plane started to shake, or stare at the back of the seat in front to try and hypnotize himself into calmness when the plane touched the tarmac and the pilot slammed on the brakes so hard that Frank felt his false teeth move. And when they were taxiing towards the arrivals gate and the same passengers who couldn't wait to get on the plane at Heathrow ignored the flight attendant's instructions and unfastened their seat belts and switched their phones on, Frank followed Dustin's lead. There was no hurry. Less haste more speed. Relax. While other passengers rushed to get their hand luggage out of the overhead lockers Frank looked positively Zen.

Inside he was having kittens.

What if he didn't make it through customs?

What if his suitcase was lost?

What if Beth wasn't waiting for him?

What if she'd forgotten that he was coming?

What if Beth was there but didn't recognize him?

What if he didn't recognize her?

What if during the flight there had been a coup in Fullwind-on-Sea and he wasn't allowed to leave the airport, like Tom Hanks in *Terminal*?

The door at the front of the plane opened and everyone started to shuffle down the aisle towards it. Dustin stood up and Frank gathered his belongings together. He took the bag of complimentary items the flight attendant had given him at the start of the flight out of the seat pocket: the eye mask, earplugs, socks, toothpaste and toothbrush and a charity envelope (even at thirty thousand feet off the ground they'd managed to find him). He offered the toothbrush to Dustin.

'I do mine in a glass of water,' Frank said.

Dustin put the toothbrush in the top pocket of his suit jacket.

'Have a good holiday,' he said. 'I hope it's not too hot for you.'

Frank thanked him even though he hated always being asked whether he was hot or cold, tired or confused. He wished Dustin luck with his new media sales conference, because that was what he did; he wasn't a hit man or a private eye. Frank stood up. He felt like he'd been folded in half in an airing cupboard for a month. He put a hand on each side of his waist and pressed his thumbs into his lower back and straightened himself out. He took his bag down from the overhead locker. He checked his passport was in the front pocket of his shirt and then made his way to the front of the plane, letting a couple of passengers get between him and Dustin to avoid awkwardly having to say hello again so soon after they'd said goodbye.

He walked through Premium and through Upper Class – which looked like the morning after a businessmen's sleepover. There were newspapers, pillows, disposable eye masks and headphones left on the seats and thrown on the floor between the seats. You can't buy class, Frank thought.

He said goodbye to the flight attendants and they wished him a pleasant stay. He stepped out of the plane and onto the walkway between the plane and the terminal building, which deprived him of the Beatles moment at the top of the aircraft steps that he'd been hoping for, and, after a lot of queuing and walking, he made it through immigration and into the United States of America where he collected his suitcase and carried it through customs.

He looked for Beth in the busy airport and suddenly felt overwhelmed. He was lost and alone in a way that he hadn't been at Heathrow. He looked around the airport at the people arriving and leaving, meeting friends, hugging each other and sharing out the burden of their luggage. He hoped that he might see Dustin Hoffman in *Rain Man*, who could at least show him how to use a pay phone if he couldn't find Beth. He had her telephone number and address in his address book, which was in the front pocket of his overnight bag. He could always get a taxi. Or a bus. Could he even walk? He had no idea how far from the airport Beth lived or how big Los Angeles was. She could live a hundred miles away or just around the corner. If he called out her name she might have heard him from her kitchen or garden.

He thought for a moment that he saw Beth. But she was far too young. She waved. She was so Beth-like. It was Laura. It had to be Laura. Of course. She was so much like her mother. Even though Laura was obviously younger and her hair and clothes were no doubt different to her mother's, the similarity and hence the familiarity for Frank was palpable. She was dressed in black jeans and T-shirt, with black Converse shoes and brown hair that was so dark that it was almost blacker than actual black. All the colour was in her eyes; one was blue and the other was green with a swirl of brown and yellow like the inside of a marble or cream poured on coffee. Laura's mismatched eyes were the result of a recent cycling accident; that was as much as Frank knew and although Beth had described them to Frank before, it hadn't prepared him. It was like watching the Hollywood production of a radio play, filmed in glorious Technicolor. Frank tried not to stare or mouth the word 'wow'.

They hugged. Frank's shirt of many colours was a firework display on the night sky of Laura's black T-shirt. His trousers, meanwhile, were quite literally a desert storm.

'Mom's sorry,' Laura said in the midst of the hug. 'She didn't think she'd get away from work in time. So you've got me.' They parted and Laura said, 'Shall we go to the car?'

'All right,' Frank said, keeping his thought that she was still ten years old and too young to drive to himself.

'Shall I get a trolley for your luggage?' she said.

'All right,' Frank said, not sure that it was a question. Laura spoke with the same monotone voice that he knew from the telephone, only without the distance or the crackle of his old BT line. He was so used to the crackle that it had become part of her voice and hearing her now in person was like listening to a CD of a song that he'd only ever heard on a scratched vinyl record. He was surprised how nervous he felt seeing Laura in person after all their email exchanges. It was like meeting a lifelong pen pal for the first time.

Laura came back with a trolley and together they lifted Frank's suitcase onto it. He put the overnight bag on top.

'I need to go to the cargo building,' he said.

'Okay,' Laura said.

'I've got to pick something up.'

'Uh huh.'

'It was going to be a surprise for your mother.'

'Will it fit in the car?' Laura asked, seemingly unconcerned or uninterested in what 'it' was.

'Oh yes,' Frank said. 'Do you know where to go?' He showed her a piece of paper with the address on.

'I think we need to drive there,' she said.

With Laura pushing the trolley they started walking to the car lot.

'I didn't realize Beth was back at work?' Frank said.

'Yep.'

In the car lot Laura pressed a key fob and the headlights of a black (naturally) car flashed. The car was so small and close to the ground that Frank wondered whether they'd even fit his overnight bag into it.

'I'll pop the trunk,' Laura said. It was the most American thing that Frank had ever heard outside of a film.

Laura put the suitcase in the small boot space and they both climbed into the front seat of the car. When Frank moved his head his hair brushed the roof. It was a sports car or a coupé. There was a rear seat but it was more of a parcel shelf and Frank couldn't imagine anyone larger than a box of tissues sitting there.

'It's less like a Tardis than I was expecting,' he said.

'What's that?' Laura asked.

'Your car. It's small on the inside too.'

'It's Jimmy's,' Laura said. 'He left it behind.' She typed the cargo building address into the sat nav and they drove out of the parking lot and into heavy airport traffic. The roads widened with every turn or fork and then the traffic cleared. Laura switched the radio on.

'Is that too loud?' she said.

Frank said that it was fine, even though he had to practically shout it.

'Is this a song you like?' he said.

'This?' Laura said. 'It's okay.'

'What sort of music do you like?' Frank said.

'Good music.' She named a few bands and singers that Frank had never heard of.

'I don't think I know any of those,' he said. 'But I like good music as well, so maybe I'd like them too.'

'They're all pretty loud,' Laura said.

'I'm going a bit deaf. They'd probably sound a lot quieter to me.' The radio DJ back-announced the previous two songs and introduced the next one. Frank didn't recognize any of those bands either. 'I suppose everything can be a bit loud if you turn it up,' Frank said.

'It can be *really* loud.' Laura's emphasis of the word 'really' was an uncharacteristic break from her almost hypnotic monotone. She seemed keen to defend the high volume of the music that she liked.

It was around two miles to the cargo building and all the way there Frank had to stop himself from shouting Billboard! Cop car! Yellow school bus! Chevy! Cadillac! Stars and Stripes flag! U-Haul truck! They drove along the widest roads that he'd ever seen: he counted eight lanes on one. Some of the roads were lined by the tallest palm trees and then there were the names on the road signs and the interchanges, the boulevards, the hotels, the huge metal LAX sign, the music on the radio, the disc jockeys, the side of the road they were driving on and his granddaughter – everything was so American.

'I think this is the place,' Laura said. The sat nav confirmed it and she turned off the road and parked outside the cargo building. The trucks outside the building were big and long; they were trucks that would form convoys. The drivers would spit tobacco out of the window and warn other truck drivers of speed traps and cop cars over their CB radios.

They went inside the building and found the correct place. Frank showed his documents to a woman who was made up like Joan or Jackie Collins. She was standing behind a counter almost as high as her hair. She called Frank 'honey'. The woman went through an open door at the back of the office and, after a minute or so, she returned carrying a plastic box. She put the box on the counter and asked Frank for his passport. While she filled out a form, Frank looked through the grille in the door on the front of the plastic box and he saw the same inscrutable, impenetrable, unchangeable but recognizable face looking back at him:

And where the bloody hell do you think you've been?

CHAPTER 11

Laura seemed to be completely unfazed by Frank flying halfway across the world with a cat. While the woman with the Joan or Jackie hair completed some paperwork, Laura looked in through the grille at the front of the cat box.

'Is that Bill?' she said. 'You brought Bill. Do you want any candy?'

She walked across the room to a vending machine and made her selection. Her phone rang. Frank recognized the ringtone from a Disney cartoon. He would have expected a loud rock guitar riff.

'Hi, Mom. Yes. We're just collecting something. No, we're still at the airport. No, it was on time. Do you want to speak to him? Okay. We shouldn't be too long now. Bye.'

Laura ended the phone call and threaded another dollar bill into the vending machine.

'What shall I get you, Frank?' she called out.

He looked over at the machine and he chose a Milky Way as it was the only thing that he thought he recognized. Joan or Jackie Collins handed him both his and Bill's passports. Laura came over and gave Frank a Milky Way.

'That was Mom,' she said. 'She can't wait to see you. She didn't want to speak to you on the phone because it would spoil the moment.' She rolled her eyes as if to show how soppy she thought her mother was.

'How is she today?' Frank said.

Laura thought for a moment. 'Sandra Bullock,' she said.

'Which is good, isn't it?' Frank said.

Laura nodded. She looked at the two passports Frank was holding – one human and one pet.

'Does Bill have a photograph?' she said.

Frank showed her the blank space on the pet passport where the photograph would have been. Laura seemed disappointed. The pet passport photograph had been optional and Frank had left it blank. Getting Bill to sit high enough and still enough on the stool in the photo booth at the big Sainsbury's probably would have proved impossible. Getting him to pull the correct neutral expression, however, would have been a lot easier. Bill had a face for passports.

Flying a cat to America wasn't cheap, but Frank didn't want to leave Bill behind and he couldn't put him in a cattery. Not again. He wasn't sure that Bill had ever fully forgiven him for the last time. When Frank had found out that Kelly Christmas – who brought in the light and the motivation to put his teeth in – was allergic to cats, he was terrified that she might sneeze and not come to see him any more. And so Frank had put Bill into a cat's home for a month. It was an act of betrayal towards his friend that Frank didn't want to repeat.

To get Bill on the flight Frank had to have him microchipped, vaccinated against rabies and certified as fit to travel by a vet who must surely have been one of the richest men in Fullwind. Bill's plane ticket was more expensive than Frank's and he'd needed to be in a plastic travel box that was ventilated, lockable and large enough for Bill to be able to stand up, turn around and lie down in. Bill had more legroom on the plane than Frank.

Frank thanked the woman behind the counter and he walked back to the car with Laura who carried the cat box. At the car Frank held the box while Laura tipped the front seat forward and squeezed the box onto the backseat.

'Will he be okay back there?' Laura said.

'As long as we don't try to swing him.'

'Mom says that about our house. Why would anyone swing a cat?'

'I think it's a Navy saying.'

'Were you in the Navy?'

'No.' Frank expected Laura to start asking questions about the war and his role in it but they never came. At last, a generation that wasn't interested.

They climbed into the car. Laura selected the 'home' preset on the sat nav and they pulled out of the parking lot. They didn't speak all that much on the drive to Santa Monica. Frank was suddenly very tired. He looked out of the window. More boulevards, highways and freeways, liquor stores, gun shops and drive-thrus and barely a single pedestrian apart from an old homeless man pushing a shopping trolley full of old TV sets past a KFC. He was hungry. He tore open the wrapper of the Milky Way and bit into it.

'Oh,' he said. He put his hand to his jaw. 'This Milky Way is a Mars bar.' He removed the chocolate bar from his mouth and looked at the layer of chewy caramel that had almost torn the dentures from his mouth.

Everything was so American.

CHAPTER 12

Frank must have looked at his family's Los Angeles home a dozen times or more since Christmas on the computers in the library. He'd viewed the house from a satellite high above the earth and looked at it from 360 different panoramic degrees, walking virtually along the street, zooming in close enough to read the slogan on a jogger's shirt and the number on the roof of a passing police car. The jogger and the cop car were always there every time he looked. When Laura drove Jimmy's car onto Euclid Street, Frank felt like he knew it as well as the one on which he lived. The jogger and the cop car weren't there and he hadn't noticed before quite how many of the buildings were bungalows and in the online version of the street, Beth wasn't standing outside the open front door of hers waiting for him. She was wearing a baggy grey sweatshirt and matching trousers. She was barefoot.

Laura pulled the car up in front of the house and Beth came round to the passenger side of the car. She helped Frank out and she hugged him. At first he held back from fully reciprocating the hug, fearing that she might have been so thin from the cancer or the radiation that she would have fallen apart in his arms. When the plane had landed, he'd been concerned that he might not recognize Beth when he first saw her in the airport – what he was really most afraid of was that it would have been the illness that had changed her and made her unrecognizable. But, thankfully, she barely looked any different to when he'd last seen her, and she didn't disintegrate in his arms.

'How was the flight?' Beth asked, still holding on to him.

'It wasn't too bad.' Frank couldn't help checking Beth's head for signs of hair loss.

Laura said hi to her mother and walked around to the back of the car.

'I'll get your bags, Frank,' she said.

'Thank you, Laura,' Frank said, and then to Beth, 'I don't know if I'll ever get used to her calling me Frank.'

'I know,' Beth said, finally releasing him from the hug but still with a hand on his arm. 'I was Beth for a while. I'm Mom again now. Are you hungry? You must be exhausted.' He looked at her face properly for the first time. She didn't look particularly pale or drained.

Laura walked by with Frank's overnight bag over her shoulder and carrying his suitcase in two hands.

'Don't forget,' she said to Frank. She gestured with a nod of her head towards the car.

'What's that?' Beth said.

'Just a minute,' Frank said. He bent down and found the lever that tipped the car seat forward. He leaned inside and lifted the cat box out.

'Dad?' Beth said. 'Tell me it isn't Bill.'

There was a meow from inside the cat box as though Bill was answering Beth. It was a short meow. He'd never been a particularly verbose cat but, like his expressionless face, his meows could sometimes speak volumes:

Yes, it's me. Who did you expect? Why does everyone keep asking if it's me? Who did you all think it would be? And by the way, if Frank isn't hungry, I certainly am. I'm starving. And exhausted? Why not ask me if I'm exhausted? I've spent most of the day in a plastic box. I've been shut in the dark with everybody's suitcases and a hell of a lot of noisy dogs. So yes, let's all go inside, shall we, so I can get out of this sodding box.

Beth hadn't been quite as thrilled by Bill's surprise appearance as Frank had hoped she would be.

'What were you thinking, Dad?' she said. 'Keeping pets is against the terms of our lease agreement. We could lose our home.'

Frank apologized. He said that he'd thought that it would be an unexpected surprise for her. She said that she'd had enough unexpected surprises; what she needed was some dull predictability. He said that he really hadn't known what else to do with Bill.

'Catteries,' Beth had said. 'Cat hotels. A cat sitter?

You could have paid somebody to come to your flat and feed him every day for however much it must have cost to fly him here. How much did it even cost?'

Frank knocked £200 off the price of Bill's plane ticket and rounded it down another twenty pounds, hoping a more moderate price tag would help his argument.

'I wish you'd think things through,' Beth said.

'I know,' Frank said. 'You're right. I never do.' Which wasn't true. For two months he'd thought about Bill running around Beth's garden, chasing a ball of wool and bothering all the American mice – Mickey, Minnie, Jerry. What he hadn't thought through was that there might be no fence around the garden or that Bill wouldn't be allowed in the garden because of the terms of Beth's lease agreement. Beth took a deep breath, she held it for five seconds and when she exhaled, the anger seemed to leave her body. It looked like a method that someone had been paid an hourly fee to teach her.

'Well, obviously there isn't anything we can do now,' she said. 'Bill is here. We'll just have to keep him indoors and hope he doesn't pee on everything.'

They agreed to start the holiday over again. Beth made Frank go outside, she shut the door and then opened it and welcomed him into her home as though he'd just that minute arrived. She hugged him and even though the cat box was already in the house she pretended to be surprised to see it.

'And you brought Bill with you!' she said.

She led Frank to the sofa and they both sat down.

'Shall I make coffee?' Laura said, slightly weary at the lame display from two generations of old folks. 'Or tea? Mom's bought English Blend.'

'Could I have a cup of coffee please?' Frank said. Beth looked surprised by his request, perhaps because she didn't remember him ever liking coffee, and she was right, but Frank didn't want to be seen as an unadventurous Englishman abroad with a suitcase full of PG Tips, pork pies and Union Jack clothing. Laura made the coffee and Frank pretended to like it. Bill was less tactful, impolitely staring at the saucer of soy milk when Laura put it on the kitchen floor in front of him:

Soy milk! Not even soya. What the hell is soy milk?

Laura found a plastic paint roller tray and filled it with torn-up strips of newspaper and, like Frank, Bill must have been avoiding going to the toilet on the plane too, because he immediately filled the makeshift litter tray. And then he drank the soy milk.

Beth showed Frank where the bathroom was and Laura's bedroom, where he'd be sleeping. He was surprised how small the house was. There were two bedrooms, a bathroom, a living room and a tiny kitchen. The front door of the house opened directly into the living room. With the door open you could watch the TV from across the street. There was a small tree on the grass to the side of the house. The house was detached and from the outside it looked like a children's painting: a front door with a window on each side and a tree. It reminded Frank of the prefab that he'd lived in with his parents after the war.

They all sat together in the living room. They watched TV and then Frank told them about his flight, about the food and the films and Dustin Hoffman in *Rain Man* and the woman with the make-up and hair at the cargo building and how a Milky Way was a Mars bar. He asked what the time was in England and Beth said that it was about four in the morning and when she saw that Frank was struggling to keep his eyes open, she suggested he should go to bed. Laura took Frank's suitcase and overnight bag into her bedroom for him. Frank said that he would have been fine in the living room sleeping on the sofa or the floor. But it had already been decided. Laura was going to sleep on the air bed in the living room. She often stayed up late watching TV anyway. Frank had said all right but only if Laura was really sure; he said that he would be happy to sleep in a tent in the garden and Beth called out from the living room, 'Let's deal with one lease agreement violation at a time, Dad.'

Frank said goodnight to Laura and closed the bedroom door, then took a few things out of his overnight bag and his pyjamas out of the suitcase. He put them on and went to bed. Even though he was incredibly tired he couldn't get to sleep. It was almost time for the first aircraft of the day and time to get up back at home. He listened to the sound of Laura pumping up the air bed in the living room until she was breathing heavily in sync with the foot pump. Soon Frank couldn't distinguish between the two sounds as they eventually soothed him into a deep sleep.

EUCLID

Frank woke up the next morning with no idea what the time was or even if it was the morning. He was incredibly hungry. His stomach rumbled. His four clocks were over on the dressing table on the far side of the bedroom, like the New York, London, Paris and Berlin clocks on the wall of a city bank or advertising firm. He was in Laura's bedroom. Bette Davis was looking at him from the opposite wall above the row of clocks. It was a framed poster advertising bourbon whiskey. Bette was smiling with a cigarette on the go.

He listened for aeroplanes. Nothing. He heard a car drive slowly by outside. There was a radio playing somewhere in the house and a female voice quietly singing along with it. He couldn't tell if it was Beth or Laura.

He'd had a dream that he was in a taxi, returning home from the airport. It had been snowing and then it had rained and Fullwind was covered in an uneven layer of dirty grey slush. As the taxi drove through the village, Frank noticed changes. Apart from everywhere looking like the inside of

124

a broken snow globe, the charity shop was now called PoundaMental! and the nativity scene had been the victim of a barn burning. His flat was gone. In its place was a huge Tesco superstore.

He reached across to the bedside table for his glasses but there was no bedside table there. He needed to go to the toilet and he really had to eat something soon or he thought he might throw up. He lay on his back to take the weight off his empty stomach and looked up at the square tiles of the false ceiling above. He pictured a bank robber moving one of the tiles to one side to hide a bag of money or drugs in the roof space, like in a film.

Frank drifted back in and out of sleep for a while and then he got out of bed. His legs ached and they felt stiff. He sat on the edge of the bed and pulled the bottoms of his pyjama trousers up and looked for swelling and redness. No blood clots. Just his usual pale chicken legs. He stood up, slowly, not wanting to lose his balance and fall over in an unfamiliar room. He walked over to the dressing table. It was 8.15 a.m. in New York, London and Berlin. In Paris it was already five in the afternoon.

He lifted a few slats of the venetian blind and the sun shone in his eyes, a ray of warm Schadenfreude as he imagined what the weather might be like at home.

He opened the bedroom door slowly. Even though he was in his daughter's home he felt like a trespasser or an unwelcome guest. There was nobody in the living room. The blow-up bed had been deflated and folded into a shape that would never fit back inside the drawstring bag that it had come from. There was a folded quilt and a pillow on the deflated bed and on the top of it all Bill was fast asleep and purring. He could hear the sound of Beth or Laura in the kitchen, duetting with Jon Bon Jovi. There were no other sounds of life in the house. The sun shone through the living-room window. Frank didn't ever want to go home.

He walked to the doorway of the kitchen.

'Good morning,' Beth said, almost singing the words and incorporating them into the song playing on the radio. 'Tea? Unless you'd prefer coffee?'

'Could I have coffee please.' If Beth offered him breakfast he would ask for eggs over easy and a stack of pancakes. 'I've just remembered,' he said. 'I've got a present for you. It's in my case.'

'As long as it's not another cat,' Beth said with a smile. Then, more serious, 'It's *not* another cat, is it?'

'Just a minute,' Frank said and he went into Laura's bedroom. He came back to the kitchen with the two boxes of Matchmakers. He gave them to Beth. She was almost overcome.

'Thank you, Dad,' she said. 'I'm so glad you're here.'

She hugged him again, not releasing him from the hug for a long time and Frank made no effort to escape. He tried to recall if she had always been so tactile. It annoyed him that it made him feel even the slightest bit uncomfortable.

'And there's something for *you* on the table in the living room,' Beth said. 'From Laura.'

Frank went into the living room and sat down at the small table.

'There's an unscheduled grocery trip because of Bill,' Beth called out.

He picked up the pile of stapled-together sheets of A4 paper from the table and looked at the front page. The first page was a title page with *'Frankie Comes to Hollywood'* across the centre.

Beth came in with the coffee and she sat down at the table next to Frank. He flicked through the pages of the itinerary that Laura had made. There was a page for each day and each page had a film-related title and a paragraph or more of related facts or trivia. Frank read the beginning of today's page out loud.

'*The Sting:* Drive to Santa Monica Pier and the beach – Visit Paul Newman's grifter home and discover what it's like to be in Tom Hanks's shoes. Movies filmed at these locations include: *The Sting, Forrest Gump, Hancock, Bean, Elmer Gantry, Rocky III, Iron Man, Hannah Montana: The Movie.* Dinner at the Cheesecake Factory.'

'That's all going to be with me, I'm afraid,' Beth said. 'The official tour guide will be looking after you tomorrow.' Frank looked at her. He was alarmed that Beth might have actually hired a professional tour guide. 'Laura,' she said to reassure him. 'They've been great at work,' she said, 'but there's one less paycheck coming in now so I don't want to push my luck. I feel terrible, Dad, I'm really sorry, but Laura still has some vacation time left. She's going to show you the sights for a couple of days while I'm at work and also while I'm at my follow-up.'

'What's that?' Frank said.

'Follow-up care,' Beth said. 'I have to go to see the doctor and check that everything is okay and so on.'

'Everything *is* okay,' Frank said, 'isn't it?'

'Oh yes. Although the side effects have been worse now the radiation is over. I was warned that might happen but it still caught me out. Tiredness, mainly, but that won't last. I hope. Anyway, forget about all that, I'm yours in the evenings and from the weekend onwards. We can do the less exciting stuff together, although I'm sure Laura has something planned for us.' She gestured at the itinerary.

'I really don't want to be a burden,' Frank said. 'You should carry on as normal and just pretend I'm not here. I'll be all right on my own. I doubt that Laura wants to spend her holiday time with a daft old man.'

'That's *why* she's taking the time off, Dad,' Beth said. 'To spend it with a daft old man and you are *not* a burden. Except when you say you're a burden. That's the only time that you're a burden.'

After breakfast they drove to a nearby grocery

store. Beth's car was larger than Jimmy's black sports car but it was still small and Frank's expectations for enormous American houses with acres of land and cars as long as trains had not yet materialized.

At the grocery store Beth bought cat food, a litter box and a carton of whole milk for Bill. The litter box had a filtered lid and a cat flap at the front end. At the store's checkout there was a man around Frank's age who packed their groceries into bags. Frank was both glad that he no longer had to work and at the same time envious of the man for still having a job. When Frank had retired it hadn't been entirely voluntarily. He hadn't been ready and he still felt fit and well enough to do his job. It simply happened because it was officially time. He was sixty-five years old and he was withdrawn from circulation like an old pound note. Frank and the man packing the groceries exchanged nods, acknowledging each like passing Volkswagen Beetle drivers. Beth gave the man a tip and they left.

When they got back to the house, Frank had to keep lookout while Beth snuck the cat-litter box in like a boyfriend at a college dorm. They fed Bill and Beth covered the sofa with a bed sheet and closed all the doors to confine the cat to the kitchen and the living room, in case he decided to mark his new territory. Ten minutes later Bill had christened his new toilet and was asleep in the living room on the pile of bedding.

After a small lunch they went back out. They drove along Santa Monica Boulevard, counting down the streets as they crossed them – 12th Street, 11th Street, 10th and 9th Streets. Frank asked why Euclid Street wasn't called 13th Street.

'It must be superstition,' Beth said. 'I don't know why the name Euclid though.'

They drove across Lincoln Boulevard, between 9th and 7th Streets. There was no 8th Street.

'Is eight an unlucky number as well?' Frank said.

Beth looked in her rear-view mirror. 'Perhaps they lost a street. Or miscounted.'

Frank thought that he could see the ocean at the end of the road up ahead. He lifted his clip-on sunglasses to see if it was the same shade of blue that he knew from Beth's photographs. If anything it was bluer.

'Euclid Street is still the thirteenth street,' he said. He flipped the clip-on shades back down. 'It isn't on the signs but it is still the thirteenth street. People make the same mistake with buildings when they don't have a thirteenth floor because it's unlucky. They think they're getting off on the fourteenth floor but they're still actually getting off on the thirteenth.'

'Maybe that explains the year I've had,' Beth said.

They passed 2nd Street and turned onto Ocean Avenue, every new road now sounding to Frank like the title of a song.

'There's no First Street either,' Beth said, noticing

it for the first time in the ten years that she'd lived there.

She parked in a large car park and they walked onto Santa Monica pier. The pier was as familiar to Frank from cinema and television shows as Euclid Street was from the maps on the library computers. They went into the Looff Hippodrome building where there was a carousel. Steam organ music played on the merry-go-round's calliope and Frank couldn't help tapping his hand on his leg in time with the music.

'I think this is where Paul Newman lived in *The Sting*,' Frank said. He took the folded itinerary out of his trouser pocket and looked at the page for today. 'Yes,' he said. 'It is.'

He looked for the door at the back of the building where he half expected to see Robert Redford on his way to see a hungover Paul Newman breaking a block of ice in a washbasin.

The merry-go-round stopped and a few tourists climbed off.

'Do you want to ride a wooden horse?' Beth said.

'Oh, no thank you,' Frank said.

'I think there's a goat if you don't like horses.'

'I get dizzy in a revolving door these days.'

They watched the merry-go-round turn again for a while and then walked along the pier. Outside the Bubba Gump Shrimp Company restaurant Frank sat on the bench and put his feet into the huge *Forrest Gump* running shoes that were stuck to the floor. Beth tried to take his photograph with his digital camera but the batteries were flat, so she took one with her phone instead. Frank felt the strongest urge to do his Forrest Gump impression but he managed to resist in case it was misinterpreted as racist – or worse. In the amusement arcade there was a Zoltar fortune-telling machine like the one in the Tom Hanks film, *Big*. Inside a glass-fronted case Zoltar was wearing a gold turban with a red feather in it, he had pirate's hoop earrings and there was a necklace of solid plastic around his neck. Beth fed a dollar bill into the machine.

'Make a wish,' she said. She stepped aside and Frank wished to himself that his daughter would never be ill again.

Zoltar's hand moved over a crystal ball inside the glass case. His eyes lit up and his mouth moved up and down between his Salvador Dali moustache and his ducktail beard. He told Frank something about destiny not being about chance but about achievement and other stuff that Frank didn't remember from the film. Zoltar's script must have been updated with legal provisos and caveats, terms and conditions just in case anyone ever tried to sue the amusement arcade for a billion dollars for not making their wish come true. There was a glissando of musical notes and the machine released a piece of paper with Frank's fortune on. Frank read it out loud.

'Your wish has been granted.'

'I hope it was a good wish,' Beth said.

'I wished that I was young again,' he lied.

'Don't tell me or it won't come true,' Beth said. They walked away from the Zoltar machine and out of the amusements arcade. 'Isn't that how the movie ends?' Beth said.

'Thanks.' Frank looked disappointed. 'I was really looking forward to seeing it as well.'

'Oh, God, I'm sorry, Dad.'

Frank smiled – the mischievous smile of a man who'd seen *Big* about twenty times. Beth gave him a soft punch on the arm and then she took hold of the same punched arm and they walked to the end of the pier. Beth bought ice creams and they stood together and looked at the ocean. It seemed so blue to Frank that he wondered what colour the sand beneath it was. Seagulls hovered close to the pier and Frank tightened the grip on his ice cream.

'I've seen a lot of TV video mishap shows,' he said.

One of the gulls swooped down to the surface of the water and came back up again with a fish in its beak. The anglers with their fishing rods leaning over the side of the pier watched the bird with envy as it flew away across the sea. Frank looked at the people down on the beach by the side of the pier. He watched a man run across the sand towards the ocean. As soon as he was in the water he dived and disappeared under a wave without stopping.

'I think your mother would have liked it here,' Frank said. 'You'd be too young to remember but she used to swim out to sea for miles. There was no pier to stand on and watch her and I'd lose sight of her. Just as I'd be thinking of calling the coastguard she'd appear along the beach, not even out of breath, dragged almost to the Isle of Wight by the sideways currents. I was always terrified that one day she wouldn't make it back.'

'I do remember,' Beth said. 'It scared me as well.'

A sea breeze blew Frank's long hair across his glasses; he pushed it away and hooked the hair behind his ear. He finished his ice cream and leaned into the pier rail and lifted his arms out at his sides.

'No spitting over the side, Leonardo,' Beth said.

A man stood next to them at the end of the pier. He took a pack of cigarettes from his trouser pocket, took out a cigarette and put it in his mouth. He searched his pockets for a lighter or matches. Frank wanted to show the man the nearby NO SMOKING sign and read him the health warning on the packet. He wanted to tell him to not spoil a lovely sunny day. He wanted to show him his daughter standing next to him. Tell the man what she'd been through. He wanted to force the man to smoke every single cigarette in the packet until he turned green and threw up and vowed never to smoke again, just as Frank had seen happen in a number of films. The man found a book of matches and attempted to light the cigarette but the breeze blew out the match. If he tried again Frank would blow out the next match himself. A blue light on the Bluetooth headset hooked onto the man's ear flickered on and off. Frank wanted to reach over and screw the flickering bulb back in place like one of the fairy lights on his Christmas tree.

'Shall we walk down to the beach?' Beth said. She gestured towards a TV crew that had roped off an area nearby, setting up to film a scene for a TV show. 'I don't want to end up in that dumb show.'

As they walked away Frank thought about pushing the smoker over the rail and into the sea. He imagined the splash and the swooping gulls pecking at the man like he was Tippi Hedren, the blue light still flickering on and off on his ear.

They went back along the pier and walked down the ramp to the sand. After about fifty yards they sat down. Two joggers ran along the beach down at the water's edge. Frank looked at the itinerary.

'It says here that the obligatory *Rocky III* training montage was shot here. Perhaps they're filming now.' They watched the joggers until they were out of sight.

Beth put a hand under her armpit. Frank had noticed her do the same thing on the pier. He wondered if she was checking for new lumps or to make sure that the lump was definitely gone. He wanted to ask her whether it had hurt or if it still did but he was also reminded of when she was very young and he had tried to teach her to make armpit fart sounds. No matter how many times Beth had tried, with her hand pushed tighter and tighter into her armpit as she flapped like a one-winged rooster, she couldn't produce an audible raspberry. The harder she tried and failed the angrier it would make her, which, in turn, would make Frank laugh more uncontrollably, until Beth would storm out of the room sulking and he would eventually have to go and apologize. Beth couldn't waggle her ears or flare her nostrils either or play a pop tune by opening her mouth and slapping herself on the cheeks and she soon realized that the only way that she would ever follow in her father's footsteps was by standing on his feet and holding onto his hands while he walked her around the room.

'Do you think you'll get divorced?' Frank said.

It was an unexpected question, somewhat out of the blue and possibly one that nobody had asked her yet. It at least distracted her from 'Lump' as she considered it for a while. 'I don't really know,' she said. 'I might have the grounds but I don't have the willpower at the moment. Jimmy's American, I've got dual nationality, we were married in the UK but we're both US residents, there's a child – an almost twenty-one-year-old child – but still, it's complicated, Dad. There's no pre-nup and I've got enough admin to do at work as it is.'

Beth could see that Frank didn't know what a pre-nup was, or possibly admin either and she explained about pre-nups, giving him a few recent famous multi-million-dollar celebrity examples.

'Me and your mother didn't have one of those,' Frank said.

'I think you and Mum were pre-pre-nup.'

'Not that we had anything that was worth arguing over anyway. I do feel sorry for the rich and successful. Do you want me to talk to him?'

'Jimmy? Dad, God, no, of course not.' The idea seemed to horrify her.

'Thank Christ for that,' Frank said. 'I wouldn't know what to say.'

A speedboat overtook the joggers and bounced along the water behind the pier.

'It's like watching an episode of *Baywatch*,' Frank said. 'Was that filmed here?' He pretended to consult the itinerary.

'Actually yes,' Beth said. 'Just along the beach a bit. Did you want to go there? You might meet Pamela Anderson. She sometimes comes out of her hut and saves a drowning child in slow motion.' Beth smiled in the same way that Frank had done when he'd claimed never to have seen *Big*.

'I could shoot him, if you like?' Frank said. 'I understand you can buy a gun in Woolworth's over here.'

'Yes, shoot Jimmy for me,' Beth said. 'Thank you, Dad. That would be a great help.' After Frank didn't answer for ten seconds, just for clarification, Beth said, 'I'm joking, by the way. Don't shoot Jimmy.'

'Maybe you'll get back together instead,' Frank said.

'Wow, Dad. You should be a marriage guidance counsellor.'

'What's the pay like?'

Beth laughed and she put her hand on Frank's leg.

'It's good to see you,' she said.

They sat together watching more joggers and beach gymnasts and the speedboat making its return trip along the water. When Frank started to get cramp and backache Beth helped him up and they walked slowly back to the car and drove along the coast to meet Laura for an early dinner.

At the restaurant Beth paid a man dressed like a snooker player to park the car and they went inside where a waiter showed them to a table on the patio overlooking the marina and the yachts and power-boats. A different waiter introduced himself as Curtis and he took their drink orders. Frank ordered a beer, justifying his choice to Beth, who hadn't questioned it, by saying, 'I am on holiday.'

Beth asked Frank if the sun was too bright for him and if he wanted to swap places with her or go and sit inside instead.

'I'm fine here, thank you,' he said. He hated being fussed over by everyone but Beth. 'I was hoping to go home with at least a little bit of souvenir sunburn.'

Laura arrived. She was dressed in black from her shoes to the sunglasses perched on top of her head. She said 'hi' and sat down. Curtis came back and Laura completed her look with a black iced tea and then they all ordered food. Frank had a California omelette, which came with avocado, mushrooms, onions, tomato, garlic and shallots, Jack Cheddar and Swiss cheese. There was a slice of orange on the side of the plate. Frank had never seen fruit on the same plate as an omelette before and he thought that possibly it could have fallen from another customer's dessert as the waiter had walked by. He wasn't sure whether to eat the orange, squeeze the juice onto the omelette, or leave it on the side of the plate because it was just there for decorative purposes. It might not even have been sliced from a real orange.

Beth asked him whether he was feeling any of the effects of jetlag yet and he said that he didn't think so. When he was in the library researching deep-vein thrombosis, he'd read about the symptoms of jetlag: the indigestion, constipation and diarrhoea, the nausea, the loss of appetite, the difficulty in concentrating, the feeling disorientated, anxious and irritable, the memory problems, the clumsiness, the lethargy, the lightheadedness, the confusion and the headaches, the muscle soreness and generally feeling unwell, and he'd concluded that he might not notice if he even had jetlag. It would be as different to how he normally felt as Christmas Day was to every other day of the year.

'What would you be doing now? If you were at home?' Laura asked.

'What day is it?' Frank asked.

'Tuesday,' Laura said.

'It might already be Wednesday in England,' Beth said.

'You'd be mistaken for thinking that at my age it doesn't matter,' Frank said. 'But if it's Tuesday, Tuesday is over-seventies cocktails night at the village hall. I would have had a few Martinis by now. There's usually some dancing, salsa or tango, a couple more Martinis, and then a fight in the car park before Midnight Blue Movies Club starts at the library: nothing too strong by today's standards, more nostalgia than pornography, although it does attract a few perverts. But if it's Wednesday, that's my night off. Sod all happens on Wednesday.'

Laura laughed and Beth sighed.

After the main course Frank looked up and down the long list of cheesecake options. There were over thirty different types and he couldn't decide which one to have. By the time he'd read the last one on the menu he'd forgotten what all the others were before it and he had to start again at the top of the list.

'What time is your flight home?' Laura said and Frank tried to remember until he realized that she was being sarcastic.

He said that he'd only ever eaten cheesecake once before. It was a frozen one that he'd bought from Fullwind Food & Wine where they only had the one flavour. Cheesecake flavour. He'd been going through a period of eating almost exclusively puddings and desserts. Food had become boring for him. He didn't really cook. He opened tins and heated up the contents. He ate spaghetti in hoops, letters, numbers and dinosaurs. Food manufactured for fussy children. But he still enjoyed desserts. So often he skipped straight to the mousses, ice cream, sorbets and caramel puddings, the lemon meringue pies and trifles.

'Shall I pick one for you?' Laura said and she chose a banana cheesecake. It arrived covered in whipped cream and slices of banana and again Frank was not sure where the food ended and the garnish began. He was too full to eat even half of the cheesecake and Laura leaned across the table and cleared his plate for him a spoonful at a time.

After the meal Curtis came to the table with a Hot Fudge Sundae in a shot glass and a candle at its centre. He placed the glass on the table and lit the candle and he and the other waiters and waitresses started to sing 'Happy Birthday'. It wasn't Laura's birthday for another five days but Frank mumbled along like he was in an English church. He looked at Laura who seemed to be singing happy birthday to herself but when the song reached the line with her name in, and Frank finally found his voice to loudly join in and sing

'Laura', Beth and the Cheesecake Factory workers sang 'dear Fra-ank' instead, and then quite a few of the other diners joined in for the final 'to you', complete with harmonies. In order to stop everyone from staring at him Frank blew out the single candle and accepted the applause. The diners returned to their meals and the staff went back to serving them.

'Happy birthday!' Laura said.

'Yes, happy considerably belated or early birthday, Dad.' Beth raised her glass of tap water.

'I presumed it was for you,' Frank said to Laura.

'God, no way,' Laura said. 'I don't like surprises.'

Frank looked at the tiny glass with the lone candle, still smoking.

'You'll have to imagine the other candles,' Beth said.

'They'd certainly need a larger glass,' Frank said.

'And the fire department on standby,' Laura said.

Laura had to eat Frank's birthday surprise and because he had never felt quite so full he wished that he'd worn his loose-fitting cargo pants. Beth paid for the meal, refusing money from Frank when he offered it. After they left the restaurant two snooker players brought both cars round to the entrance. Beth asked which car Frank wanted to go back to the house in.

'I don't know,' he said. 'I don't mind. Really.'

'Come on, Frank,' Laura said. She clapped her hands to hurry him up. 'It's not *Sophie's Choice*.' Beth shook her head. 'Poor taste?' Laura said.

'Always,' Beth said.

Laura had to make Frank's decision for him again and they drove back to the house in convoy, Beth and Frank up front with Laura following behind. They drove as near to the beach as they could so that Frank could see the pier at night with the lights on and he thought again how everything he'd seen since he'd been here had been like a movie. Today there had been the old men playing chess on the beach, the gymnasts, the people jogging and cycling along the boardwalk, the middle-aged couple on Segways, the woman on roller skates towing a chihuahua behind her on a skateboard, the man doing tai chi, the yoga class, the weightlifters and the beach volleyballers. They were all the movie's background actors.

Even the pier didn't look real. The bright play-school colours of the Ferris wheel and the roller coaster and rides of the amusement park that had looked like an enormous Mouse Trap board game in the daylight were now lit up like a pinball machine. Frank thought that in a few days' time, when filming on the pier was finished for the 'dumb show' that Beth was keen not to appear on, Hollywood Teamsters would arrive to dismantle the amusement park and the pier and they'd load everything onto trucks to be packed away in a props warehouse. They'd deflate the hills in the distance like Laura's air bed and all the gymnasts, the beach volley-ballers and the Segway riders, all the street performers, trapeze artists and the old men leaning over the sides of the pier fishing for halibut, even the man with the Bluetooth and the cigarette; they would all go back to their day jobs in hotel bars and cheesecake factories.

CHAPTER 14

Aviator*: Drive to Hollywood Boulevard and the Chinese Theatre to see the footprints and handprints of the stars. Discover what it's like to be in Tom Hanks's shoes again and also his gloves. Followed by a 'Homes of the Hollywood Stars Luxury Minibus Tour'.*

Movies filmed at these locations include: Gangster Squad, Forrest Gump, Twins, Italian Job *(lame remake)*, The Aviator, Iron Man 3.

Today's Fact: *The Chinese Theatre has changed its name three times: from Grauman's Chinese Theatre to Mann's Chinese Theatre and finally to TCL Chinese Theatre, which may be the least Hollywood-sounding of the three, but unlike all the other owners, they were at least actually Chinese.*

Laura was wearing black again, different clothes but the same colour. On the drive to Hollywood, Frank asked her if she was a goth. The question surprised Laura. It sounded so unusual coming from the mouth of her eighty-two-year-old grandfather that she didn't notice a red light and nearly drove into the car in front.

'Am I a *goth*?' she said. 'Wow. No, I'm not a goth.'

Frank loosened his grip on the passenger seat, which he'd squeezed tightly when Laura had slammed on the brakes.

'An emo, then?' he asked.

Laura turned to look at Frank. The extent of her grandfather's knowledge of youth subcultures had caused her to temporarily forget how to drive. The lights were now green. A driver behind honked their horn.

'I'm not an emo either,' she said, remembering where the accelerator pedal was and moving forward. 'I don't really like labels.'

'Wait till you get to my age,' Frank said. 'You're really going to hate it. Pensioner, OAP, the aged, the elderly—' a moment of silence passed while Frank thought, before continuing – 'old codger, geriatric.'

'Old timer,' Laura joined in.

'Past it,' Frank said.

'Senior Citizen.'

'Wrinkly.'

'Old coot.'

They both were silent, thinking up synonyms.

'Old fart,' Laura said.

Frank pretended to be offended.

'Now that's just rude.'

Laura parked the car in a mall car park and they

146

walked to Hollywood Boulevard. Outside the Chinese Theatre Frank looked at the hand- and footprints of the film stars in the cement and he couldn't get over how so many great people had all stood or knelt in this one small area of the world. And now here he was too. He put his feet in the prints left by his favourite actors. He almost refused to believe that they could all be genuine and suspected that at least some of the prints might have been created by lookalikes in borrowed shoes, like the people dressed as movie superheroes posing for tourist cameras and handing out flyers outside the theatre.

Laura left Frank alone to marvel at the prints in the cement while she went to a kiosk to collect tickets for the 'Homes of the Hollywood Stars Luxury Minibus Tour'.

When she came back Frank said, 'People had smaller feet in the old days.' And then he remembered that he was from the old days too.

The driver and guide on the minibus tour, Robert something-unpronounceable, which was possibly a made-up name, was a working actor. He said so a number of times during his 'Homes of the Hollywood Stars Luxury Minibus Tour' patter. One day, he said, he would put his hands in the wet cement outside the Chinese Theatre and have his name cast in brass at the centre of a terrazzo star on the Walk of Fame on Hollywood Boulevard and Vine Street.

Jack Nicholson. I worked on a movie with a friend

of his. Great guy. Is anybody here going to Universal Studios? Look over there, right in the heart of the San Fernando Valley. There are sixteen cities within the city of Los Angeles . . .

Robert something-unpronounceable-and-possibly-madeup showed them the houses of the rich and famous. Some of them were so large and extravagant that Frank thought they couldn't possibly be real. He thought that up close the houses would turn out to be half or a quarter the actual life size and if anyone genuinely lived there they would need to duck to enter through the front door. Or perhaps the buildings were hollow balsa wood shells or two-dimensional pictures like the huge billboards that he'd seen by the side of the highway. He saw no people going in or coming out of any of the houses on the tour to give him any idea of scale and disprove his scepticism.

Robert knew a lot about the homes of the stars and during the tour he also sang songs, told jokes and played snatches of related movie and TV theme tunes through the bus's stereo. Outside a house that had been built on the site of the home that James Stewart had lived in for almost fifty years, Robert demonstrated one of a number of his impressions.

'It's not as good as mine,' Frank whispered to Laura.

'Go on, then,' Laura said.

Frank shook his head. 'No.'

148

'Go on,' Laura said. 'Show us your Jimmy Stewart.'

'I haven't warmed my voice up,' Frank said.

'Yeah, sure.'

Robert passed blurred photographs around the minibus of some of the stars that he'd 'papped' while driving past their homes and he rated them out of ten for how normal or 'nutso' he thought they were.

It was an entertaining tour. Frank liked the way Robert pronounced certain words – ve-heer-cle, the-ay-ter – and he enjoyed the jokes and the celebrity gossip and all the facts and figures about the houses that he would forget the minute that he climbed out of the ve-heer-cle when the tour was over.

Elvis Presley's first home, blah blah blah, an acre and a half of land, blah blah, fifty-one million dollars on the market right now. Where are you guys from? England? I've got Scotch ancestors.

Robert stopped the bus outside the gates of the vast Greystone Mansion for more statistics.

Fifty-five rooms, forty-six thousand square feet, sixteen acres. He reeled off a few of the films that had been shot there. *National Treasure, X-Men, The Muppets, Ghostbusters, Batman and Robin, There Will Be Blood, The Witches of Eastwick, Dead Ringer.*

'I love that movie,' Laura said.

'Is that the film with two Bette Davises?'

Laura nodded. 'We should definitely go there tomorrow.' She took out her own copy of the itinerary. She unfolded it and wrote, 'Visit Greystone Mansion' in black (naturally) pen.

Robert drove on.

The Osbournes, did you guys see when Sharon threw a ham over the wall? Tom Cruise, Frank Sinatra, guess who lives here now? Thirty million dollars, the oldest home in Beverley Hills, Shirley Temple lived here from the age of five until her late teens. Lana Turner, gangsters, murder, sex, scandal, George Clooney, Madonna's real estate? More like unreal estate? Opulence. Extravagance. Decadence. Who here is a fan of The Fresh Prince of Bel-Air? *That's right sir, the* actual *house. Any fans of Neil Diamond on the bus? Sweet Caroline, ba ba da. Rodeo Drive, here you go now, ladies, Coco Chanel, diamonds, Prada, the* Pretty Woman *hotel over there, one night is over ten grand, how are you guys from Germany at the back there?*

When the tour was over everyone applauded Robert. Laura tipped him. Frank offered to give her some money but she refused to take it. They went to a diner nearby and Frank ate a burger, disappointed that the portions weren't quite as enormous as he was planning on telling everyone in his post-holiday anecdotes.

'I might start my own tour when I get home. The homes of the stars of Fullwind,' he said.

'Does anyone famous live there?'

'There's the woman in the charity shop with the lazy eyes.'

He attempted to demonstrate by staring into two different distances.

'Ow,' he said. He took his glasses off and rubbed his eyes. 'That must hurt, doing that all day.'

'Who else is famous in Fullwind?' Laura said. 'Apart from the woman with the googly eyes?'

'Eyes Facing South-West,' Frank said. 'That's her Sioux name.'

'Is she Native American?'

'I don't think so.'

Frank told Laura about Washes His Car Too Much, Picks Up Litter and Trims His Lawn With Nail Scissors and all the other people he'd renamed after seeing *Dances With Wolves* on television.

'What's my Native American name?' Laura said.

He thought for a while.

'I don't know yet. I'll let you know when I think of it. You can't rush these things. You don't want to end up with the wrong name.' He shifted in his seat. 'For my tour I think I'll have to make my luxury minibus more luxurious. My back is killing me.'

Frank found Laura very easy to talk to. Their shared love of films made the age gap immaterial. Frank asked about her job and Laura took a business card out of her pocket and passed it across the table. In gothic text at the card's centre it read: *Venice Slice – Laura, Junior Stylist.*

'The journey to work must be a nightmare,' Frank said. 'All the way to Italy and back every day.'

'Ha ha,' Laura said. 'It's near Venice Beach,' she said. 'That's California. We do haircuts and pizza slices.'

'In the same place?' Frank said. 'Isn't that unhygienic?'

'I eat there all the time and it hasn't done me any harm,' Laura said, and she tilted her head and her mismatched eyes seemed to fall sideways inside her skull in a more accurate Eyes Facing South-West impression than Frank's earlier attempt.

He handed the business card back.

'You can keep it,' Laura said. 'In case you ever need a haircut. Or a pizza.'

He put the card in the front pocket of his shirt.

'How is your project going?' Frank said. 'Are you still brainwashing your mother?'

'I like to think of it as heart-washing,' Laura said. 'But yes, the Reunion Project is still on. You know, on the first night you were here,' she said, 'we watched the last ever episode of *Friends*. I remember Mom and Jimmy watching it when it was first on TV and Mom crying and Jimmy hugging her. I teased them at the time. That movie we saw last night? A bad movie. But one of their favourites. And you know how those waiters sung happy birthday to you?'

'Yes,' Frank said.

'Mom arranged that for Jimmy once. On his birthday. He had banana cheesecake.' She shook her head. 'I've had to sit through a lot of really cheesy movies. But somebody has to make Mom realize that she and Jimmy belong together. Neither of them is going to make the first move otherwise. Mom's too proud and Jimmy's too polite. He won't make the move even though he really wants to.'

'You still see Jimmy?' Frank said.

Laura nodded. 'And he's been round to the house a couple of times. When Mom's out.'

'And Beth doesn't know?'

'No. Please don't tell her. Although Jimmy does have the annoying habit of tidying up when he's round. Mom's noticed that but she hasn't worked it out that it was him. He's always liked things to be tidy, which was great before because Mom and I both hate housework. I seriously worry about what a dump we'll be living in, in a few months' time. We'll be under a foot of dust and won't know where the vacuum is. Mom definitely noticed it was tidier after last time Jimmy'd been round. A picture was straightened up and some books were put away, the CDs were back in the right cases and the chairs mysteriously parallel with the table. She thought we had a poltergeist. Rather than believe that I could possibly have tidied up she'd sooner believe in ghosts. It was like we'd been burgled by chambermaids.'

'Does Jimmy know about your project?'

'No way,' Laura said. 'He'd be horrified.'

Frank didn't know what to make of it all. He wasn't sure if it was a good or a bad thing. Should he be telling Laura off?

'Why did Jimmy leave?' he said. 'He did leave, didn't he? I don't really know why they separated. I didn't want to pry too much. Did they argue?

Is one of them to blame? I'm sorry. I shouldn't be asking you all this. It's probably upsetting.'

Laura shrugged. She didn't seem upset at all.

'I wish they had argued, to be honest. They did argue a bit but mostly without actually saying anything. The silences were worse. I used to go and sit in my room because it was too quiet. If one of them had stormed out of the house or they'd thrown a few pots and pans at each other, it would have been better. Exciting at least. I'm joking. But no, I don't think either of them were to blame though. Scratch that. *Both* of them are to blame.'

A thought occurred to Frank.

'Does Jimmy still not know that Beth has been ill?'

Laura shook her head.

'And you haven't told him?'

'It's up to Mom,' Laura said. 'I don't want it to be the reason why they get back together. I don't want Jimmy coming back because he feels sorry for Mom. She doesn't need a nurse. He definitely would have been there in the hospital with her. Even if she didn't want him there. But I don't think Mom wanted to feel like she was helpless without him and to admit that she needed him, holding her hand in the hospital and passing her Kleenex when she was all teary. Keeping Lump to herself was even a bit selfish. If that doesn't sound dumb?'

Frank thought about the time that he'd spent by

Sheila's hospital bed holding her hand and how he would have felt if she'd kept her illness a secret from him. For a long time Sheila had done exactly that. She did it out of kindness to Frank. Maybe Beth was doing Jimmy a favour by not telling him. Frank had hated going to the hospital. He'd grown used to, but was never ever comfortable with, the smells and the sounds of sickness and cure, the miracles and the normality. He always felt like he was getting in the way of the nurses and was forever apologizing and standing up when they came to the bed to check her blood pressure or take yet another sample. And yet when he left the ward to go to the toilet or to get a cup of tea from the machine or a breath of fresh air with all the smokers hooked up to bags on wheels outside the hospital, he felt so guilty. When he left the hospital in the evening, he was glad that the strict visiting hours had given him an excuse to be able to leave. He'd take the bus home and sleep alone, knowing that he might never lie next to his wife again. Even though she'd always complained how he was hogging the bed and she'd sometimes kick him because he was keeping her awake with his repertoire of snores: the 'pig with asthma' and the snore that sounded like somebody dragging an old cooker down a garden path. His 'snorgasbord', Sheila had called it.

Frank was at the hospital with Sheila when the doctors and consultants had run out of miracles and then there were just different shifts of overworked nursing staff keeping her comfortable until the inevitable. Frank stayed with her then because he didn't want to miss the awful moment that he was both dreading and at times looking forward to. He'd wished that he could have taken Sheila home while she remembered who he was. While she would still think that he was rescuing rather than kidnapping her. When finally it was all over, it wasn't all over. He still had to tell everyone and get the death certificates so that he could remove her name from their joint bank account. He then had to choose the right flowers, even though he knew nothing about flowers, and pick a coffin from a catalogue, selecting the colour and the type of wood before choosing suitable music to accompany the coffin's entrance into and exit out of the crematorium chapel. He also found a humanist minister to conduct the service because Sheila would have hated for religion to play a role in her death, after she'd managed to avoid it for most of her life.

Frank thought of all of that and, in spite of how dreadful it had all been, he would have hated to have been denied any of it. Perhaps if Laura did manage to bring her parents back together, it wouldn't be too late for Beth to tell Jimmy about her illness without it immediately breaking them apart again.

He asked Laura if she worried that her plan might somehow end up making things worse. She said she had to try.

'But do you honestly think it could work?' Frank said.

'This is Hollywood,' Laura said. 'Of course it can. I'm going to create a happy ending for Mom and Jimmy. Are you in?'

'Am I in?'

'Will you help me?'

'I don't know. How?'

'You'll think of something.'

The waitress came and cleared their table and asked them if they wanted anything else. Laura asked for the check. When the waitress came back Frank insisted on paying for the food. Laura had to help him choose the right banknotes.

'They all look the same to me,' he said. He smiled at the waitress, who looked like she might have been an actual Native American, and he was horrified that she might have thought that he was referring to her when he'd said that all the money looked the same. The waitress took the money and went away again. Frank wondered what her name was. When she brought the change he saw the badge on her uniform: Debbie.

In the evening, when Beth was back from work, the three of them sat at the living-room table and played Scrabble. While Beth was deep in thought, looking for a word to play, Laura said to Frank, 'What age did you meet Grandma?'

'What age? I can't remember. I'm not good with numbers and dates.' Frank counted years in his head. 'I imagine I was probably around your age. Although this was the early 1950s, so we were both already practically middle-aged.'

'That doesn't make any sense,' Laura said. 'If you were middle-aged when you were twenty, you would have died when you were forty. Unless you're a vampire. You're not a vampire, are you?'

'I'm not a vampire,' Frank said. 'I did say I wasn't good with numbers. We left school a lot younger, though, and went straight to work. Average life expectancy was about seventy or thereabouts. If you lived to a hundred you'd get a telegram from the Queen and it would be on the news. These days everyone expects to live until they're at least a hundred and fifty. I'm sorry, I seem to have got a bit sidetracked. What was the question?'

'Was Grandma your first love?' Laura said.

Frank blushed. 'I suppose she was.'

'And your last?'

'Well, I don't want to count my chickens, so I can't say for sure quite yet.' Beth looked up from her letters at Frank. 'Yes,' he said. 'Let's say yes.'

'So you and Grandma were made for each other? Soulmates and life partners?' Laura said.

'You do become very close to someone after forty years,' Frank said. 'I don't think either of us would leave the room without telling each other where we were going. Even if it was just to go to the kitchen or the toilet.'

Beth looked at him again. She was either surprised

at how candid her father was being or waiting for him to be quiet because she couldn't concentrate on finding a good Scrabble word.

'Mom has told me she had some terrible boyfriends when she was growing up,' Laura said.

'Oh yes,' Frank said. 'She certainly did.' Beth watched, virtually open-mouthed, as Frank told Laura about some of the self-centred and boorish boys and the rude, slovenly and thoughtless boys that Beth had dated.

'Treble word. Seventy-one,' Beth said. 'Now give me the letters bag, Laura, and you, dear Father, can stop critiquing my love life.'

Beth won the game and Frank came last, although he protested that he would have beaten Laura if he wasn't all of a sudden suffering from jetlag after all and if she'd spelled 'agonise' the proper way with an 's' instead of a 'z', and if he'd been allowed 'flavour' rather than 'flavor'.

'This is America, Frank,' Laura said. 'Them's the rules.'

After the game they watched *The Truman Show* on a movie channel and Frank wondered what significance the film played in Beth's and Jimmy's relationship. In a really long ad break Beth tried to explain to Frank for the fourth or fifth time exactly what her job involved but no matter how she described it and what it entailed – abstractor, facilitator, functional activator, micro management, credentialling coordination, expeditor, pagination system operator – it still didn't sound like a real job to him. He accused her of making up words to use in their next game of Scrabble.

When Frank was in the bathroom, taking his dentures out before bed, he kept breaking into involuntary bursts of laughter. He didn't know at what. They'd all laughed so much tonight that he just couldn't seem to stop. It was as though the air-conditioning unit might be pumping nitrous oxide into the house. If he'd died in his sleep that night and somebody had stood in a church and said that it was what he would have wanted, it wouldn't have been entirely nonsense. It was the sort of thing that was often said about entertainers after they'd finished the punch line to their greatest ever joke or literally sung their heart out before dropping down dead on stage mid-curtain call, with the sound of the audience's laughter and applause ringing in their dying eardrums. Frank had always thought it was a corny show business cliché, but, after just a few days with his family, it wouldn't have been the worst time to triumphantly leave the stage in a box. He didn't want to go back to Fullwind. There was nothing waiting for him there other than money problems and inclement weather. He had no great attachment to anything that he'd left behind. All that he loved in the world was here with him now.

CHAPTER 15

There was a new updated itinerary printed and left out on the living-room table for Frank when he got up the next morning:

Batman & Robin *(Revised)*: *Drive back to Hollywood to Greystone Mansion. Gasp at the Tudor-style mansion and stroll around the landscaped gardens.*

Movies filmed at Greystone Mansion include: The Big Lebowski, The Bodyguard, Batman & Robin, Death Becomes Her, Spider-Man(s), X-Men.

Today's Fact: *Built by Edward L. Doheny (the inspiration for Daniel Day-Lewis's character in* There Will Be Blood*) as a gift for his son (Ed L. Doheny's, not Dan D-Lewis's)*

On the drive to Greystone Mansion, Frank and Laura shared traffic accident anecdotes like scars. Laura told Frank about how she'd cycled into a tree branch three years ago, resulting in her almost losing her sight and ending up with two different-coloured eyes. Frank knew about the tree and the bicycle but he didn't know about the boy.

'I was dating this guy who turned out to be an idiot, but a romantic one,' Laura said. 'He rented a tandem for us and because he was the guy, he had to go at the front, even though my legs were probably stronger. Anyhow, we ended up on some side street on this dumb bicycle made for two and he steered us under a tree and instead of shouting "duck" or doing the chivalrous thing and protecting me from the branch by taking it full in *his* face, *he* ducked. What a hero. It's called heterochromia,' Laura said, referring to her eye condition. 'Kiefer Sutherland and Robert Downey Junior have it too and David Bowie and Alexander the Great. It's mostly dogs who get it, though. Tell me about your accident. It was a milkman, right?'

'Yes. I was walking and he was driving a milk float. I was probably going faster than him. He drove into me and I ended up underneath the milk float. I broke my arm and a bone in my foot. Isn't it pronounced Bowie?' Frank said. 'Like Joey.'

'Bowie,' Laura repeated, in a transatlantic cockney accent that was not dissimilar to that of David Bowie himself. 'What exactly is a milk float? I thought it was something to do with parades?'

'That's just a float,' Frank said. 'A milk float is a van for delivering milk. They're electric and they're very slow. It's probably the most embarrassing thing you can be run over by. You have milkmen in Los Angeles, don't you?'

Laura nodded.

'I expect your milkmen are a lot different to ours,' Frank said. 'They probably look like film stars. More glamorous than Benny Hill.'

'He's that guy who gets chased around by women all the time, right?' Laura asked.

Frank was as surprised that a twenty-year-old American girl would have heard of Benny Hill as Laura had been that an eighty-two-year-old English man would know what a goth or an emo was, or that he would be the one to teach her the correct way to pronounce the names of rock stars.

They drove in through the gates of Greystone Mansion and up the steep hill to the car park. They walked slowly around the vast public park, through courtyards and gardens, stopping to sit on benches by fountains and ponds and to look through the windows of the gothic neoclassical Tudor-style concrete seven-chimneyed folly of a building at the black-and-white marble floor inside. Bette Davis had once walked down the stairs holding that hand-carved oak banister. Batman lived here. They talked about the other films that had been shot on location there, competing with each other for who had seen the most. Laura asked whether Frank had ever seen a TV movie that Bette Davis was in with James Stewart. He hadn't heard of the film and he was sure that Laura had only mentioned it so that she could ask him again to do his James Stewart impression. Frank still refused. He said that it would probably come out

163

sounding more like Sean Connery. She asked him
to do Sean Connery instead and see what happened.
Frank looked up at the faux Tudor mansion that
they were sitting in front of and something dawned
on him.

'Do you remember my friend John?'

'I haven't forgotten about Jimmy Stewart yet,'
Laura said.

'My friend Smelly John . . .'

'Smelly John?' Laura said, thinking she'd misheard
him.

'Yes. Smelly John lived in sheltered housing. Do
you have sheltered housing in America?'

'I don't think so.' Laura was still eager to find
out what made John smelly.

'It's a sort of warden-assisted home. For retired
people mainly,' Frank said.

'Like a retirement community?'

'A retirement community. That makes it sound
more romantic. John's retirement community was
a place called Greyflick House. The coincidence
has only just occurred to me. Greyflick House and
Greystone Mansion. It wasn't quite as posh as
this, I'm afraid,' he said. He thought about the
communal lounge and the armchairs, the broken
lights, the noisy plumbing and the sticky carpeted
corridors of the plain rectangular brick building
that was Greyflick House. 'It was really just a box
for old people and I don't think many films were
made there. I won't include it in my bus tour.'

Frank lifted the zip-up travel document pouch

out from inside his trousers, where it was attached to his belt so that nobody could steal it. He unzipped the pouch and took out his wallet. He opened the wallet and found an old postcard of Smelly John that he kept in the wallet like a picture of a war bride or a lovechild. When he removed the postcard the cheque from the landlord came out with it. The cheque still wasn't torn up; that was the extent of Frank's escape plan. That he might somehow still be able to cash the worthless piece of paper or give it back to the landlord in exchange for his home. He poked the cheque back into the wallet and unfolded the postcard and gave it to Laura. The postcard picture of Smelly John was taken in the 1970s when he was a young punk rocker. His hair was green and shaped into spikes and there was a Coke-can ring pull hanging from his left earlobe. On the postcard, Smelly John was standing next to a red telephone box and a London policeman. It was like a still from a Hollywood film that was set in London. Smelly John, the policeman and the phone box were the equivalent of the joggers and the gymnasts and the other LA props on Santa Monica Beach.

'He's a punk?' Laura said.

'*Labels*,' Frank said and he shook his head. 'But yes. That's why he's called Smelly John.'

'Cool. How old is he now?'

'He *was* sixty-four. He died about a year and a half ago.'

'I'm sorry,' Laura said. She gave Frank the postcard.

'He left me this in his will,' Frank said. 'Not just the postcard. He left me some other things too. Some old records, but I've got nothing to play them on. He left me his hats. He had quite a small head, it turns out. There were a few other things as well. No great fortune, sadly.'

'No treasure map?'

'No treasure map.' Frank put the postcard back in his wallet. 'I could send you the records, if you like. I saw you have an old record player in your room. You'd probably like the music more than I would. Do you like the Sex Pistols?'

Even after goth, emo and David Bowie, Laura could still be surprised by her grandfather. She was intrigued and perhaps a little fearful of what he might say next.

Frank told Laura how Smelly John had been to the first ever Sex Pistols concert and how he'd always said that he was going to have their music played at his funeral. When he died Frank hadn't made it to the funeral and didn't know whether anybody would know what music John had wanted played or if they would have been true to his wishes.

'A few weeks after the funeral I went to the cemetery. Even though John wasn't buried there, because he'd been cremated. But still, I found the most neglected-looking gravestone right over the far side of the cemetery. The name on the gravestone was illegible and it was broken and overgrown by weeds. I pretended that was where John's body was. It was the most punk rock-looking gravestone there. This all sounds silly when I say it out loud.' He looked like he was going to abandon the story.

'Go on,' Laura said.

'I took a cassette recorder with me. I'd originally bought it to play a Spanish language tape on. I never got round to that, but anyway, I had to record John's music from a CD onto the tape.'

He told Laura how he'd put the cassette recorder on the ground by the gravestone and waited until he was sure that there was nobody else around and then he'd played 'Pretty Vacant' by the Sex Pistols for Smelly John. The song had been accompanied on the cassette tape by the distant barking of a neighbour's dog and halfway through there was the sound of a backwards doorbell. When the music was finished a man's voice said, '*¿Puede darme algo contra el mareo una piscina?*' Which, if Frank had ever played the tape before, he might have learned meant, 'Can you give me something for sea-sickness?'

'That's a nice story,' Laura said. 'Funny/sad. I could do your hair like that for you, if you like? Spike it up and dye it green. We could get a pretty spectacular Mohawk out of your hair.'

Frank said that he would think about it. He said that he hadn't been in a hairdresser's for a very, very long time and Laura said that, as a trained hairstylist, she had already managed to work that out. She said that he had the longest hair of anyone she knew, male or female. Frank asked if they did old-fashioned shaves at her salon. He said that it was one of the things that he'd regretted never having experienced.

'That and water skiing,' he said.

'We should write a list.'

On the walk back to the car, Laura said, 'You know how you said Grandma was your first and last love?' Frank nodded. 'Mom's never gonna meet her Mr Right because she already has – and he's in Pasadena staying with his brother. Sooner or later she's going to start dating again and I don't want her to end up with another one of those bad boyfriends you talked about. I don't want a racist or a car thief for a stepfather, Frank. Most men are idiots. No offence.'

'None taken.'

'Mom is not going to be able to pick and choose any more. She's an old woman. No offence.'

'None taken. Perhaps we should presume I won't be offended by anything you say,' Frank said.

'Deal. Now do your Jimmy Stewart.'

When they got back to the house Frank was tired. Considering he was in a city where nobody ever walked, he'd done a hell of a lot of walking. Beth wasn't back from work yet and he went for a lie-down in Laura's room. He closed his eyes and he must have fallen asleep because when he opened them again he could hear Beth talking to

168

Laura, their voices coming from different rooms in the house.

'Did you tidy the kitchen cupboard?' Beth said.

'No. Why?'

'I don't remember all the cans being in such neat rows.'

'You'd better check the bathroom towels,' Laura said.

Frank presumed that Jimmy had tidied the cupboard when he'd last been there or that he'd been to the house today while they were all out. He tried to remember what film Laura was making reference to. He was sure that Julia Roberts was in it. It was probably another of Beth's and Jimmy's date movies. Maybe Laura had tidied the cupboard to remind her of it. He closed his eyes and fell asleep again. The next time he woke the house was quiet, it was dark and everyone had gone to bed.

CHAPTER 16

Rebel Without a Cause: *Visit the Griffith Observatory to watch the planetarium show. Pose like tourists in front of the Hollywood sign and next to James Dean's head. American astronomy joke for Frank: How can you tell when the moon is broke? When it is down to its last quarter.*

Movies filmed at these locations include: Rebel Without a Cause, The Terminator, Dragnet, Jurassic Park, Yes Man, The Spy With My Face, Flesh Gordon.

Frank woke up, unsure for a moment again where or when he was. Instinctively, he felt around with his feet at the end of the bed for his hot water bottle. When he was at home, besides listening for the first aeroplane to fly over his flat in the morning, in the winter he'd also learned to tell the time by the temperature of his hot water bottle – the cooler the rubber, the later it was.

There was no hot water bottle. He wasn't at home. He looked around the room. Bette Davis was there, still smoking and advertising whiskey. There were photographs of Laura and her friends, arranged in a circle on one wall. Concert and cinema ticket stubs were pinned to a cork notice-board on another wall beside a large yellow foam hand with a pointing finger and the words 'Number 1' on it. The room was tidy. Perhaps too tidy for a busy twenty-year-old. Frank thought it had been tidied for his benefit. The only mess in the room was his; a shirt thrown on top of his open suitcase and a pair of his trousers with one leg in the case and the other out, as though they were attempting to escape. One of Frank's socks was on the floor next to his upturned shoes, he'd spilled coffee on the bed sheet and there was a circular cup stain on the dressing table, the same as the one that he'd pictured on his non-existent Premium Bonds envelope.

He thought about the far greater mess that he'd left behind at home. Not just the drawers that he'd tipped out in the living room when he'd forgotten where he'd put his passport at the last minute or the clothes that he'd thrown on the bed during one final suitcase repack. And not even the smells from the open carton of milk he'd left in the fridge or the rubbish that he'd forgotten to empty from the kitchen bin, but the life mess that he'd left behind: his unpaid bills and impending homelessness.

Frank had told a lot of people that he was going on holiday. He'd told Eyes Facing South-West in

171

the charity shop, he'd told the librarian, the woman in the post office, the man cleaning the photo booth and the child peeking through the curtain, he'd told the travel agent in the big Sainsbury's and customs officers and airport security staff on both sides of the Atlantic. But he hadn't informed any of his neighbours, he hadn't told the postman, or even his landlord. He wondered how long it would be before somebody – Hilary, the head of the Neighbourhood Watch, perhaps – noticed he was missing and called the police, who would get no answer when they rang Frank's questioning doorbell and they would have to kick the front door in.

He tried to put all thoughts of home out of his mind. He wondered how late it was. Even though he was still incredibly tired, he felt as though he'd slept for a long time. He was worried that he might even have slept through an entire day. The thought of losing that much of his time here made him feel sick. He thought he could feel the heat of the sun shining through the window but he wasn't yet familiar enough with that for it to be a reliable means of telling the time.

He got up. His joints were certainly creaking and protesting like they did in the morning. He went into the living room. Beth had already left for her follow-up appointment and Laura was sitting on the sofa watching TV. Bill was asleep next to her.

'Morning,' Laura said. She got up from the sofa.

As if to prove how she could not be pigeonholed and perhaps as a result of Frank thinking that she might be a goth or an emo, she was wearing a sand-coloured suede skirt and a bright blue T-shirt. If she'd been standing on the beach, Frank might have lost sight of her.

She asked if he wanted some breakfast and he said would it be all right for him to have a shower and a shave first? Laura gave him fresh towels and lined up bottles of shower gel, shampoo and conditioner along the side of the bath. She gave him some expensive-looking aftershave balm and left him alone while she went to start breakfast.

The shower and the shave woke Frank up but by the end of breakfast he was full and tired again. He would have loved a lazy day on the sofa watching television and catching up on what Bill had been up to but Laura had drawn up an itinerary and taken the time off work to be with him. He could chat with Bill anytime. And what had television done for him since the 1970s?

It took over an hour to drive to Griffith Park. They hardly spoke in the car because Frank was so tired. By the time they arrived at the observatory he was more awake. Laura parked the car and they walked back down the hill a short way so that Frank could have his picture taken with the Hollywood sign in the background. Laura stood back to fit Frank and the sign in the photograph. Frank was distracted by something and Laura called out, 'Gaga! Say cheese!' A nearby couple looked over, perhaps thinking that Lady Gaga might be at the Observatory. When they saw that Laura was talking to an old man, because of his long white hair and his eclectic clothing style, they weren't entirely sure that he wasn't Lady Gaga and so they took his picture just in case.

Inside the observatory building, Laura bought tickets for the planetarium show and while they waited for the start time they walked around some of the observatory exhibits. They looked at the Camera Obscura's 360-degree view of Los Angeles, trying unsuccessfully to find Euclid Street and the jogger or the passing police car that Frank had seen on the computers in Fullwind library. They watched the caged Tesla Coil spark and crackle and the gently swaying brass ball of the Foucault Pendulum – which Frank was convinced was the name of a Vincent Price film. When they were standing by an eight-foot glass model of the Milky Way he said to Laura, 'It's called the Mars bar in England.'

Just before the planetarium show was due to begin Frank sat on a bench next to a bronze statue of Albert Einstein and Laura took their photograph. Frank said it would go with the Forrest Gump bench picture that Beth had taken on the pier and he asked if Laura knew of any other celebrity benches in Los Angeles? She said that there was a bench in downtown LA that featured in the film *(500) Days of Summer* but the grassy knoll where the bench was had been fenced off and closed due to state cutbacks. It was the first time that Frank had heard anyone use the phrase 'grassy knoll' when it wasn't in relation to the assassination of President Kennedy.

In the planetarium Frank sat back in the seat that, according to Laura, could have been the very same seat that James Dean had sat in in *Rebel Without a Cause* and he looked up at the screen on the ceiling of the inside of the dome. He thought that he might fall asleep. But once the show began he was completely captivated. It wasn't just the lasers and the sunsets, the big bangs and shooting stars. The man giving the lecture, who reminded Frank of Troy McClure from *The Simpsons*, told the story so well. It was entertaining, funny and educational – even though, much like the minibus tour or the safety demonstration on the flight over, Frank would forget everything he'd learned as soon as Troy had stopped talking.

After the show they went to the observatory cafe. In the queue for the cash register a woman heard Frank say the word 'tomato' to Laura and she asked him if he was Australian. He said he was from England and another woman in the queue sighed, presumably thinking that Frank was Hugh Grant, which is what Dustin Hoffman in *Rain Man* had told Frank would almost certainly happen to him when he was in America.

They sat at a table and ate lunch and Laura gave Frank a chocolate bar.

'What's that?' he said.

'Try it.'

He unwrapped the chocolate and took a small bite.

'*This* is a Milky Way,' he said. He overplayed his surprise, his face frozen and open mouthed. 'It's a Milky Way disguised as—' he peeled the wrapper back to read it – 'a . . . Three Musketeers?'

He asked whether Beth had passed on everything that he'd taught her about how to best and most enjoyably eat chocolate bars. Laura shook her head.

'For instance, with a Milky Way,' he looked at the wrapper again, 'or a Three Musketeers, you first bite the chocolate from the end. And then the same with the sides.' He bit the chocolate from the ends and then the sides of the bar. 'Then, carefully, try and get the top layer of chocolate off in one piece.' He removed the top layer of chocolate. 'You then roll the nougat into a ball.' He rolled the nougat between his fingers like Plasticine and then he put it into his mouth.

'That's gross,' Laura said.

'I've made myself feel a bit sick now,' Frank said.

When his stomach had settled he told Laura the correct methods for eating other chocolate bars, including a Twix, a Kit Kat, an Aero, a Crunchie and a Bounty. He realized that with the exception of a Cadbury's Creme Egg and a Walnut Whip, all his methods were the same and involved carefully removing the chocolate to expose the filling inside. His area of expertise suddenly seemed quite negligible.

When Laura went to the restroom (Frank was already picking up the language) he watched her walk away and then he turned to look out of the window of the cafe at the hills and the sky the colour of Laura's T-shirt and at the Californian sunshine and the Hollywood sign, and he thought about his place in the universe, trying to remember what Troy McClure had told him that was, and not for the first time since he'd arrived in America he wondered how he was ever going to get on the plane back home.

When she came back, Laura tipped three chocolate bars onto the table: a Butterfinger bar, a Hershey and something in a bright orange packet with the word 'Reese's' in yellow lettering across the centre. Frank still felt a bit sick and didn't want to eat any more chocolate but he opened the wrapper of the Hershey.

'Hmm. There isn't much I can teach you with this,' he said. 'You could melt it in front of a fire or freeze it and smash it with a hammer, I suppose. Let me get back to this one later on.' He put the Hershey bar to one side on the table and tore open the Reese's wrapper. He took out one of the two peanut butter cups and examined it, turning it around in the palm of his hand as though he were pricing up a diamond. 'I think what we have here is a cupcake,' he said. And he stuffed it into his mouth whole.

The peanut butter was incredibly salty. He moved his mouth from side to side. He took his glasses off. He looked a bit unwell.

'You don't have a peanut allergy, do you?' Laura said.

Frank held his open palm up and shook his head. 'Just a minute,' he said. He swallowed the last of the gooey peanut butter and he sat back in his seat.

'Silly old sod,' he said.

They went to the gift shop where Frank bought a sweatshirt with planets on the front for himself, an Albert Einstein doll for Beth and a cat collar with stars and stripes on it for Bill. He said that Laura could have anything in the shop that she wanted. She chose a pencil. It was the cheapest thing on sale.

Before they went back to the car Frank posed for a picture by the James Dean statue and then they drove back towards Hollywood. Laura asked Frank if he was too tired to go to the cinema but he knew that she'd already bought the tickets and even though he was sure that if he'd closed his eyes for a second he would have fallen fast asleep, he insisted that he was wide awake and that he was really looking forward to seeing *Rear Window* in a cinema for the first time.

The film was introduced by an enthusiastic young man who told the equally enthusiastic audience about the making of the film and its more recent restoration; then, after a long round of applause, with whooping and loud cheering, the audience fell silent and the film began.

James Stewart's name appeared on the screen and everyone cheered and applauded again. Laura nudged Frank.

'Do your impression,' she whispered.

The audience cheered once more for Alfred Hitchcock's on-screen director's credit and then there was absolute silence as they watched the film.

After twenty-five minutes, Hitchcock made his cameo appearance winding up a clock in the apartment opposite James Stewart's and the audience in the cinema cheered and applauded. At the end of the film they clapped again. Some people stood. Everyone stayed until the credits for the film and also for its restoration had both finished and the house lights were switched on.

On the drive back to Santa Monica Frank told Laura how much he'd loved seeing the film in a cinema. He'd watched it so many times on television. It was one of his favourite films – which she already knew as it was the reason why she had bought the tickets. He told her that when he was stuck in his flat after being run over by the milk float he would sit at his living-room window and pretend to be Jimmy Stewart in *Rear Window*. He was still too shy to demonstrate it when Laura asked him to.

He thought about the cinema that he'd always planned on building in his garden back at home.

He decided that if he went back to Fullwind – *if* he went back – he would definitely start building the cinema. He wanted his garden cinema experience to be like the one he'd just been a part of.

If someone had stood up and made a rabble-rousing speech before a film in England and if the audience cheered every time an actor's name appeared on screen Frank would have found the enthusiasm phoney and annoying; people would have complained to the cinema management, but it was different here. The man introducing *Rear Window*, Troy McClure in the planetarium, the minibus tour guide, even the voice on the sat nav. Frank loved everyone's sense of show business.

He'd only been here for a few days but he liked America a lot and he liked the people. He wished that he'd come over sooner. He was really enjoying himself. He hadn't seen enough of Beth yet but that would change tomorrow and it had been great to spend time with Laura. She didn't seem embarrassed to be seen with him, even when he was showing off with chocolate.

Frank looked out of the car window at his new favourite city. He liked how the freeway they were on was as wide as any of the roads in Fullwind were long and the way that every new road sign reminded him of the cinema or television or somebody famous: Long Beach and Sacramento, Cloverfield, Century City, Palm Beach and Sunset Boulevard, Rosa Parks, Kennedy, Franklin and

Roosevelt, and his favourite: Christopher Columbus Transcontinental Highway.

He liked the way everywhere they went seemed to have been a movie location at some point. He liked the impressive-looking tall office blocks and the apartment buildings of Downtown LA that they'd driven past even though he couldn't help being reminded of the Croydon skyline that Beth and Laura had travelled so far to get away from.

As he watched it all pass by he started to feel a bit carsick. He was nauseous from the chocolate and the peanut butter and from the popcorn and the bucket of soda in the cinema that had both at last lived up to his expectation American-size wise. But he was also giddy from everything that had happened in the past few days. Like a child he was tired but he didn't want to ever go to bed in case he missed something. His brain was sparking and fizzing like a Tesla coil. He stared at the road ahead until the nausea passed. When they were back on Euclid Street, Laura parked the car and Frank thanked her for such a great day. She switched the engine off and turned to face him.

'Listen, Frank. Jimmy might be here.'

'What?'

Laura took a deep puff from her inhaler. Frank didn't even know that she had asthma. She shook it and took another puff.

'He wanted to bring me something for my birthday. I told him to just get me some wine and flowers and bring them round. I neglected to tell him that I would be out and Mom would be in. I thought if she saw him on the doorstep with flowers and a bottle of expensive wine, she'd think they were for her and invite him in. It would be a start. They'd have to say something to each other. Even if they argued or if Mom threw the flowers in his face or hit him over the head with the bottle, at least it would be a start. If he's here, you should talk to him.'

'Me?' Frank said. 'What?' The car had stopped moving but his motion sickness had returned. 'I don't think I should interfere.'

'You definitely should.'

Laura opened the car door and climbed out before Frank could protest further. She'd spoken in such a hurry and left him no space for excuses. He considered locking all the doors and staying in the car until it was time to fly back home. He liked Jimmy and he wanted him and Beth to be together again and he wanted Laura's project to be successful but this wasn't in any of the brochures or on the itinerary. Right now he felt like he'd been ambushed in the middle of his holiday and Jimmy's sudden appearance felt like an outbreak of legionnaires' disease in the hotel pool.

Frank slowly followed Laura to the house. She was already inside before he stepped onto the grass. He wondered if he should tell her that she'd forgotten to lock the car doors. Maybe it would be best if he stayed here and guarded the unlocked car. When he went into the house, the living room

182

was empty apart from Bill. He'd made no attempt to escape while the front door was open. In just a few days of being confined to the indoors Bill had become institutionalized. Frank could hear voices coming from Beth's room. She was talking to Laura. He hoped that he hadn't heard crying.

On the living-room table there was a bunch of flowers wrapped in cellophane. Frank had no idea what type of flowers they were. Next to the flowers there was a bottle of wine. On the label it said, 'Laura's Red'. He wondered if Jimmy had had the wine specially labelled and bottled or if it was just a happy coincidence. He picked up the open card from the table next to the wine.

Happy birthday, Laura. This is Laura's Red.
What a fortuitous find.
It's a 2010 union of Cabernet Sauvignon,
Merlot, Malbec and Shiraz.
It's got black pepper, herb and dark fruit flavors.

Jimmy appeared to be selling the wine to Laura rather than giving it to her as a birthday present. He'd signed the card: 'All my love, Dad'. Frank didn't understand the significance of the flavours or of the wine's year but he thought that Laura would like it because it was in a black bottle.

He put the card back on the table and sat on the sofa waiting for something to happen. He suddenly remembered how tired he was. He couldn't sit far enough back into the sofa to properly relax. His body was both heavy and weightless at the same time. Beth came out of her bedroom. She'd tied her hair back and removed her make-up and any evidence that she might have been crying. If Frank hadn't understood before what Laura had meant by undercurrents of Audrey Hepburn, he knew now.

'I should make dinner,' Beth said.

'I'm not actually all that hungry,' Frank said, trying to help by not making her cook when she was upset. 'I ate half a pound of peanut butter at the observatory.'

'That's nice,' Beth said. She sounded as exhausted as he was. She sat on the sofa next to him and put her head on his shoulder. Frank listened to the sound of her breathing. He thought she might already be asleep.

'How was it today?' he said. 'At the hospital.'

'Everything is fine,' Beth said. 'I'm fine. Lump is gone. Do you mind if we don't talk about it tonight?' Frank didn't know if she meant the follow-up care, Jimmy, or both, but either way, it suited him as much as it did Beth. 'I'm knackered,' she said. She tried so hard to find her old voice that instead she sounded like Dick Van Dyke in *Mary Poppins*.

The house was very quiet. Frank wondered what Laura was doing. He listened to Beth breathing next to him. He tried to detect an audible change in her breathing as a result of the radiation. Shorter or deeper breaths or a rasp or a wheeze. He didn't know what to look for. He wanted to stroke her hair.

'A woman at the observatory asked me if I was Australian,' he said.

'That stops after you've been here for a couple of years.'

Laura came out of Beth's bedroom. She picked up the flowers and took them into the kitchen and brought them back in a vase and put the vase on the table. She read the card and looked at the wine and then at Frank and her mother, who had now definitely fallen asleep on his shoulder. Laura must have been crushed by this failure of her project but then she smiled at Frank and shrugged as if to say, 'Oh well.'

Later on they ate pasta and salad from plates on their laps and watched *While You Were Sleeping* with Sandra Bullock. Frank was distracted from the story by constantly looking from the TV to Beth and trying to compare the actress's mood with his daughter's and hoping to see a likeness. After the film they were all yawning and it was agreed that the day had nothing left to offer other than sleep and so they prepared for bed. Beth went to the bathroom to brush her teeth and Frank put his in a glass while Laura unfolded the air bed and prepared a place on the floor for Bill. When they were all in their separate rooms they called out goodnight to each other like the

Waltons. Frank closed his eyes, the sound of Laura inflating the air bed like bronchial whale song eventually soothing him into a deep sleep again.

CHAPTER 17

In the morning Laura couldn't get the doors of Jimmy's car to open.

'You're going to have to ring him,' she said but Beth said that she didn't want to.

'I'm going to be late.'

Frank watched from the doorstep as Laura tried to persuade Beth to phone Jimmy so that he could contact the car company and get them to unlock the car via their computer. He was thinking how much simpler things were when cars had keys, one for the door and another for the ignition, but he kept the thought to himself because he didn't want to be that old person who said those old-person things. Laura would have joked about starting handles and a man walking in front of the car waving a red flag, then all his hard work namedropping David Bowie and the Sex Pistols would be for nothing. He watched Laura trying to open each of the car's doors unsuccessfully and he couldn't help thinking that he was witnessing another phase of the Reunion Project and that Laura had deliberately disabled the car's computer somehow. Like a nun in a modern day remake of *The Sound of Music*.

Still refusing to ring Jimmy, Beth offered to drive Laura to work in her car instead. She told Frank that she wouldn't be long and he watched from the doorstep as Beth and Laura drove away along Euclid Street, which was actually 13th Street, and thought that, considering Jimmy's obsession about things being in order, it must have made living on it something of a nightmare for Jimmy. When the car was out of sight Frank listened to the sound of the engine fading until the street was almost silent. A dog barked in the distance and he heard either a woodpecker or somebody hammering a picture onto a wall and the constant hum of traffic on a highway somewhere. Or it may have been an air conditioning unit in the house next door. Frank went back inside.

Last night he'd dreamed that he was involved in a game of chicken with Jimmy. They were both driving towards the edge of a cliff when Frank's shirt somehow got tangled around the handle of his car door and he couldn't get the door open. Just as he was about to drive over the cliff, Frank woke up. It took him a moment to realize that the dream wasn't familiar because it was a recurring one, but because it was a scene from *Rebel Without a Cause*. Now he wondered if the locked car door aspect of the dream had been a premonition or a form of déjà vu.

In the real world, of course, Frank wouldn't have even known how to start the car. He'd never learned how to drive. It was one of those things that he'd always meant to do, like getting a professional shave. What was it that people said about learning to drive? It takes one lesson for every year of your life before you were ready to pass your driving test? Frank would now need eighty-two driving lessons. Not only could he not drive but he also couldn't change a tyre or put petrol in the car either. He didn't know how to light a barbecue or set up a snooker table. He couldn't grout or glaze, fire a rifle or put up a tent without help. If there genuinely had been something wrong with Jimmy's car he would have been of no help.

He brought a chair over from under the table and sat down at the living-room window. Bill was next to him on the window sill and the two of them watched, waiting for Beth to return. Passing drivers might have thought that Bill was stuffed if his otherwise fixed stare hadn't followed them as they drove by the house.

Since arriving in America, Bill hadn't exactly seen the sights but he'd been stroked by Beth and Laura more times than Frank had ever managed. Frank and Bill had been living alone together as a couple for so long that there was very little physical contact between them any more. Laura would tickle Bill's belly and wave her hands around in front of his face for him to try and pat with his paws. He'd never been so fussed over. Bill probably didn't want to go home either.

After fifteen minutes at the window, Frank started to feel himself getting cramp in his leg and he left Bill to keep a lookout while he went for a short walk to stretch his legs. In the kitchen he filled the kettle. He was developing a taste for coffee and wondered if he would still like it when he got back home, or if it would turn out to be one of those holiday drinks like ouzo or grappa that became undrinkable when the holiday was over. He took a cup down from the shelf and opened the cupboard above and looked at the neat rows of tins. *Sleeping With the Enemy*. That was the name of the film that he'd been trying to remember. He would have to wait until he got back to Fullwind and the library before he could find out the name of the actor who tidied the kitchen cupboard and straightened Julia Roberts's towels so terrifyingly in the film.

There was a calendar on the kitchen wall. On the last day of his holiday Beth had written 'Dad goes home' in red pen. He wondered how she'd felt when she'd written it and tried to detect traces of relief or sadness in the pen strokes and check for hidden asides in invisible brackets: (thank God) or (at long last).

While the kettle boiled he switched the TV on to drown out his internal monologue that seemed desperate to discuss going home. On the local news a freak hailstorm had covered a small area on the other side of Los Angeles in a layer of what looked like snow. Children were having a snowball fight on an outdoor basketball court while their parents were interviewed on camera in the foreground.

The freak weather was so unusual that the children had to wear oven gloves and plastic carrier bags taped over their hands to pick up the snowballs because they didn't own any gloves. Frank looked out of the window. There wasn't a cloud in the sky.

He watched the rest of the news and a few advertisements with their speedily read terms and conditions that invalidated all the claims made that preceded them. There was an advert for 'senior assisted living' in a luxury retirement beachside home that showed a lot of very happy retired people walking around the gardens and sitting by fountains and under palm trees. A full calendar of events and activities was promised for the residents. T'ai chi, bridge, chess and opera. Movies, fitness and computer classes, mini golf, dog shows, makeovers and chair volleyball. There was a pool and a sauna. Frank thought of Greyflick House with its armchairs in a circle and the smell of school dinners and everyone looking bored. Even though Greyflick House was less than a quarter of a mile from the beach, the sea view was obscured by a housing estate and an incinerator.

Frank thought about his flat. He pictured prospective buyers being shown around and criticizing his furniture, turning their noses up at the smell that he'd left behind and laughing at the bedroom wallpaper that Sheila had chosen and spent over a year talking Frank into putting up. He thought that perhaps nobody had been round to view the flat at all because the building was wrapped in crime-scene tape and the garden was full of television-news camera crews while a long line of police and concerned members of the community spread out across and all the way along Sea Lane, conducting a fingertip search for clues to Frank Derrick's whereabouts. Frogmen were suiting up. Putting on their flippers and spitting into their goggles, preparing to drag the pond on the green behind the library.

He saw himself in the near future, pushing a shopping trolley full of old TV sets past a KFC or saying the words, '*Big Issue*' to passing shoppers ignoring him outside the big Sainsbury's. He'd steal shoes and a winter coat from a cardboard box left on the pavement by the door of the charity shop and find past-its-sell-by-date food in the bins behind Fullwind Food & Wine.

He switched the television off, made a cup of coffee and walked around the house. There were items of furniture and books and pictures in the living room that he recognized that Beth must have brought with her from England. The living-room desk was a present from Frank and Sheila when she'd first moved into her own home in Croydon.

Beth's bedroom door was open and he went inside. The blind was closed and he switched on the light. It was the largest room in the house but still not particularly spacious. Beth's clothes were draped on every available surface as though she'd been trying on a number of outfits before leaving in a hurry for a party. The double bed was unmade on one side and unslept-in on the other.

On what was technically the far side of the room there was a glass-fronted display cabinet. It took up almost the full length of the wall. Inside the cabinet there were various superhero action figures, all still in their boxes and wrapped in cellophane. They were arranged in the cabinet by size, character and movie franchise. They obviously belonged to Jimmy. Frank was reminded of the unplayed-with and consequently unhappy toys that he'd seen on the *Toy Story* DVD but also of his own collection of figurines on the mantelpiece at home. His mishmash collection was displayed with less care and attention to order and detail than Jimmy's and was likely of considerably less financial worth. Above the cabinet there was a bookcase full of comic books and graphic novels arranged by size, the colour of their spines and then in alphabetical order.

There was an old-fashioned record player in the bedroom but no records. Frank wondered if it had ever been used, or if the turntable had never turned and was as sad about that as the still-boxed action figures were for having never seen any action.

Beth leaving Jimmy's boxed superheroes and the comic books on display was like the actions of a parent of a missing child keeping the room of their lost loved one exactly as it had been left just in case the child should ever return. Beth had left at least one side of the bedroom untouched. And tidy too. It was like a shrine to Jimmy. She hadn't put everything away or into storage and she hadn't thrown his record player out of the window and Frank suspected that if he opened the sliding doors of the wardrobe he would find that she hadn't cut all of Jimmy's shirts up either. Frank wanted to ring Laura and tell her of the evidence that he'd found but she obviously already knew.

He switched the light off and came out of the bedroom. He went back to the window where he slipped into his James Stewart impression, reciting lines from *Rear Window*. The street was too wide and there were trees in the way so he wasn't able to spy effectively on the neighbours. If there was a romance or a murder taking place in any of the houses opposite he couldn't see it. He looked at Bill on the window sill beside him and he thought that Grace Kelly had let herself go.

When Beth came back, cat beat man to the door to welcome her. Bill nuzzled at Beth's legs and purred while she spoke gibberish to him in a high baby voice that Frank had always felt too self-conscious to use, even when he was completely alone with the cat. Frank called Bill in from the garden as though he was trying to get the attention of a waiter at the end of a meal. Beth crouched down to stroke Bill and he arched his back, pushing his face into her palm, his purr now like an idling steam tractor.

When Beth and Frank left a few minutes later,

as they drove away, Frank saw Bill sitting at the window, watching.

'Should I have moved him?' Frank said. 'Or shut the blind?'

'If the neighbours haven't noticed him by now they never will,' Beth said.

They counted down the streets until they reached the Third Street Promenade and its shops. Beth was going to help Frank find a birthday present for Laura. He'd never given much thought in the past to what to buy either Laura or Beth for their birthdays or Christmas. When Sheila was alive she'd always made those decisions and Frank's contribution had rarely extended beyond writing 'and Dad' on a card. In the years following Sheila's death he would post a cheque for their birthdays and send another cheque at Christmas. If he had ever read his bank statements he would have seen that the cheques were never cashed. Frank treated his bank statements in the same way as his utility bills. He thought that if he didn't open the envelopes then the contents had no real power.

They walked along the pedestrianized street – possibly the only one in LA – looking in shop windows and when they went inside one of the shops, Frank tried his best not to give off any signals of boredom. He'd never enjoyed shopping but he was glad to be spending time with his daughter. He would have been just as happy if they were getting their nails done or sitting in a beauty salon with their feet in a pool of fish.

They went into a movie memorabilia shop where he didn't need to fake his interest in the things on sale. He looked at the posters and the signed photographs and action figures, and Beth seemed to become entranced, or at least distracted, by the rows of superheroes and villains.

When Frank had almost forgotten why they'd gone into the shop, he found a book that was written by Bette Davis. On the cover she was dressed in black and smoking a cigarette. Frank opened the book to the first page and he saw that it was signed.

'I'm going to buy this,' he said, a little too loudly and pleased with himself.

'How much is it?' Beth said.

Frank looked at the price. The difference in emotions from first discovering the book to seeing how much it cost was exactly the reason he didn't open his bank statements.

'That's a lot of money,' Beth said.

Frank thought about it. He asked Beth how many dollars there were to the pound. It was the third or fourth time that he'd asked her since his arrival. Almost as many times as he'd asked her what the time would be in England.

'I've hardly spent anything since I've been here,' he said. 'And Laura must have spent a fortune on me this week.'

'Well, it's up to you,' Beth said.

'I'll get it.'

At the counter a man in an old green cardigan

told Frank and Beth that the book had been published not long after a book written by Bette Davis's daughter.

'That book was not particularly complimentary. Not the hagiography one might expect from one's own child,' the man said. He was American but he had more of an English accent than Frank. Frank wondered if it was just his work accent and whether the man took his English accent off with his cardigan when he got home.

'The final chapter,' the man said.

'Spoiler alert,' Beth said but the man continued.

'It takes the form of a letter from Bette Davis to her daughter. It expresses her sense of betrayal at the book written by her daughter. The tension between mother and daughter was, I'm afraid, exploited to market both books. Do you have any daughters?'

Frank and Beth both answered yes in unison.

'I have two sons. William and Benjamin. Shall I gift-wrap it?' the man said.

Beth said yes before Frank could answer, guessing (correctly) that her father might be about to tell the man that he had once had two cats named Bill and Ben, until Ben was killed in a car accident.

The man wrapped the book. The folds and joins of the wrapping paper were perfect and he used the smallest amount of Sellotape so that it could barely be seen. When he handed the wrapped book to Frank the paper around it was as tight as the sheets on a hospital bed.

They left the shop and Beth repeated her concern that it had been a lot of money for a book. She said that she would be coming back to see whether the man had replaced it on the shelf with another 'unique signed copy'. She asked Frank if he wanted to get an ice cream and when he said yes, she said, 'Get me one too. I need to find a bathroom. I'll have a single scoop Rocky Road.'

'A single what what what?' Frank said.

'A single scoop Rocky Road.'

Frank repeated it to himself.

'Wait until I get back, if you like.'

'I've bought ice cream before,' Frank said with what he hoped was casual bravado. In reality he was scared by the prospect. 'What do I do?'

'Go up and ask for the ice creams and give them the money.'

'The same as at home?'

'The same. If they're a bit friendlier don't let it freak you out.'

'Should I give them a tip?'

'Give them a couple of bucks. Do you have enough money?'

'I think so,' he said. He checked his pocket. 'What was it you wanted again?'

'Single scoop Rocky Road. Meet me over there.'

Beth pointed to a seated area and went to look for a bathroom.

Frank walked up to the ice-cream stall, repeating single scoop Rocky Road to himself along the way.

'Yes, sir, what can I do for you today?' a young man in a white shirt and black bow tie said.

Frank ordered two single scoops of Rocky Road.

'That's a single scoop two times?' the man said.

'Yes please.'

'Two separate ice creams?'

'Yes, thank you very much.'

The man asked what cones Frank wanted. He looked back to see if Beth was back yet but she wasn't, so he chose the first one on the left.

'Are you from Australia?' the man said as he scooped the ice cream.

'England,' Frank said.

'Whereabouts?'

'Sussex.'

'Sussex,' the man said, unconsciously mimicking Frank's accent. 'Vacation?' He then asked a question about ice-cream toppings and Frank still couldn't see Beth so he said 'yes' to the vacation question and 'no thank you' to whatever the other thing the man had said was.

He walked over to the seated area with the ice creams and waited for Beth. There was a small crowd watching a man break-dancing. Beth came back.

'How did you get on?' she said.

Frank gave her one of the ice creams, noticeably pleased with himself.

'The man thought I was Australian. I'm beginning to doubt my own past.'

'Did you tip?'

'I told him not to tie his shoelaces in a revolving door.'

'That's a very good tip.'

'Thank you.'

They sat down on the edge of a man-made pond and ate ice cream, watching the break-dancer spinning on his head on a flattened-out cardboard box.

'Let me know if you're tired,' Beth said. 'We can always go back to the house.'

'I'm fine.'

'Okay, but if you are tired just say. Okay?'

'Okay.'

The break-dancer climbed an invisible wall.

'When I was in the hospital,' Frank said, 'after the accident, the doctor told me I had the heart of an ox, which I presumed was a good thing.'

'Perhaps it depends on the ox,' Beth said.

'He said I had good blood too. They took so much of it when I was in hospital I was surprised I had any left. I had an arm like a heroin addict by the time I was discharged.'

Beth had been hearing her father's stories for a lot longer than Laura but she would probably never fully get used to some of the things he said.

'The same doctor described my facial injuries to a group of medical students by saying I looked like a wasp chewing a bulldog.'

'I think you mean a bulldog chewing a wasp.'

'That's what I said. But the doctor said, no, definitely a wasp chewing a bulldog and he passed me a mirror. He was one of those laughter-is-the-best-medicine doctors you mentioned.'

'Did I?' Beth said.

'You were talking about Laura and the way she dealt with illness.'

The break-dancer ended his routine and the watching crowd applauded. He folded up his cardboard dance floor and was replaced by a busker who plugged in an electric guitar to a small amplifier.

Frank asked Beth, if she didn't mind talking about it, what had happened yesterday when Jimmy had come to the house. She said that he was dropping off a present for Laura and he hadn't realized that she would be in.

'He seemed more embarrassed than anything. He just wanted to leave the wine and the flowers and go.'

'Did you tell him why you were there?' Frank said. 'Because you'd just been at the hospital?'

Beth shook her head.

'If you wait too long you'll never tell him,' Frank said, feeling strange to be the one offering anyone advice. It wasn't something that he was used to. He was a hypocrite too as he hadn't told Beth the truth yet about how he'd paid for his flights. He had planned to tell her and he didn't want to take the secret home with him. He didn't want to spoil things now, though, and he decided to tell her everything in the next few days. Or on the way to the airport. Maybe he would wait until he was thousands of feet in the air after a couple of complimentary airline gin and tonics. He could write it on a tiny paper cocktail napkin and slot it into the napkin pile on the flight attendant's drinks trolley. He'd seen Warren Beatty do something like that in the film *The Parallax View*. Frank really needed to stop thinking of everything in terms of film scenes. Perhaps Hollywood wasn't the best place to begin.

The guitarist was playing a Jimi Hendrix song, complete with facial grimaces of ecstasy on the high notes.

'Elizabeth,' Frank said. The use of her full name often came before something weighty or serious.

'Yes, Father.'

'Have I ever let you down?'

'Have you let me down? No. How?'

'Oh, I don't know. In any way, I suppose.'

'No, Dad, you haven't let me down.'

'Right,' Frank said. 'You would say so though?'

'Dad.'

'Right. Sorry.'

Jimi Hendrix was really showboating now. He was down on his knees in the tree-lined pedestrian shopping street playing the guitar with his teeth and Beth suggested they leave because she hated a show-off. She dropped a couple of dollars in his open guitar case anyway and they walked back to the car and drove to the grocery store, where they bought pizzas and a birthday cake.

Looking at the selection of potato chips Frank

said, 'I know America isn't so different to England any more. Your cars are smaller now and our supermarkets are bigger. But I think we win on crisps.'

At the checkout the same man from earlier in the week packed their shopping. He used every inch of available space in the bag before opening out a new one. The shopping was packed as perfectly and tightly as the Bette Davis book. Frank exchanged Volkswagen-driver nods with the man again and Beth gave him a tip. On the way out of the shop Frank decided to give him the name Old Man Packing Bags.

Back at the house Frank sat on the sofa and nodded off. When he woke up it was almost 7 p.m. Beth had been out without him waking and had picked Laura up from work and they were both in the kitchen. Music was playing on a CD player as the two women prepared food, swapping places in the small space, swerving to avoid each other and passing cutlery back and forth as though their movements were choreographed.

Frank wondered what significance the song playing had for Beth. Whether it was the first song that she'd heard when she'd met Jimmy or the last song that was playing when they broke up. He watched his daughter and granddaughter moving around the kitchen to the music like Morecambe and Wise. It was striking how alike they were when they were together. And not just to each other; Frank could see Sheila in both of them. He could see nothing of himself physically in Beth's face or any of Laura's father's in hers. It was all Sheila. Sheila's nose and Sheila's ears and, if Laura hadn't cycled into a tree, Sheila's eyes.

Sheila.

That would be Laura's Native American name and it would be Beth's too.

Frank was suddenly overcome with how good it felt to be in a house with his loved ones and at the same time how much he missed his wife. In Fullwind, where they'd lived together for so many years, many of Sheila's things were still there to remind him of her, just like Beth with Jimmy's toy collection. Sheila's things were in the backs of drawers and at the bottom of cupboards, they were hanging on the walls and the paint colours and wallpaper patterns were the ones that Sheila had chosen. But in spite of all the physical reminders Frank didn't think of his late wife when he was at home anywhere near as often and as powerfully as he had since he'd been in America. Even just in the last few minutes watching Beth and Laura in the kitchen, he felt like he was watching a home movie of Sheila. Frank thought how she would have loved to be here now, dancing around the kitchen with her doppelgängers, the three of them together like Russian dolls or a set of matching suitcases.

On the top of the deflated air bed, Bill stirred from one of his many naps. He stood up and arched his back like a gymnast and he meowed. There'd been no obvious change in Bill as a result of his short time in the US. He was still stonier-faced than Mount Rushmore but there was an unfamiliar twang to his meow:

Are you just gonna sit here in the parlor all the live-long day, Frank, or are you gonna go out and fix me some goddam food?

They ate the pizzas that Beth and Frank had bought and drank the wine that Jimmy had left as a birthday present. When Beth had seen the label with Laura's name on it she'd remarked, 'That was thoughtful,' and Laura and Frank had exchanged a conspiratorial grin, both of them regarding the remark as a chink in Beth's armour and a possible breakthrough for the project. Beth lit the twenty-one candles, she carried the cake into the living room and Frank joined her in singing happy birthday to Laura. She opened her presents, almost screaming when she saw that the book that Frank had bought her was signed. She said that it was too much but also refused to give it back. After 9 p.m. one of Laura's friends came to pick her up and she went out to celebrate her birthday with people of her own age.

Beth washed the dishes and then she found a long ball of string and tied one end of the string to Bill's new cat collar. She switched off the security light above the front door and opened the door just wide enough to let Bill through. At first he was unsure, not moving away from the door, but then he slowly strolled further across the grass as Beth unravelled more of the ball of string.

They peeked through the gap in the door, keeping an eye out for neighbours and stifling their laughter at Bill on the other end of the ball of string like a kite. He walked under the tree and then started to circle it until the string was too taut for him to go any further without turning back on himself. Bill sat down under the tree. A dog barked nearby. Bill went to the toilet beneath the tree.

'Somebody's going to have to pick that up,' Beth whispered to Frank.

'Don't look at me. I'm a guest.'

'We could tie a ribbon around it or attach a balloon to the poop,' Beth said. 'Leave it for Laura as a birthday present.'

After a while Beth had to sneak out and unravel Bill and bring him back indoors. She then went back out and picked up Laura's stinky birthday present in a thick wad of paper napkins. She put it in the dustbin and came back inside.

They watched some more TV and speculated what Laura might be doing. Beth hoped that she wasn't attempting something called 'Twenty-one Drinks' that involved drinking twenty-one different drinks.

'She's great, isn't she?' Frank said. 'Laura.'

'I guess she is. I suppose I've been very lucky.'

'It isn't luck,' Frank said.

'Shucks,' she said, and then, 'Hang on. You do mean because I'm such a great parent, don't you?'

Frank nodded.

'It runs in the family. And I don't mean on my side,' he said.

'You aren't so bad,' Beth said.

'Oh I don't know about that. Most of the important parenting decisions with you were made by your mother. I was very much watching from the sidelines, occasionally making unhelpful daft remarks or pulling silly faces. If anything I was a hindrance.'

'Silly faces and daft remarks are important too. Don't be so hard on yourself. You are at the very least okay as a dad.'

'Thanks very much,' Frank said. 'And you've been an adequate daughter.'

'Thanks right back at you. What's the first thing you're going to do when you get home?' Beth asked.

'You make it sound like I've been in a coma,' Frank said. He changed his voice to what he imagined a man coming out of a coma might sound like. 'I'm going to drink a pint of beer in a pub and eat a pork pie.'

'I wonder if anything's changed,' Beth said. 'I hate coming back after a vacation to find that everything's exactly the same. No new houses or stores. Nobody's died or got married or moved away. It makes me feel as though the whole world stops when I'm away and nothing can happen unless I'm there. I don't want that responsibility.'

'I had a dream that the flat had been knocked down and turned into a supermarket,' Frank said.

'If it comes true, I'll have to come and live with you.'

'Okay.'

He knew that she was only saying that because nothing they were saying right now was to be taken seriously and she had nothing to fear. But to Frank, the offer of him living with Beth sounded so irresistible. He let himself imagine that it was true. He pictured himself at the Griffith Observatory and walking around the grounds of Greystone Mansion with Beth and Laura and them all going to the cinema together every week. He'd buy warm pastries and pizzas at the grocery store where he'd become friends with Old Man Packing Bags. They'd meet up and sit in an empty bar in the middle of the day when it was too hot outside, drinking bottled Budweiser beer, eating peanuts from a bowl and watching baseball on a TV behind the bar. They'd play pool and darts and go for wet shaves together at Venice Slice. Frank would spend his weekends on the beach with Beth and Laura. He'd never wear long trousers and he'd learn how to play beach chess – and he wouldn't have any gloves or a hot water bottle or an umbrella.

Bill would be so much happier here too. Beth and Laura would stroke him and paw spar with him. And even if he was never allowed in the front yard, Frank would sneak him out and take him to the beach where he'd walk Bill on a lead attached to his stars-and-stripes collar. He'd seen a woman on the news walking down the street with a ferret on a lead and nobody had seemed to bat an eyelid. Frank would take Bill out on a lead. Or a leash. He'd need to learn the language. Leash, board-walk, trash can, candy and potato chips, popsicle and ladybug. He'd have to get used to walking on the sidewalk instead of the pavement (which was the road). He'd eat tomaytoes, eggplant and zucchini, all from aloominum cans. He'd wear pants, the pockets filled with cents, quarters, bits and dollars. He'd have a zip code and a cell phone and in an emergency he'd call nine-one-one.

It was gone eleven when Beth said that she was tired and Frank had to admit that he was as well. They took turns to pump up the air bed so that it was ready for Laura when she came in and then said goodnight and went into their separate rooms. It took Frank longer to fall asleep without the reassuring sound of Laura inflating the bed, but once he was asleep he was too tired to dream.

CHAPTER 18

Beth sent a text message asking Jimmy to speak to the car company who did something magical and the car doors unlocked and all three of them squeezed into the black sports car because, as Laura said, 'I don't want to throw up in Mom's car.'

Even though she was suffering from her first legal hangover, she was still pleased that Beth had made this small step towards Jimmy. And when he in turn had acknowledged it with his own text to say that the car would need to go in for a service, they were practically courting again. Frank, meanwhile, was surprised that Laura hadn't disabled the locks or simply pretended to not be able to open the doors and that there was something wrong with the car after all.

Laura folded her sweatshirt into a pillow and folded herself into the back seat. She put her head on the folded sweatshirt and Beth drove them to the beach. Laura asked Beth to turn the radio on and then she asked her to turn the volume down. Beth hummed along to songs on the radio unaware that Laura had re-tuned it to a station that played hits from the era when Beth had dated Jimmy.

At the beach they hired a quadricycle. It had four wheels, seats, headlights and two steering wheels. It was only an engine short of being a car. It was a bigger car than the one that they'd driven to the beach in. When the man in the beach hire shop referred to the quadricycle as a 'Surrey', Frank had asked whether it would have a fringe on top. It did. The quadricycle had a roof like the awning outside a tearoom. The awning was striped like toothpaste and it was indeed fringed. As they cycled along the beach bike trail that ran for twenty-two miles all the way from Malibu to Torrance, the fringe blew gently in the breeze all the way.

Beth and Laura sat in the front of the quadricycle, pedalling while Frank relaxed in the back like he was the King of Siam. He offered to pedal so that Laura could recover from her hangover in the back but she said that she was feeling better already. Frank was relieved because, after pumping up the air bed the night before, his right calf ached as though he'd hopped a marathon.

The quadricycle was the widest of the pedalled transport on the bike trail. It cast an impressive shadow on the path in front of them. It was also the slowest and they were overtaken by tandems, trikes, unicycles, beach cruisers, high-handlebar choppers, tag-a-longs, kiddy carts, rollerblades and parents on roller skates pushing baby buggies.

Frank looked at the beach to his right and at the usual mix of joggers, sun-seekers and show-offs. He looked up at the sky. He wondered if he would eventually start to miss clouds. A plane flew over the ocean towards Hawaii or Australia. A walkout by the National Air Traffic Controllers Association or the Fullwind coup that he'd feared when he'd first arrived at LAX now seemed like a wonderful notion.

'That's where I work,' Laura said. She had to shout to be heard above the noise of the pedals. She took her hands off the steering wheel and pointed over to the left. 'Up that street and over a bit. Pedal faster, Mom. I called in sick.'

They both pedalled harder. They were laughing. The whir of the chain and the wheels grew louder in volume but they didn't noticeably go any faster. A rollerblader glided past Frank thought that the music playing in his large headphones couldn't have been good for the skater's hearing but he didn't share the thought because he still worried about pigeonholing himself.

They parked the 'quike' on the sand to the side of the bike trail. Beth went to buy some cold drinks and Frank and Laura sat under the shade of a palm tree and watched the world cycle by, locals and tourists, young and old, whole families riding by in convoy.

'Do you cycle a lot?' Frank asked. 'I hope the accident on the tandem didn't put you off.'

'Not so much lately. But not because I'm scared,'

Laura said. 'I don't have a bike any more. I might have to get one, though, once Jimmy has his car back. An extra incentive to make the Reunion Project a success.'

'I used to cycle everywhere,' Frank said.

'What made you stop?'

'The brakes.'

'Ha ha.'

'Oh sorry, that was *how* I stopped. Do you remember when your grandmother was ill,' Frank said, 'and she was a bit forgetful?'

'It's called Alzheimer's,' Laura said. 'I do know.'

'Yes of course,' Frank said, 'Alzheimer's.' It was possibly the very first time that he'd spoken the word out loud in direct relation to Sheila. Doctors had said it to him and he'd read it in her medical notes but he'd never said it out loud. 'When your grandmother couldn't remember people's names or how to hold a fork she still knew how to ride a bike,' he said. 'So I suppose that thing they say must be true, that you never forget how to ride a bike. Do they say that here too?'

'I think it's an international idiom,' Laura said.

'Right. An idiom. Well, I worried about all the other things she had forgotten. She could ride a bike but what if she forgot what traffic lights were or what side of the road to cycle on? Or what a road was. But she did really love cycling. Almost as much as swimming. She'd cycle to the beach or the shops and sometimes to nowhere in particular, just riding her bike for the sake of it. So I didn't want to be the one who had to try and stop her.' He cleared his throat, surprising himself how emotional the anecdote had made him. 'And this is the really awful part, I put an advert in the newspaper and sold her bicycle. That's awful of me, isn't it?'

'Not if you were only looking out for her,' Laura said.

'But I didn't tell her that I was selling her bike. When someone bought it, I told her it had been stolen.' He shook his head, disgusted with himself for lying to Sheila. 'I ended up selling my bike too because I couldn't really carry on riding it when I'd taken that simple thrill away from her. That would have been too bloody unfair. Anyway,' Frank said, looking for a lighter tone in his voice, 'I don't think I could go fast enough to be able to balance now.'

'You could get stabilizers fitted,' Laura said.

Frank wanted to say that Sheila had been his stabilizers but, luckily, the sight of Beth in the distance returning with three canned drinks stopped him from making more of a sentimental fool of himself than he felt he had already done.

'Your mother still had stabilizers on her bike almost into her teens,' he said.

'Interesting. Tell me more,' Laura said.

'I wish we'd had a video camera. I could still be living off the fees from *You've Been Framed!*' Frank realized that Laura might not know what *You've Been Framed!* was. He started to explain.

'Yes, I know,' Laura interrupted him. 'Like *America's Funniest Home Videos*. Details, Frank,' she said. 'Dish the dirt on Mom's terrible cycling.'

Beth was getting closer to them.

'She just couldn't stay upright,' Frank said. 'There were a lot of grazed knees and tears before that happened. And lots of sulking. Your mum could sulk for England. The first time we ever heard Elizabeth swear was after she'd fallen off her bike. She must have been only five or six.'

Beth was about twenty yards away now.

'What did she say?'

'I can't remember. It would have needed bleeping out on the television though.'

Frank remembered exactly what Beth had said but he didn't want to repeat it in front of his granddaughter. He could remember it like it was yesterday. Beth picking herself up from the grass, swearing and kicking the still-spinning back wheel of the fallen bike.

'Thank God there was no one else around because your grandmother and I would have looked like the worst parents in the world, trying not to laugh at our crying and possibly injured child because she'd said a rude word. *Two* rude words.'

'I though you couldn't remember what she said,' Laura said.

'I remember the amount, not the actual words.'

'She still sulks,' Laura said. 'For America now but she still sulks. And she swears.' She tutted. 'She's a terrible mother.'

Beth was five feet away.

'And here she comes,' Laura said.

'What's that?' Beth said.

'Frank was telling me about how you used to fall off your bike. And what a potty-mouthed child you were.'

'Any rude words I used must have been picked up from somewhere,' Beth said. 'And it certainly wasn't Mum.'

Frank held up his hands to protest his innocence. Beth put a drink can in one of his outstretched hands. She gave another drink to Laura and sat down. They opened the drinks. Frank looked out at the sea.

'What's on the other side?' he said. 'If you swam and kept on going where would you eventually end up?'

'Hawaii,' Beth said.

'Where your people come from,' Laura said, gesturing at his shirt with its elaborate fruit-and-flowers pattern. Her sarcasm was even sharper with a hangover. Frank looked down at the shirt. Laura and Beth laughed.

'Don't you like it?' Frank said.

'It's great, Dad,' Beth said.

'It's like it's rebelling against the pants' desire to not be seen,' Laura laughed and Frank looked at his camouflage cargo pants.

'They are a bit ridiculous, aren't they?' Frank said. 'I don't know what I was thinking. I was blinded by all the pockets.'

When a circle of drummers started loudly banging plastic oil drums and dustbin lids close by Laura held her head in her hands as if she was in pain.

'How are you enjoying being twenty-one?' Beth said.

'I will never drink again,' Laura said. 'One more reason why it isn't a happy number.'

'Have you told Dad about happy numbers?' Beth said.

Laura took her hands away from the sides of her head. She told Frank how there were happy numbers and unhappy numbers and twenty-one was unhappy.

'Recreational math,' she said.

'Right,' Frank said.

'Okay,' Laura said. 'So, you pick a number and then square each of that number's digits, add the answers and repeat. Keep doing the same until you're left with one and that means the number you started with is happy. Eighty-two is a happy number.'

'Is it?' Frank said.

'Yes,' Laura said. 'To find out if it's happy, you split the two digits of eighty-two so you have an eight and a two. With me so far?'

'Yes,' Frank said.

'Multiply the eight by itself, which is sixty-four, and multiply the two by itself, which is four. Still with me?'

'I think so.'

'Add those two answers together, sixty-four plus four equals sixty-eight. Do the same again. Separate the two digits of sixty-eight and multiply. Six multiplied by six is thirty-six and eight multiplied by eight is sixty-four. Add them together and that gives you a hundred. Now split the one hundred into single digits. One, zero and zero. One multiplied by one is one, zero multiplied by zero is zero, and the other zero multiplied by zero is zero. You've reached your final answer of one. Which means that eighty-two is a happy number.'

Frank didn't say anything.

'I've got a headache now,' Beth groaned and put a hand on her forehead.

'If you apply that equation to twenty-one you'll never reach the number one. So that makes it unhappy,' Laura said. 'I've got to wait until I'm twenty-three for my next happy number.'

Frank said that he thought that he understood but Laura didn't believe him and she explained it again, this time drawing the sums in the sand with her finger which didn't really help as the sand was too fine and dry to read what she was writing.

'When is my next happy number?' Frank said.

Laura thought about it for a while and then she said, 'Ninety-one. Mom's is unhappy too.'

'Oh great, thanks,' Beth said. 'How many years do I have to wait to be a happy number again?'

While Laura worked it out Frank told them both about the toys that weren't played with and suitcases that had never been on holiday. The formula was simpler and he didn't need to draw it in the sand. He didn't mention Jimmy's unopened action figures who'd never seen any action though. He didn't want to admit to snooping around the house and going into Beth's room, or, until she cut his shirts up and put his toys in storage, 'Beth and Jimmy's room'.

'Sixty-seven,' Laura said. 'Your next happy number, Mom.'

'I demand a recount,' Beth said.

When the drum circle became too much for Laura's hangover, they quadricycled back along the beach. On a stretch of the trail that was wide enough to not cause a traffic jam Frank and Laura swapped places and Frank pedalled. It was hard work but it felt good to not be a passenger for a change. After they'd cycled about fifty yards he felt like he'd completed his second marathon in as many days.

Later, at the house, Beth and Laura disagreed over who should drive Jimmy's car to Pasadena for its service. Laura said that it would make more sense if she kept it for another day and then Beth could drive the car to work the day after and meet Jimmy for lunch. Frank imagined that Laura would have somehow made sure that the lunch took place in a candlelit restaurant, where she would arrange for a violinist to stand by their table and serenade them with familiar songs from their past before a man selling single red roses showed up. After the candlelit dinner – which would be in a

Chinese restaurant – two fortune cookies would appear with the bill. In one cookie the message would say that *Love would find a way* and in the other fortune cookie there would be a ring. By this time it would be late and Jimmy would have had too much to drink (in Frank's imagined scenario he'd forgotten that Jimmy was practically teetotal) and he wouldn't be able to drive Beth home and they'd have to book into a hotel. Frank thought that he might have been right in the first place when he'd believed that Laura had deliberately *Sound of Music*'d the car.

Beth said categorically no and Laura begrudgingly agreed that she would drive the car 'all the way to Pasadena' after work the next day, when she'd be 'so tired from work that she'd probably crash it'. She'd have to take a detour through 'the heaviest traffic known to man' to Silver Lake where she would meet a couple of her friends who 'would be massively put out' but would then follow her to Pasadena in their car. Laura would drop the little black car off with Jimmy and then drive 'all the way back through the heaviest traffic known to man' to Silver Lake in her friend's car. Laura would then go out for a drink with her friends and they'd give her a lift back home. It was, Laura said, with one final attempt to change Beth's mind, such an overcomplicated ass-about-face way of dropping the car off that she might not be back to say goodbye to Frank before it was time for him to go home or, if she was back in time, she might not recognize him as he would have grown such a very long beard by then.

'It's up to you, Mom,' she said.

'It's okay,' Beth said. 'You can take the car back.'

CHAPTER 19

Laura drove to work in Jimmy's car the next morning leaving Beth time to spend the whole day with Frank. They looked at the newspapers together over breakfast. At lunch-time, they went round to the side of the house and to the rear of the building where, leaning against the wall, next to a bright green child's bicycle, there were two folded garden chairs with toothpaste stripes the same colour as the fringed awning on the beach quadricycle. Beth brought the chairs over to the tree on the grass of the communal front yard and leaned the chairs against it. She put a blanket on the grass.

'Open the chairs out, Dad,' she said and went inside to get the picnic. 'And mind your fingers.'

Frank picked up one of the chairs and struggled to unfold it. It was a simple task but Beth had undermined his confidence and made it seem more complicated or hazardous than it was. He still hadn't managed to unfold the first chair by the time Beth came back with a tray full of food. She put the tray down on the blanket.

'Here.' She held out her hand and Frank passed

her the chair. Beth opened it out like an origami swan and put it on the grass next to the blanket. She did the same with the other chair and they both sat down.

Beth had dusted off a teapot that sat unused at the back of the kitchen cupboard and she'd brought out two teacups on saucers and a jug of milk. Not soy or half and half but milk from a plastic carton with a picture of a mooing cow on the label.

'Shall I be mother?' Frank said, reaching for the teapot.

'Be careful, it's hot.'

'I don't know what I'll do without you,' Frank said. 'I'll be burning myself and pinching my fingers.'

When he sat back in the chair he spilled hot tea on the back of his hand. He didn't cry out and he wiped his hand on his trouser leg, hoping that Beth hadn't noticed, validating her constant need to warn him against the dangers he posed to himself.

They sat under the tree and drank tea from teacups and ate white bread sandwiches as though they were in the same exaggerated Hollywood version of England as the postcard images of Smelly John, the red telephone box and the London policeman.

Frank very rarely sat in the garden at home. One of his neighbours would always appear and start talking to him while he was trying to read the paper or lose himself in his own thoughts. He'd not seen any of Beth's neighbours since he'd been here. Perhaps it was a neighbourhood where everyone 'liked to keep themselves to themselves', which – with present company excepted – sounded to Frank like utopia.

He flipped the shades down on his glasses and watched the sun flickering between the branches and twigs of the tree. There was the gentlest of breezes and a helicopter hovered somewhere in the distance. A car horn sounded and a bird was singing a tune that sounded familiar, possibly from one of Laura's Reunion Project mix tapes. Frank wondered whether Laura had enlisted the help of local wildlife in her project. Now that he thought about it, he had noticed Laura yesterday whistling one of the mix-tape songs in an absent-minded, but probably deliberate way.

Frank and Beth talked about how Sheila used to feed the birds in their garden.

'It was the first thing she did every morning,' Frank said. 'Go outside and top up all the bird feeders she had hanging from the trees. We didn't own our own house but we had about six different bird houses. I think they were eating better than we were too. I was jealous of that robin.'

'I remember writing any new birds we saw on the calendar,' Beth said. 'You called her the Bird Mum of Alcatraz.'

'I did, didn't I,' Frank said. 'I'd completely forgotten that.'

When Sheila became too unwell to feed the birds,

Frank had tried to take over the job but he would forget, or there was never enough food, and one by one the birds stopped coming to the garden. The pigeons and seagulls stayed but they were more annoying than welcome.

'The only birds I get in the garden now are Bill's murder victims,' Frank said.

Beth put some sunscreen on her arms and her face and then handed the tube of cream to Frank.

'Put it on your arms and your face at least,' she said.

Frank put too much of the sunscreen on. Beth stood up and leaned over him to rub the cream into his face. She sat back down. 'Don't you have any short pants?'

Frank looked at his trousers. He was wearing a beige pair of what Laura had described as 'old guy's comfortable pants'. The waist was elasticated and the pockets Velcroed shut. He looked at Beth who was putting sunscreen on her legs. She was wearing frayed denim shorts that might once have been a full pair of jeans.

'There's a time in a man's life when it's better for everyone if he keeps his skin under wraps,' Frank said.

They sat outside for almost an hour. They talked about other gardens that they'd sat in in the past. At their homes in Croydon and Fullwind and on holiday in cottages on Hayling Island and the Isle of Wight. They talked about ice cream sodas and dandelion and burdock, which led on to Tizer and

Tango and singing the R White's Lemonade jingle. They sang a few more old TV jingles and then tried to name all the birds that Sheila had fed in their garden: blue tits and coal tits, robins, jays and magpies, blackbirds and nuthatches. Beth wondered whether families in Britain could still be divided into those who got their TV listings from the *Radio Times* and those who got theirs from the *TV Times*. Frank said that yes, he thought they could be and that he and Bill still lived in a *Radio Times* household. Frank remembered the photo albums that he had in his suitcase. Laura had asked him to bring family photographs with him and he'd forgotten all about them. He hoped that she wouldn't mind him showing them to Beth first. He told Beth and they agreed to look at them a little later on.

When Beth went inside to get some cold drinks and to make a couple of work phone calls she said, 'Do you want to stay here?'

'I should probably go home eventually,' Frank said. 'The charity shop will go out of business.'

Beth tutted and picked up the lunch tray and went indoors. Frank pulled the shutters down on his glasses; he closed his eyes and returned to his American daydream from a day or so ago. He pictured himself now living in the beachside retirement home that he'd seen advertised on the television. He was sitting on the balcony drinking a Martini, watching the beach volleyballers and surfers on the sand below. He looked at the sea in the distance. It was even bluer in his mind's eye. A plane flew across the cloudless sky. 'You'll never get me up in one of those,' he said to the other retirement-home residents on the balcony with him and they all laughed hysterically and a little wearily because Frank was the home's joker. Old Man Packing Bags was there and there was a married couple whom Frank had named Laughs All The Time and Smiles Every Day and two women whom he called Jane Fonda and Brigitte Bardot. All the men on the balcony, Frank included, Frank especially, were dressed in Hawaiian shirts and Bermuda shorts. The women wore flowery summer dresses and sun hats or green croupier visors.

When the Californian sunshine became too much for Frank, he'd go and sit under a palm tree or take the elevator down to the swimming pool. It was kidney-shaped, next to a smaller heart-shaped hot tub. Everyone was either relaxing around the pool or in the water on lilos and inflatable alligators, drinking cocktails or dive-bombing each other. Frank wondered if he had enough money left for a return trip to America. From the moment he stepped through the airport security scanner at LAX in a few days' time until whenever he came back again would just be holiday taint.

He sensed that he wasn't alone any more. He opened his eyes expecting to see Beth with cold drinks but, instead, there was a small boy, about six years old; Mexican, he thought. He was standing over by the bright green children's bicycle staring at the old guy in his garden. Frank smiled to reassure the boy that there was no stranger danger here.

'Hello.' The boy didn't answer and Frank looked around for his parents. 'Is that your bicycle?' The boy's trance held. 'My daughter – Beth,' Frank pointed at the house. 'She's the lady who lives here. She had a bike a little like yours. She was a terrible cyclist when she was your age though. I imagine you're a lot better than she was. I see you've taken the stabilizers off already.'

The boy didn't say anything but he was checking Frank out, looking at his long hair and his convertible sunglasses. Frank playfully flipped the sunshades up and down.

'I hope I'm not stopping you from doing anything. Did you want to ride your bike? Just pretend I'm not here.' The boy remained silent and still. 'I'll be going home in a few days. On an aeroplane.' Frank didn't know if the boy could understand what he was saying. He looked over at the front door, hoping for Beth. He wished that he'd listened to his Spanish-language tape before recording the Sex Pistols over it. If he mimed an aeroplane with his arms out at his sides like wings would it be patronizing, even for such a small child? It might even be mistaken for a Leonardo DiCaprio impression. 'If my home is still there, of course. I think I might have given it away. My *casa*,' he said, remembering one of the few Spanish words that he knew. Frank had lowered his voice conspiratorially. 'I haven't told my daughter yet, and I don't think she'll be too happy about it when I do, but I don't want to upset her because she's just getting better after being ill. I just want her to be well again. I'm sorry, I'm going on a bit, aren't I? Perhaps I should let you get on with what you're doing and go back to my siesta.' A second Spanish word; Frank was more fluent than he realized. He flipped the shades on his glasses down and closed his eyes but he could still feel that the boy was staring at him. He opened his eyes to see him still standing there and so he carried on talking as though he was having a conversation with his cat. 'I thought I might not see her again, which terrified me, if I'm honest. But she's better now. Although Laura, that's my granddaughter, Beth's daughter – she's the lady who dresses in black, but don't ask her if she's a goth; I made that mistake – Laura thinks that Elizabeth misses Jimmy. He's the man with the . . .' Frank realized that he didn't know what Jimmy currently looked like and so couldn't describe him. 'Laura is trying to get her mum and dad back together again.'

Frank was mercifully interrupted by the door of one of the bungalows behind Beth's house opening. A woman came out.

'Hello,' Frank said. He started to get up and the woman quickened her pace slightly as she walked towards the boy. Frank settled back into the chair.

'I'm Beth's father,' he said, and then, thinking

that the woman was closer to Laura's age, 'Laura's grandfather.'

The woman put a protective arm around the boy's shoulders.

'Hi,' she said.

'I'm on holiday. Vacation.'

And now what? Frank thought. Jimmy Stewart impression? 'Right,' he said. He looked at the sun and mimed wiping the sweat from his brow with the back of his hand. He looked at an imaginary wristwatch. 'I should go in now. Beth will be wondering where I am. It was very nice to meet you.'

The woman said goodbye and wished Frank a pleasant stay in America. After a struggle Frank managed to get up from the chair. When he was confident that he wouldn't keel over, he went inside. Beth was standing by the phone writing something down.

'I just met some of your neighbours,' he said.

'Oh, which ones?'

'A small boy. Mexican, I think. And his mother.'

'She's nice. What did they say?'

'Nothing in particular. I think they wondered who on earth I was and what on earth I was on about.'

'We've all been there, Dad.'

Later, when Laura would have been on her way back to Silver Lake from Pasadena after dropping off Jimmy's car, Frank went and got the two photo albums out of his suitcase. It was only after Frank had checked the case onto the flight at Heathrow that it had occurred to him that he could have just brought the photographs and left the albums behind. It would have made the suitcase a little lighter to carry. He brought the photo albums over to Beth where she was crouched down by the open front door, tying string to Bill's collar. The cat turned his head awkwardly away to look back at Frank with his neutral Switzerland of a face:

This again? What am I now? A dog? A ferret?

Beth and Frank didn't hide Bill from the neighbours this time as he reluctantly stepped out of the house. They left the security light on and they sat squashed close together under its halogen glow and waspish buzz on the doorstep watching Bill unenthusiastically plod across the grass.

Frank passed Beth the first photo album.

'I remember these albums,' she said. She wiped the fine layer of dust from the red tartan cover with her palm and turned to the first page and the picture of Laura taken in the hospital on only the second day of her life, with her tiny hand looking like it had been modelled from pink Plasticine, holding on to Frank's finger like old clay. Beth let out an almost broody 'aah' and continued to make appreciative noises with every new photograph as she watched her daughter growing up a year and a page at a time in this slo-mo flip book, from baby to princess and ballet dancer and then to her shy and moody teens. When the pictures ended on her sixteenth birthday with Laura glaring at the camera and refusing to say cheese, Beth said, 'Why do they stop?' She turned the blank pages, expecting to find more pictures.

'You stopped sending them to me,' Frank said. 'I thought that Laura didn't like having her picture taken any more.'

Beth thought about it for a second.

'That's true,' she said. 'I'm sure I could fill these pages for you though.'

Beth passed the photo album back to Frank, exchanging it for the second one. She wiped the dust from the cover. The pictures in the second album were arranged in no particular order. They were taken at different times, in colour and black and white and there were also a few Polaroids. There were a number of photographs taken before Beth was born. One of Frank and Sheila standing outside the church on their wedding day with other members of the family, whose names Frank couldn't remember when Beth asked, and one of Frank and Sheila in a hotel bar on their last holiday together in Portugal.

'Everything in this picture is brown,' Beth said. 'The clothes, the furniture, the curtains, you and Mum. Oh, I loved that doll,' she said, forgetting about all the brown in the picture because of another photograph of herself at the top of a slide holding onto a doll that was almost as big as she was.

'It's probably still in the loft,' Frank said.

'Really?'

'I'm one of those hoarders from the television programmes,' Frank said.

'Bill!' Beth said. 'Twins.'

The two kittens in the picture were identical, although Ben was already more animated in the photograph than Bill would ever be in real life. Beth angled the photo album up at Bill sitting under the tree. 'You look so young,' she said to the cat, who stared back über blankly.

Way to go, guys. You've kept me locked up for a week, I'm only allowed outside tied to a rope. I've been subjected to the most insipid rom coms ever made and a really tedious pop music nostalgia fest and now you're showing me pictures of my dead brother. What's next? Water boarding?

On the next page of the photo album there was a picture of Frank, Sheila and Beth sitting together on a brown leather sofa.

'Where's that?' Beth said.

'It's your place in Croydon.'

'Is it?' Beth held the album closer to her and up to the porch light and tried to bring the blurred photo into focus or see the rest of the room from a different angle like on a ludicrous crime show. 'That is an ugly pair of curtains,' she said.

'How about the sofa?' Frank said. 'I slept on it after your mum passed away. I stayed with you a few times, do you remember? Because my flat felt so empty and I couldn't seem to sleep at all. I'd never noticed all the noises it made. I thought it was in mourning too.' He apologized to Beth for being so frivolous about such a sad time. 'It is surprising how noisy a place is when you're on your own though.' He looked at the photograph again. 'Your sofa wasn't the best place to solve my sleep problems. It was too short for me and the leather made me sweat buckets.'

'Stop criticizing my furniture,' Beth said.

'You just called your curtains ugly.'

'Curtains aren't furniture.'

'I apologize. To you and your sofa.' He remembered how Laura would come downstairs really early in the morning when he slept there and she'd try to wake him up so that he could watch television with her. Beth would have told her to not wake Granddad up and Laura would have to find subtle and clever ways to accidentally wake him. She'd turn the television on really loud or pretend she had a cough.

'She sat on the carpet next to me and ate a bowl of cereal right by my ear,' Frank said. 'Until her crunching or the snap, crackle and pop had accidentally woken me up.'

Frank had watched a lot of early morning cartoons with Laura around that time and the first half of the same two or three films over and over again.

Talking about Project Wake Up Gaga made Frank want to tell Beth about Laura's latest scheme. How could she be anything other than moved or pleased? Surely she would be proud of what her daughter was trying to achieve?'

When Beth looked at the picture of Sheila in her swimming costume, taken in the garden in Fullwind she said, 'Was she ill then?'

'I think she was,' Frank said. 'But we didn't know yet. Do you remember how she always used to get everyone's names wrong? She knew so many people called what's his name and thingamabob. And her stories where every noun in the story was "thing" had been going on for years. The thing on top of the thing was stuck under the thing and so I had to use the thing. I somehow knew exactly what she was talking about, though. We had a private language. She was the only one who spoke it and only I could understand it. I just thought it was more of that. Until the senior moments that she joked about became more frequent. She must have known she wasn't well before any of the rest of us did.'

'She still looks great,' Beth said. She touched her mother's face on the photograph. 'I hope it's genetic.' She looked at Frank and he knew that she was afraid he might think that she was talking about the Alzheimer's rather than looking good in a swimming costume.

'I know,' Frank said to show that he understood.

The last photograph in the album was Frank on the short brown leather sofa under the dreadful curtains. Jimmy was sitting on the sofa next to him. They were both asleep and wearing paper Christmas hats. Frank now knew why Laura had asked him to pack photographs, 'bring memories,' she'd said. He'd certainly done that. And not just of ice cream soda and the *Radio Times*. When Beth looked at the pictures of her mother and father together Laura may have been hoping that Beth would have been reminded of her own happier times with Jimmy. But looking at Jimmy in this last photograph, the two men on the sofa asleep in their Christmas hats with their arms folded and their mouths wide open, Frank realized what Laura had meant when she'd called him her secret weapon. Beth watching Jimmy's favourite films or listening to his music and eating his food was one thing but if there was really any truth in the theory that women married men who reminded them of their fathers, then maybe Beth's father would remind her of her husband. Photographs of Jimmy would be powerful enough but Frank was the real thing. He was Jimmy in 3D. The second time that Frank heard Beth sniff he realized that she was crying.

CHAPTER 20

Home Alone: *82-year-old Frank Derrick is accidentally left behind when his family goes on vacation. After jumping on beds, eating ice cream and watching gangster movies, Frank has to protect his house from a pair of dumb burglars by setting a series of traps with hilarious consequences. Will Frank save the house and the day? Will he get his family back?*

Frank waved goodbye to Beth and Laura and watched them drive off together in Beth's car, missing them already, as people used to say here. He wished he could tie a ball of string to them both and pull them back to the house. He hoped that Beth was all right. He'd hated to see her so unhappy. A few tears were an understandable reaction to seeing the old photographs but then she'd started to really cry; she was sobbing and shaking and Frank had never felt so useless. There was hardly even enough room on the doorstep for him to put a comforting arm around her.

Frank had seen Beth cry as a child but only once as an adult. It was after Sheila's funeral. Beth had been so calm and organized up until then, helping Frank arrange everything, paying for death certificates and breaking the bad news to distant family members and friends when he couldn't bear to tell another person. Beth had kept her composure before and during the service, and even when the coffin disappeared behind the crematorium curtains, she simply bowed her head. It was only afterwards in the crematorium car park when the other mourners had set off for the wake that Beth had finally broken down. She'd wept uncontrollably, shivering and making almost inhuman sounds that terrified Frank whose immediate instinct had been to look around for Sheila. Luckily, Jimmy had been there. And he said all the right things. Frank was on his own last night. Bill was there but he didn't help. The two of them watched helplessly while Beth let it all out, rocking back and forth on the doorstep with her hands holding on to her knees. Between sobs she took deep gasps of breath that sounded so desperate and vital that Frank wondered if he should call an ambulance and, after what seemed like an eternity but was probably less than a minute, the sobbing stopped and she was crying at a less alarming level and then she began to settle. She was silent but for a few last, deep, deliberate breaths. She apologized and then almost laughed as she said, 'I'm an unhappy number living on an unlucky street.'

This morning, Frank had been desperate to speak to Laura alone so that he could inform the project leader that the latest phase of her plan had spectacularly backfired and perhaps all the sub-conscious reminiscing might actually be making Beth unhappier than she already was. He wanted to ask Laura about the photograph of him and Jimmy on the sofa in Christmas cracker hats too. He'd been puzzled by the picture. It wasn't just because of its devastating effect on Beth but because he had no recollection of it ever being in the photo album.

Beth had been quite chirpy this morning, rushing about the house, getting ready for work and making sandwiches for Frank. She'd asked him a number of times if he was sure that he'd be all right on his own all day and she told him to make sure he ate the sandwiches and to drink lots of water. She left a tube of sunscreen on the living-room desk in case Frank wanted to sit outside and she reminded him to sit in the shade under the tree if he did and to put the door on the latch or take the keys outside with him. He asked her if he could wash some of his clothes as he had run out of clean shirts and Beth quickly showed him how to use the washing machine. She put a box of washing powder on top of the machine and said that she would ring him when she was on her lunch break to check that he hadn't locked himself out or flooded the house.

'If I've locked myself out, I won't be able to answer the phone,' Frank said.

'Change of plan,' Beth said. 'Don't lock yourself out.'

She called out to Laura who was in the bathroom to hurry up, as though she was driving her to school rather than work, and then they were both in the car and Frank hadn't had the chance to speak to Laura alone.

Without them there the house suddenly seemed so quiet, as though they'd taken all the world's sounds away with them. He put on one of Laura's mix-tape CDs and sat at the table and looked at books that Laura had strategically placed around the house. Books that Beth and Jimmy had shared, Beth reading a chapter and then passing the book to Jimmy or vice versa, one of them always slightly ahead of the other in the story, like Fullwind was in relation to Los Angeles.

Frank hadn't managed to read a book for a number of years. He seemed to have lost the concentration required and now he only browsed. It was the same with newspapers and magazines. He would read the headlines and look at the pictures and draw his own conclusions.

He wasn't enjoying the music that he'd put on. It wasn't music that he would describe as 'good'. He turned the volume down and went into Laura's bedroom to get his holiday shirts. He took them into the small utility area at the back of the kitchen. He couldn't remember the last time that he'd used a washing machine and, like photo booths, they'd changed. He looked at the control panel on the front of the machine. There were three main knobs and various buttons and a display that was flashing a row of eights on and off like his DVD player at home. He had entirely forgotten the simple instructions that Beth had given him. When anyone tried to teach Frank something new or give him directions he would be listening but the information wouldn't be sticking around for long.

He looked at the numbers and symbols on the washing machine control panel and compared them to those on the label on one of the shirts. Nothing matched. None of the words on either of the shirts' labels were in English and what instructions there were on the front of the washing machine appeared to be in symbol form and hieroglyphics, apart from a few words that made little sense and appeared to be in the same dropped Scrabble board of American English as Beth's job descriptions.

He looked around the kitchen for a manual. In the cutlery drawer he moved a spoon into the fork compartment to give Jimmy something to do if he came round. He eventually found the washing machine instructions and, after ten minutes, he thought that he'd worked out how to do a simple quick wash. 'Don't mix ColorSync,' the instructions said. He looked at his shirts and he wondered how that was physically possible and he put them in the machine. He thought about putting some of Beth's and Laura's clothes in too, but he didn't want to risk shrinking them or any of the colours of his shirts running. In spite of how little a goth or an emo Laura claimed to be, Frank doubted that she would be overjoyed if he dyed all of her black clothes yellow. He closed the washing-machine door and tipped some powder into the drawer.

He pushed the on switch, the machine clicked and whirred a few times, lights flashed, and it filled up with water. There was a moment of silence as though it wasn't going to work and then the drum started to turn. Frank walked into the living room feeling pleased with himself.

'Who says you can't teach an old dog new tricks?' he said to Bill and then immediately apologized for having used the 'D word'.

Before the first rinse Frank was bored again. He turned the music back up. He was listening to more Reunion Project music and looking at more books than Beth. He'd been watching the films and TV shows and was even wearing Jimmy's aftershave; at this rate, Frank was in danger of falling in love with Jimmy himself.

He went and looked at the washing machine, staring at the dial to see if he noticed any movement as it went through its various cycles. With just his two shirts being thrown around inside the machine the shirt buttons slapped against the metal drum. He should have washed more clothes. Wasn't there a drought in California? He felt guilty for contributing to it.

Frank missed having the company that he'd just

started to get used to. Even Bill was asleep. He wondered how far it would be if he walked to the grocery store to ask Old Man Packing Bags if he wanted to go for a drink. He could quiz him on what it was like to be an old man in America. Did he have a pension and what happened if he got sick? Did he live in a retirement community with palm trees and crazy golf? How welcoming were they to old people from other countries? 'Old Man Packing Bags' could have been Frank's Native American name, too, a few weeks ago when he was folding his clothes into his suitcase, and in a few days' time it could be his name once again as he packed to go home. It made Frank want to hide his suitcase. He wondered whether it would fit through one of the ceiling-tile spaces. He went into the bedroom and started unpacking the case. He hadn't wanted to trespass on any more of Laura's personal space by using her wardrobe and chest of drawers and had left most of his clothes in the suitcase. He found the emptiest of the drawers and put in two pairs of socks and he hung a cardigan in the wardrobe. In amongst all the cool black clothes, the cardigan's beige cable knit and brown leather-look buttons were like a parent waiting to pick up their children at a school disco but unpacking a few things made Frank feel less like his holiday was over. He thought about deliberately leaving the cardigan or the socks when he went home. Sheila always used to say that when Beth had left her jacket or her purse behind after visiting them it meant that she was coming back.

The phone rang. The loud and alien ringtone surprised and unnerved Frank and he hesitated before eventually answering it. It was Beth. She couldn't concentrate at work because she'd convinced herself that he actually would flood the house. He told her that he'd managed fine with the washing machine and it was already on its final spin, which was why he was CURRENTLY SHOUTING. He asked how she was and she said that she was okay. She reminded him again about the sunscreen and the garden chairs, the latch and the door keys and she wished him a lovely relaxing day.

After Frank hung up, he saw that the speed-dial list on the phone began with: 1. DAD. He'd never won anything in his life. His bogus Premium Bonds win was the closest he'd come to a prize. And yet here he was, at the top of the US speed-dial charts. He wanted to take the big foam hand down from Laura's bedroom wall and run around the house pointing and shouting, 'I'm number one!'

Ten minutes later, he picked up the phone and pressed the number and listened to the ringtone, imagining what it sounded like at the other end of the line in his empty flat. He wondered if anyone would answer: the landlord or the estate agent or somebody who was viewing the property. Perhaps a squatter would answer the phone, or the new tenant who had already moved in: sitting on Frank's sofa, watching his television and answering his phone. Maybe the police would pick up the phone and ask him if he was a relative of Frank Derrick. Or maybe he would answer the phone himself, like in a science fiction film or an episode of *Tales of the Unexpected*. Frank thought that he might not be the 'DAD' at the top of the speed-dial charts after all and he could be ringing Jimmy. He quickly hung the phone up and, as soon as he did, it start ringing. He walked away, deciding to ignore it. He went into the kitchen and stood near the washing machine, hoping for a loud spin to drown out the sound of the telephone but the machine had finished its final cycle. The phone kept on ringing. The answer machine would surely switch on soon. If it was turned on. He went back into the living room and held his hand above the phone, trying to trick it into thinking that he was about to answer so that sod's law would cause the phone to stop ringing. Could it possibly be somebody calling him back from his home phone? What if it was Beth again? If he didn't answer it, she would worry and she'd have to drive all the way back home or call the police. If it didn't stop in two more rings, he would answer it. After a further five rings he picked up the phone.

'Hello,' he said, expecting to hear Jimmy, Beth, Laura, the police, an estate agent or his own voice from the future.

'Hi, there.' It was a young-sounding man. American. 'My name is Arnold from West Coast telemarketing. May I take up just a few moments of your time?'

'I think you probably want to speak to my daughter.'

'If I could just take up a few moments of your time?'

'I'm sorry,' Frank said. 'I don't live here.'

'That's not a problem, sir. Can I take your name?'

'It's Frank, but I—'

'Frank,' Arnold repeated.

Frank heard the sound of typing on a computer keyboard.

'Can I take your last name, Frank?'

'I'm here on holiday.'

'That's okay, sir. If I could just take your last name.'

'It's my daughter's telephone. I don't actually live here.'

'If I could just take your last name.'

'Derrick,' Frank said. He heard the sound of typing and then a pause on the other end of the line. 'D.E.R.R.I.C.K.' Frank spelled out his name for the man. There was the sound of more typing, possible backspacing and typing again.

'Like Mr Derrick,' Frank said.

'Thank you, Mr Derrick. Now—'

'He used to work with Basil Brush.'

'I'm sorry, sir?'

'Basil Brush.'

'I beg your pardon, sir?'

'He's a fox. He was on television and he always had a human straight man.'

'Yes, sir. If I could just—'

246

'There was a Mr Roy and a Mr Rodney and a Mr Derrick. I think there were others more recently. I haven't watched it for some time. It's a children's programme.'

'Yes, sir, I—'

Frank interrupted Arnold every time he tried to speak.

'He had a catchphrase.'

'Sir, if I could—'

'Boom boom. Do you have Basil Brush in America? Actually, do you have foxes?'

The past week had been the longest Frank had been without a cold call. At home, the cold callers could be the only people he spoke to for days on end. Even though he complained constantly about them, and in spite of putting his phone number on a list to stop them from calling him, sometimes when he was feeling a bit lonely, a sales pitch from an energy supplier or a market research company could feel like cognitive therapy.

'Perhaps I could call back later?' Arnold said.

'I leave on Saturday.'

After the phone call Frank took his wet shirts out of the washing machine and put them on coat hangers and hung them in front of the window of Laura's room, hoping that the sun would dry them.

When Beth came home after picking Laura up from the salon, Frank told them both that he'd done his washing without flooding or breaking anything and that the shirts were already dry and hanging in the wardrobe. It was difficult to tell who was proudest: Frank, Beth or Laura.

In a lengthy game of Scrabble after dinner, Frank lost by such a large margin that they didn't bother to add up the scores. Laura hadn't been so far ahead of him, having played low-scoring words such as 'love' and 'wed'. Even 'reunion' only scored her a seven. Frank thought that Laura must have been looking at the letters before she took them out of the green cloth bag. The game that Laura was most interested in winning wasn't Scrabble. Just how far she would go to make the project a success wasn't clear and Frank expected to see her walking around the house in her mother's wedding dress any day now.

CHAPTER 21

Home Alone 2: Lost in New York: One
day after Frank Derrick was accidentally
left home alone and fending off burglars
he accidentally ends up on vacation and
reunited with the same pair of bungling
criminals. More booby-traps and slapstick
ensues.
Also shot at this location: Home Alone.

Frank wasn't looking forward to a second day
on his own in the house. The novelty had
worn off pretty quickly. Beth left a sandwich
in the fridge again and gave him the same instructions as the day before. She told him to use the
sunscreen if he sat outside and to try not to lock
himself out. As soon as he was alone the telephone
rang. It was a different man asking the same questions as the day before but Frank wasn't in the
mood today and he put the phone down while the
man was still talking. Why had no one rung when
Beth or Laura had been in the house? It was as
though they knew when he was alone.

Frank switched the TV on and started going

through the channels but couldn't settle on anything. He felt restless. He thought that he was wasting his holiday by sitting indoors. He was in California and the sun was shining and it was hot enough to grow oranges. In a few days he'd be in England where it would be raining and everything was imported. He kept expecting the phone to ring or for someone to knock on the door to try and sell him armchair covers or a walk-in bath. It felt too much like being at home.

He went over to the window and watched the occasional car drive past. He sat on the sofa and flicked through a magazine. He moved to a chair by the table and then back to the sofa. Every time he changed position Bill looked up thinking that it was breakfast time again or lunch or dinner time. Frank would stand up and the cat would prepare to follow him into the kitchen and then Frank would sit back down again in a different seat.

What is this? Musical bloody chairs?

When Frank felt this way at home he would go for a walk. He'd been in Los Angeles for a week but he still hadn't walked anywhere that didn't begin or eventually end in a car park. He wondered if Santa Monica had a charity shop or a library and how far away they were.

He went into Laura's room and sat on the bed. His feet were bare as he'd run out of clean socks. He should have put more clothes in the washing machine. He put his Liquorice Allsorts flip-flops on and walked around the house, remembering why he never wore flip-flops. He flat-footed between rooms, going into the bathroom and rearranging the shampoo bottles and the shower gel. Ordering them by shape and size just like Jimmy would do if he was here. He went into Beth's room and looked at the action figures. He came out and then darted quickly back into her room, expecting to see the toys out of their boxes or noticeably in different positions; Superman next to Batman, Robin standing behind Captain America. He went into the kitchen, ate half a sandwich, sat on the sofa and fell asleep.

When he woke up it was the afternoon. He went over to the window to see if the Mexican boy was there. He should sit outside. It looked like a hotter day than yesterday. The phone rang. It was too hot for cold calls. Frank ignored it and went into the kitchen. He opened the cutlery drawer and took out a pair of scissors and went into Laura's room. The telephone was still ringing so he shut the bedroom door. He sat on the bed and began to cut the legs off his cargo pants. He started on the left leg, cutting about ten inches off from the bottom and then did the same with the right. He put the trousers on and stuffed his zip-up document pouch into the right trouser-leg pocket and his map of Los Angeles in the back pocket and he looked in the mirror. One leg was quite a bit longer than the other. He stood at an angle to try and even them up and almost toppled over. He took the trousers off and cut another inch or two off until he thought both legs were of equal length and he put them back on. They weren't perfect but he decided they would do as he was running out of trouser leg to cut. He sat back down on the end of the bed and put on the socks that he'd been given on the plane. They were bright red. He put his navy-blue deck shoes on. He opened the wardrobe and chose one of his loud shirts and put it on over the white T-shirt that he was wearing, leaving the buttons of the shirt unfastened.

He came out of the bedroom, put the scissors away in the kitchen, and scooped some food onto a plate for Bill. The phone wasn't ringing but he didn't remember it stopping. He picked up the door keys and took the map out of his pocket and threw it on Laura's bed because it was uncomfortable and he didn't want to look like a tourist. He stepped outside, flipped down his clip-on shades and walked across the patch of grass to the tree and then he carried on going. He stepped onto the sidewalk and, watched by people all over the world on computers in Fullwind library and through observatory telescopes and the Camera Obscura, he started walking along Euclid Street. Keener viewers would have seen that a blank-faced cat had walked out of the house behind him.

Frank didn't notice Bill and the cat didn't follow him as he walked off in the same direction that Beth had driven to the grocery store and to the beach because it was the most familiar to him.

The street was deserted. There were parked cars but no traffic. The road ahead was dead straight. He thought he could see hills or mountains. He was in California and the sun was shining; it was hot enough to grow oranges. It felt good to be walking.

A few hundred yards away from the house he stopped and bent down to pull his airline socks up. There was no elastic on the socks and they'd already slipped down into his shoes. There was a short siren blast and a flash of lights. Frank stood up. A police car had stopped next to him and two police officers climbed out, one male and one female.

'Good afternoon, sir,' the female officer said. 'Is everything okay with you today?'

'Yes, thank you very much.'

The male cop spoke into a radio on his shoulder. Frank couldn't work out what he was saying.

'Where are you off to today, sir?' the female cop said.

'Oh, nowhere really,' Frank said. 'Just going for a walk.'

'Maybe we can drop you somewhere, sir?' the male cop asked.

'Thank you but it's all right. I'm not going far.' Frank was aware that he was staring at their guns. He'd seen armed police at Heathrow Airport and at LAX but never this close up on the street. Fullwind's police community-support officer Maureen tended to leave her firearms at home when she was on duty. He tried to focus on something else. He wondered if the car was the same one that he'd seen passing by when he'd looked the street up on the Internet in Fullwind library. He couldn't see the number on the roof.

'Where are you from, sir?' the male cop said.

'England,' the female said. 'Am I right?' she asked Frank.

'Yes. West Sussex.'

'Vacationing?'

Frank thought that wasn't a word but kept it to himself. They'd been very friendly and polite so far but they were still armed.

'Yes,' he said. 'I'm staying with my daughter and my granddaughter.'

'And they live in Santa Monica?' the female cop said.

'Yes, just back there.' Frank turned and pointed back up the street. 'They're both at work today. They're probably glad to get a day off from me.'

The male officer spoke into his radio.

'We're needed,' he said to the female officer. He climbed into the car.

'Well, you take care today,' the female officer said to Frank. 'Be safe, be seen.'

'That shouldn't be too difficult in this shirt,' Frank said.

The woman laughed. 'And remember we drive on the right side of the road here.'

If Frank had been talking to Beth he would have corrected her by saying, 'I think you mean the *wrong* side.' But like Maureen, Beth didn't carry a gun.

'Have a good day, sir,' the female officer said.

'Thank you.'

The female officer climbed into the car, there was another burst of the siren, a U-turn, and the car drove off down the street. Frank watched them go. When they were out of sight he heard the siren. This time it stayed on.

Frank thought that he should go back to the house but he started walking again until he came to a crossroads. He waited to be certain the road was clear and he crossed. He decided to carry on going until he reached the end of the street and then he would turn back, but when he was at the end of the street he didn't feel that he'd been any distance at all. If he'd been at home, he wouldn't even be at the library yet. He turned right and walked along Santa Monica Boulevard in the direction of the sea. There was more traffic and occasional pedestrians going in or coming out of shops and walking back to their cars. A woman jogged by and she said hi to Frank. He imagined himself slowly picking up speed and breaking into a run to race the woman. It had been such a long time since Frank had last run. He pictured himself as the young Forrest Gump, shaking the calipers from his legs. *Run, Frank, run,* people would call out to him as he went by, picking up speed, over-taking the jogging woman with ease until he was at the end of Santa Monica Boulevard where he would run under the archway sign that led onto the pier. He'd run past himself from a few days ago, sitting on the bench outside the Bubba Gump Shrimp restaurant, having his picture taken by Beth. The woman jogged so far away ahead of him that just the thought of catching up with her made him tired.

Frank had joined Sheila a few times on one of her early morning runs around the village. He always ended up telling her to go on ahead while he stood doubled over with his hands on his knees and a stitch. Frank was always a few steps, strokes or wheel-spins behind Sheila, whenever they'd run, swum or cycled anywhere. Sheila would be halfway to France while he paddled through the seaweed at the water's edge and Sheila cycled up Fullwind's only hill at the same speed that he came down it. Sheila ran Olympic rings around Frank as she effortlessly triathloned her way through retirement.

Just past 5th Street he sat down on a bench outside a bank and wondered whether the bench had featured in any films. He looked along Santa Monica Boulevard. He could see the sea. He'd walked more than halfway to the beach, which he decided was now his destination. He'd sit for a while there and buy a cold drink before walking back to the house.

When he reached the beach, Frank sat down on a seat whittled from a tree stump next to the bike-hire shop and looked at the beach and the sea.

He was out of breath. From here the Ferris wheel and the roller coaster on the pier looked even more like a giant Mouse Trap game. It was impossible to think of Mouse Trap without also thinking of Smelly John and the times they'd played, but very rarely completed, the game together in the dimly lit communal lounge of Greyflick House. Smelly John loved board games and especially those that involved chaos or collapse: Jenga, KerPlunk or Buckaroo! Anything to disturb the peace of the other more resigned residents in the lounge of the sheltered housing complex. On the day that Frank found out that Smelly John had died, he was on his way to take John to the park to play on the huge board games that had been set up there. There was a Connect 4 as tall as a man, Jenga bricks the size of house bricks and an enormous Mouse Trap game, but it was nowhere near as large as the one that Frank was looking at now. Frank wished that John was here to see it.

He looked at the men playing chess on the beach. They must have hated having their centuries-old game of skill and strategy, the game of kings and scientists, looked down upon by the garish colours of a game renowned for its inability to ever achieve its object, to trap a mouse.

He got his breath back but he felt quite tired. Frank had once asked Sheila what would happen if she ever swam too far out to sea and was too exhausted to make it back to the shore and Sheila had said that she only ever swam half the distance that she was capable of. She always saved enough energy to get back. If she had ever miscalculated and swam past that halfway point she would just keep on going until she was in France. Frank had passed his halfway point somewhere between 9th and 8th Streets but he'd kept on walking and now he thought that he might not have left himself enough energy to walk back to the house.

He looked along the beach and back in the direction from which he'd come and he considered his options. He could sit and wait until he felt strong enough to walk to the house; with a bit of luck the police would stop him again and this time he would accept their offer of a lift. He could find a telephone and ring Beth and ask her to come and get him but he didn't have her work number. He couldn't even call the house, the one phone number that he ever rang, because even if he could remember the number, Bill didn't have the opposable thumbs to answer it.

Frank thought about hiring a bike and cycling back to the house. As it was the least sensible of his options so far he considered it in more detail, looking at the different kinds of bike outside the hire shop and wondering which would be the most suitable for him. He decided on a beach cruiser with high sit-up-and-beg handlebars shaped like a wishbone. The bike was painted in a green-and-khaki camouflage pattern, designed to blend into a different war than what was left of Frank's chocolate-chip and cookie-dough trousers. The bike had a crossbar that was wider than any crossbar on a British bicycle. It looked more like the petrol tank on a motorbike.

Frank put his hand in his pocket for his zip-up document pouch and his hand came out the other side. He looked down at the tips of his fingers sticking out from the bottom of the trouser pocket. He had obviously cut the bottom of the pocket off back at the house and the pouch had fallen out. He started to panic, wondering where it had fallen out. Had it dropped onto the floor before he'd left? Or was it somewhere between Beth's house and the whittled tree stump where he now sat? His passport was in the document pouch with his money. He should turn back now. Retrace his steps on Santa Monica Boulevard and hope that he could find it. Maybe a kind soul would have already handed it in to a shopkeeper who would have written out a 'lost wallet found' sign and stuck it in the shop window. He felt the other pockets to be certain that he had lost the document pouch. In the breast pocket of his shirt he found Laura's business card. It had been through the same wash and spin cycle as the shirt and Frank couldn't read the address or the telephone number. He looked along the beach where they'd quadricycled. 'Up that street and over a bit,' Laura had said and she'd pointed. Frank didn't know how far 'over a bit' was, of course, and she may have meant up that street and over a bit in Phoenix or in New Mexico, but the journey in the back of the quike had at least felt shorter than the walk from Euclid Street and so Frank decided to see if he could find Venice Slice and his granddaughter.

CHAPTER 22

If Frank had brought his map with him he might have found a shorter route to Venice Slice than the Ocean Front Walk that ran alongside the beach bike trail and, once he'd crossed beaches from Santa Monica to Venice, he wouldn't have needed to be concerned with looking like a tourist. In amongst all the men with no teeth, the fire eaters, sword swallowers, sand sculptors and pavement artists, the bodybuilders with skin the colour and texture of clementines, the huge men riding tiny bicycles, the tattooed and the pierced, the hippies, the stoners, the acid casualties and the Vietnam vets, the drummers, the three-stringed-guitar players, street pianists and those dancing to the music inside their own heads; in his cut-down cargo pants with one leg longer than the other, his bright red airline socks, one of which had completely disappeared into his shoe, and his long white hair and shirt of many colours open to the waist and flapping in the breeze behind him like the cape of a superhero, Frank looked like he'd lived here for years.

If he'd opened the map out on the sand of Venice

Beach and started asking people for directions they would have thought he was another street-performance artist. When he got home, if he knew the right thing to type into the Internet, he would probably find a video of himself: 'Guy Can't Fold Map Back Up', 'World's Oldest Hippy' or 'Lost Australian Dude'. It would be his Native American YouTube name, his SiouxTube name. He might even end up in one of the Venice Beach boardwalk murals.

As he walked past another tattoo parlour or medical marijuana store, somebody called out, 'Gerry Garcia man!'

He turned to see a young man in baggy jeans with holes in the knees smiling broadly at him. Until he'd seen the man smile Frank had thought Gerry Garcia might be a Spanish insult. He returned the smile and walked on, wondering what a Gerry Garcia man was. He'd already been walking for forty-five minutes looking for a land-mark, a frozen yoghurt stand or a basketball court that was recognizable from the quike ride, but everything was new to him.

He stopped to rearrange his airline socks and a woman a lot younger than him, but with hair just as white, offered to paint his portrait on a grain of rice for fifty dollars. She was standing behind one of the tabletop street stalls that lined the beach side of the boardwalk and she held her open palm out across the table to show Frank the rice that his face would be painted on. He couldn't even see the grain of rice. He said no thank you and started walking again.

His legs hurt now. His calves were stiff and his knees sore. When he'd bent down to adjust his socks it felt as though he was stretching his calves to the point where they might actually snap. His back was stiff too and he knew that when he finally sat down the change of position was going to be difficult. The discomfort of standing up again would be even worse. So he carried on walking.

He was thirsty and the only person on the board-walk without a bottle of water. He hadn't eaten anything other than half a sandwich and he was feeling hungry. Shops and stalls taunted him with their offers of ice-cold drinks, frozen yoghurts, ice creams and foot massages. He thought of his wallet lying on the living-room floor or in the hands of the local cops as they passed it around the station, laughing at his passport photograph. When he remembered that his Smelly John punk postcard was also lost, it made him feel physically sick. He regretted not turning back to look for it now. Why did he always make such bad decisions? A man cycled by wearing a Princess Leia bikini and a short fur coat. He was probably once a lost tourist. The boardwalk seemed very crowded and dangerous all of a sudden. Some of the more colourful free-spirited beach eccentrics had started to just look mad. Even without any money or a passport, Frank was nervous about being robbed. He walked past another row of tabletop stalls: a badge maker, jewellery, candles too ornate to be lit and a man making model aircraft and bicycles from drinks cans.

When he reached the outdoor beach gym he saw a small crowd had gathered to watch bodybuilders lifting their own weight in iron. Frank had at last found his landmark. A similar, smaller outdoor gym had been opened a year ago in the park on the edge of Fullwind but it was rarely used other than as a place for the bored local teenagers to sit and smoke cigarettes.

The beach gym was surrounded by a blue metal fence. A line of people stood outside the fence and watched the half a dozen men and one woman working out. It reminded Frank of the zoo. When Beth had gone to buy drinks on Sunday she'd said that she was going to 'the cafe over by Muscle Beach'. This was the closest that Frank had been to knowing where he was. He'd walked too far but if he turned around and walked one or two streets along he would be close to where Laura worked.

He went back along the boardwalk until he reached a gap between buildings and walked through it onto a short but wide pedestrian market-place, where a man tried to sell him some falafel. He went past a cafe, a sunglasses shop and a bicycle- and surfboard-hire shop until he was on a larger street. He took the business card out of his shirt pocket and tried to read the salon address. He looked up at the buildings for a street name sign to match the smudge on the business card

264

but only saw signs for tattoos and piercings, more sunglasses and bike rentals.

If the street looked familiar to Frank it was from the cinema again. Orson Welles had filmed a famously long opening tracking shot here for *Touch of Evil* which Frank was unwittingly retracing as he made his way along Windward Avenue, dipping in and out of the pillared archways to look in shop windows, hoping that the next tattoo parlour or sunglasses shop would be a hair salon and pizza parlour.

At a large crossroads the word 'VENICE' was strung between buildings in individual unlit neon letters. From Frank's point of view, the letters were in reverse like an ambulance sign. The sign marked the original Gateway to Venice Beach. Before the canals had been filled in and paved over in 1929 he would have been underwater or onboard a gondola. He was convinced that this was the street where Laura worked and decided to follow it a bit further but it soon became more residential and it seemed less likely that he would find the hair salon. He'd lost track of time. How long had he been walking for? When did he leave the house? Two hours ago? Three? He had four clocks on Laura's dressing table but no wristwatch. He thought that it might be getting dark. Or cloudy. If there was a hailstorm Beth might see him on the news and come and rescue him. He flipped the shades up on his glasses and gained an hour of daylight.

There were no other signs of life on the street now. He looked up at the sky, thinking about waving at the Camera Obscura or Google Earth. If the right person was watching he could take off his shirt and semaphore an SOS. He came to another crossroads. There was a white-painted church building on the corner opposite him. He regretted turning away so many religious evangelists and Bible thumpers from his doorstep back at home. If he knocked on the door of the church to ask for sanctuary or a lift and they slammed the door in his face it would be a form of karma. When he reached the church he found that it had been converted into apartments.

He stopped and consulted his inner compass. If he turned left he would be heading back towards Euclid Street or at least in that general direction. He walked up the street; it was shorter than the one he'd left and there was either a school playground or an empty car park at the end of it.

He brushed his cheek with the back of his hand. He had the sensation of a hair tickling his face. He picked at it with his thumb and forefinger and tried to focus his vision on the hair, his eyes facing south, west, north and east, but he couldn't see it. He brushed at his face again and pushed his bottom lip up over his top lip and blew. The hair was still there. It felt like the single thread of a spider's web that he'd walked through on his garden path on a muggy day. While he'd been concentrating on the hair Frank hadn't noticed a man walking towards him. He was walking a lot faster than Frank and in ten seconds their paths would meet. He had to decide quickly whether to ask for help or cross over to the other side of the street to avoid him. Frank assessed, judged and stereotyped the approaching man. He marked him out of ten like a gymnast or a ballroom dancer, giving him points for threat, risk and danger. When they were a few yards apart Frank was about to say hello when the man stepped off the sidewalk and crossed the road, quickening his pace away from Frank, having himself assessed the risk of the crazy-looking old dude with the long white hair and peculiar clothing, breathing heavily, staring wildly in all directions and hitting himself repeatedly in the face, and given Frank a perfect set of tens.

Frank continued to the end of the street and turned right at the playground. It was deserted but for a dog running around the perimeter of the fence trying to work out how to escape. Frank knew how he felt. He heard a siren far off in the distance and listened to it drop in volume. The cavalry weren't coming. He was alone. He stopped by the playground fence. However fiercely independent, proud and stubbornly bloody-minded he was, he had to admit it. He was lost. He could walk the streets of Los Angeles for days and never find his way back to Beth's house. He'd miss the trip to Universal Studios that he had been so looking forward to, even though on Santa Monica

Pier he'd claimed that a revolving door made him dizzy in order to avoid riding on a children's merry-go-round. He might even miss his flight home. He was the baggage handlers' dispute or Icelandic eruption that he'd wished for. He spoke to the dog behind the fence and the dog growled and started barking. Frank moved quickly away.

He'd heard horror stories about people just like him being picked up by the police when they were found aimlessly walking where they didn't belong, lost and confused with no identification. They ended up in institutions for years protesting their sanity, never to be seen again by their distraught families, who, years later, would still be out searching for them, printing leaflets and keeping their bedrooms on hold in case they ever returned. Frank might end up in an asylum or sleeping on the beach where he would need to find his signature boardwalk eccentricity, whether it was cycling up and down in a gold bikini or plucking a one-stringed banjo. When you're surrounded by crazy people the best way to make yourself invisible and to stay safe was to stand out and, based on the reaction of the man who had just passed him, Frank was already halfway there.

Halfway there. Time to turn back. Swim back to the shore where there's a towel waiting for him. Sheila.

His whole body seemed to be oozing clammy sweat now and his skin was itching. He hadn't put on the sunscreen when Beth had told him to and his skin would soon be as red as the airline socks, which had now completely disappeared inside his shoes. There was a blister forming at the back of the heel of his right foot and he'd been walking with a limp since passing under the Venice sign.

He tried to think about something positive. He thought about the beachside retirement home from the TV and the sun setting over the sea while he drank Martinis on the balcony. Old Man Packing Bags had started a conga around the pool and Frank took the elevator down to join on to the back of it as they snaked their way around the pool, picking up more pensioners along the way, high-kicking and shouting 'hey' and 'la la la la' on their route between the palm trees and around the fountains in their Hawaiians and Bermudas. Assisted living. That was what he needed right now.

He'd always expected that it would be Alzheimer's, Parkinson's, pneumonia or a stroke which would be the name of his downfall. Diabetes, maybe, heart failure, osteoporosis or some new strain of flu. A peanut stuck in his throat, even. But not this. He hadn't anticipated that popping out for a walk and getting lost would be the cause of his demise. If someone had stood at the front of a church and said that this was what he would have wanted, it would have been untrue.

Frank hadn't written a will. Of course he hadn't written a will. He hadn't quite got around to it. He'd left no instructions for how he should be buried or cremated or where his remains should be scattered. He hadn't asked to be buried at sea or fired into space in a rocket. There was no Frank Derrick exit-music playlist. Something loud, he now thought. One of Laura's favourite bands. Loud enough to literally wake the dead. He hated the idea of Beth having to choose between an oak or an elm coffin or to be made to feel like the worst person in all the world by selecting the cheaper option of a chipboard veneered casket with only 'brass-look' handles.

He worried about what would happen to Britain's largest mantelpiece zoo. Would it be bulldozed and paved over with the rest of his flat, like the Venice Beach canals in whatever year that was? He couldn't remember. His worldly goods might not be worth a great deal but he would have liked to have known that they might at least have formed the basis of a new charity-shop window display. Even Smelly John had left a will and all he had were a few old punk rock records, a postcard and some small hats. Frank wished that he had a pencil and a piece of paper so that he could write something now. He didn't have a lot to bequeath but he could at least say goodbye to Beth and Laura and write down his name for whoever discovered his exhausted, sunburned skeleton.

He wasn't doing so well at thinking positive thoughts.

Frank had been walking for such a long time now. He was panting like a puppy in a locked car and the waves of nausea had become more frequent and turbulent with every step further into the unknown. The streets that had looked so mathematically and geometrically mapped out on the computer in Fullwind library felt like a maze. He wondered how long jetlag took to really establish itself. Could he be experiencing the symptoms this far into his time in the new time zone? His mouth was watering and he felt sick. He was having difficulty concentrating, he was lightheaded and he was disorientated and anxious. The clumsiness was already there before he'd left the house and the muscle soreness had just become more pronounced. Would he feel this way until he reset his body clock by going home? As lost and alone as he currently felt, the thought of going home was still one he didn't relish.

He'd walked onto a street that looked like a dead end. He turned back and started walking in the direction that he'd just come. His inner compass had been shaken up and stamped on and someone was holding a magnet over it. He had no idea where he was going at all now. Another man was walking towards him and he decided definitely to ask for help but, before he could speak, the two men had bumped into each other. There was a sound of breaking glass.

'What the fuck.' The man, who Frank could now see looked as crazy as he probably did, was staring wildly at him. 'You smashed my drink. Now what you gonna do?'

Frank looked at the brown paper bag on the

ground and the broken glass at the open end. There was a trickle of yellowish liquid.

'I'm sorry,' Frank said.

'Are you going to pay for my drink now? Is that it?' The man was very close to Frank. He had hair the colour and texture of a scouring pad and a face that was also purple and grey. The man smelled of cheese.

'I'm sorry,' Frank said. 'I don't have any money.' He put his hand in his pocket and out through the other side. It seemed to confuse the man, who looked at Frank's fingers that he waggled through the hole in his pocket like the 'Sooty in the nude' joke that he used to do for Beth when she was a child. The man with the pots-and-pans face said something unintelligible and shook his head; he might have spat and then walked away. Frank did the same, in the opposite direction and as fast as his tired, blistered feet would allow. He turned the corner and crossed the road, trying to put some distance between him and the angry man. Even in his disoriented state Frank knew that he was being scammed and the broken bottle was full of something the same colour as whiskey that may have started life as whiskey but wasn't whiskey any more and the man had bumped into him on purpose. Years of practice with people on the phone and at his front door attempting to sell him walk-in baths and Jesus had hardened him to grifters.

The single thread of spider's silk was now a full

web. He thought that he was going blind. He took his glasses off and wiped them on his shirt to remove the blurriness but when he put the glasses back on his vision was just as blurred. He wiped the glasses again. He saw spots. Sheila used to get migraines. He missed her so much. He was going to start feeding the birds again when he got home. There was a ringing in his ears that he hadn't noticed before. He would write the names of the birds on the calendar. He had fierce heartburn and his mouth was watering. He felt like he'd been eating Opal Fruits. *Made to make your mouth water.* He'd sung that jingle in the garden with Beth. Up ahead he thought that he saw Laura driving towards him in Jimmy's black sports car. *Patrick Bergin!* he suddenly thought. That was the name of the actor in *Sleeping with the Enemy*, and then his vision changed from emo to goth and he collapsed like a Glasgow tower block. When he hit the ground, a nearby bicycle fell over. LA's butterfly effect.

CHAPTER 23

There was no hot water bottle and there were no planes overhead to tell him what time it was. He looked for the smoking Bette Davis and his four clocks on the dressing table: New York, London, Paris and Berlin, but they weren't there. He couldn't see the foam finger and he didn't feel like number one of anything at the moment. Although lying flat on his back on the pavement – no, on the sidewalk – he felt marginally better than he had when he'd been walking. It was a relief not to be moving. He waited for his life to flash before him. Eighty-two years was a long time. Would it take longer to flash by than if he'd died ten years earlier or would his life montage flash by really quickly? He waited to see himself being born and growing up and meeting Sheila and Beth being born and Laura and Smelly John and the women in the charity shop and on the bus to the big Sainsbury's. He'd watch himself make all his ill-considered and ill-conceived mistakes all over again until today's final spectacular blunder before he was reunited with Sheila like dead

Leonardo DiCaprio and old Kate Winslet on the sunk *Titanic* at the end of the film.

The sky was so blue and everything seemed so still. It wasn't as dark as he'd thought it was. There were sounds and a siren, this time increasing in volume. Frank looked up at the man looking down at him. Was this God? He really should have been more patient with those missionaries on his doorstep. Or was this an out-of-body experience? He looked up at his departing soul looking down on his empty body like he was scrolling through the streets of Los Angeles on the computer in the library when he was still alive. He was confused. Where was the tunnel, where was the light? The man looking down at him had such a friendly face. Concerned but smiling. It was a reassuring face. He had a beard, like God's, but not so white. The few white hairs in his beard were the only real signs that he had aged in the five years since Frank had last seen Jimmy. He was holding a cell phone to the side of his friendly, smiling, concerned, and yet reassuring, face.

'It's okay,' he said. 'I've found him.'

CHAPTER 24

Beth would later tell Frank how she had rung three times in half an hour with no answer and so she'd left work and driven back to an empty house. She'd found the sunscreen on the desk and the half-sandwich and the document pouch containing Frank's wallet and passport on the floor of Laura's bedroom. On the bed there was a map of Los Angeles, a pair of flip-flops and the legs from Frank's cargo pants. Beth had panicked. She didn't know what to think. Frank hadn't left a note, just a series of random clues. There was a pen next to a pad of paper on the living-room desk with the sunscreen. Surely he would have left her a note. She checked the other rooms, looking under the beds and, for some reason, inside the washing machine. All she found was one of Frank's wet socks and the smell of a spring meadow. At least he'd used fabric softener.

Beth searched outside. There was nowhere to hide in the space. She looked up at the branches of the tree because you never really knew with her father. She knocked on her neighbours' doors and asked if they'd seen him. The Mexican woman said that she'd met him the day before but had not seen him since. Beth walked up and down the street, not wanting to go too far in case she missed Frank returning to the house. She looked in gardens and called out his name as though she was looking for a lost cat or a dog. She was so worried about Frank that she hadn't noticed that Bill wasn't there either.

She rang Laura, who was in the middle of cutting somebody's hair, to see if Frank was with her. Laura told her to call the police. Thirty minutes had passed since Beth had come home; after another ten, she rang the police. And then she called Jimmy. It took him just over an hour to find Frank. He'd been more than lucky. He'd tried searching the streets using an ordered system and by a process of calm elimination, but traffic restrictions and one-way systems had made that difficult and soon he was driving up and down the same streets again and again. He might have missed Frank completely if he hadn't been so easy to spot. Even though he was partly dressed in camouflage, his shirt stood out like dandruff under a UV disco light, and Frank was walking. Jimmy had joked about that later, how Frank was the only pedestrian in the city, which had made him easier to find. Frank had thought that he'd seen Jimmy's car and then he'd lost consciousness and fallen to the ground, knocking over a bicycle. It was the sound of the bicycle hitting the sidewalk that drew Jimmy's attention to his father-in-law lying unconscious next to it.

Jimmy had known exactly what to do. He'd checked for any visible injuries. He'd loosened Frank's belt and found an old cardboard box that he'd plumped up like a pillow to raise his legs off the ground so that he could direct the blood flow to his brain. Beth would later question whether Frank possessed such a thing. Jimmy had made sure that Frank's airway was clear and he'd called 911.

Frank was already feeling a lot better by the time he was lifted into the back of the ambulance on a gurney and he enjoyed the ride to the hospital almost as though it was a planned part of his holiday. He'd never been inside a vehicle with a siren on before. He was surprised that it wasn't a lot louder. He joked with the paramedics, one of whom was originally from just a few miles away from where Frank lived. When the paramedic said that Disney was right and it really was a small world after all, Frank agreed but said that he wouldn't want to paint it. The paramedic, who had been born and brought up in Worthing and then lived in Manchester before moving to LA, spoke with a strange hybrid accent that reminded Frank of a Premier League football manager.

Jimmy followed the ambulance to the hospital and he walked by the side of the gurney as it was wheeled into the emergency room. By now Frank was feeling perfectly well and he'd begun to think that he was wasting everyone's valuable time when they should be saving lives and buying and selling fine wines. He looked up at Jimmy walking beside him. He had hardly changed at all. Five minutes with a razor could literally shave off as many years. Frank tried to see himself in Jimmy's features, to see if there was any truth in the theory about women choosing men who looked like their fathers. He imagined Jimmy without the beard, expecting to see his own face looking back at him as though he was wiping the steam from a bathroom mirror. He'd seen a television documentary a while ago that he thought touched on the subject of the whole daughter/father/husband thing. The only part that he could fully recall from the documentary was a panda that refused to mate with the other pandas but was sexually attracted to the zookeeper who'd raised it. The thought made him feel nauseous and faint again and he closed his eyes until the queasiness passed.

He was parked in a curtained-off cubicle and Jimmy stayed with him while the emergency-room staff took Frank's blood pressure and his temperature and checked his heart rate. They talked to each other in abbreviations that sounded to Frank as if they were as made up by Hollywood as the people using them looked.

In between tests, Jimmy and Frank chatted like old friends and when a doctor came and spoke to Jimmy, thinking that he was Frank's son, Frank didn't protest. If he'd had another child, he would have been happy to have had a son like Jimmy. Jimmy suggested that they should wait until Beth arrived before the doctor gave a diagnosis. She should be here soon. When Beth arrived, it was with mixed emotions. Distress, concern, anxiety, bewilderment, anger, despair, relief, resignation, embarrassment, awkwardness and gratitude because Jimmy was there, along with the familiarity of having been in and out of the same hospital thirty times or more. She opened with a line that she must have thought of on the drive there about a truth universally acknowledged that all men were numpties and that her father was king of the numpties. Beth couldn't thank Jimmy enough but she gave it her best shot. Frank looked for the warm glow of a rekindled flame in either of them. Jimmy offered to step out into the hall so that Beth could talk to Frank alone.

'I'll get some coffee,' he said.

Beth sat down on the end of Frank's bed.

'I was hoping I wouldn't be back here quite so soon,' she said.

'I'm sorry,' Frank said. 'I'm an awful pain in the arse, aren't I?'

'Yes, Dad. You're an awful pain in the arse.' Beth tried so hard to pronounce the word 'arse' in an English accent that she ended up sounding like a pirate. He saw that she was looking at his cut-down cargo pants.

'It was hot,' he said. He put his hand in the pocket and poked his fingertips through the hole. 'I cut the pocket off by mistake. I kept the legs.'

'I saw,' Beth said. 'I'm not sewing them back on.'

'What if there's another war?'

'*Really?*' Beth said. 'You're cracking jokes?' She shook her head with exasperation. 'Where the hell were you going?'

'Nowhere. Anywhere. I wanted to surprise my granddaughter at work. It seemed a lot closer in the car and you are always asking me if I'm getting enough exercise.'

'Don't try making this my fault,' Beth said.

Frank said, 'I'm sorry. I just went for a walk. Like Captain Oates.'

'Who the hell is Captain Oates?'

'You remember. You did it at school. He was the Antarctic explorer who famously went out for a walk?'

Beth thought about it. 'Wasn't he also famous for leaving a note?' she said.

'I think he actually just told everyone he was going out,' Frank said. 'I really wasn't planning on being out long enough to leave a note. I was interrupted by the police and so I walked a little further. Once I was at the end of the road, I just kept going.'

'You're not Forrest Gump, Dad,' Beth said. 'And what? The police?'

Frank wanted to tell her how, coincidentally, as he'd been walking down Santa Monica Boulevard, he had imagined that he was Forrest Gump.

'They were very nice,' Frank said. 'They offered me a lift back to the house.'

'And you didn't take it! Jesus, Dad, the police.'

'I'd only walked about ten yards by then and they had a more urgent call on the radio.'

Beth put her face in her hands. She couldn't bear to hear any more.

'And I guess you didn't use sunscreen?' Beth said, taking her hands away from her face.

Frank considered lying but Jimmy had shown him his red nose and forehead in the mirror.

'When I saw the sea it looked so inviting,' Frank said. 'Did you find my wallet? And my passport?'

'Yes, I did. You don't get out of going home that easily.'

'Do you want me to go home?' Frank said.

'At this precise moment – yes.' Beth sighed heavily. 'No, of course I don't want you to go home.'

She asked him where he'd walked exactly and he tried his best to tell her, but once he'd left Muscle Beach he really had no idea.

'I'm not very good with directions,' he said.

'You don't say.'

There were raised voices and the sound of urgency nearby. People in different-coloured uniforms rushed by the cubicle. Frank had been in hospitals before but it was somehow more exciting here. He imagined gunshot wounds, gangland hits and drive-bys. When the controlled hubbub had passed, Beth and Frank looked at each other.

'I didn't know you had numpties in America,' Frank said.

'We didn't until last Monday.'

Jimmy came back with coffee and Laura arrived

shortly after. She appeared from behind the hospital curtain like the child in the supermarket photo booth. She saw Beth and Jimmy having coffee together and smiled in a carefree way that she hadn't managed since her ninth or tenth birthday. She turned the smile to Frank and nodded. He thought that surely she didn't actually believe that he would have gone missing deliberately for the sake of her project. Laura answered his question when she walked over and kissed him on the head and whispered something about 'taking one for the team' before opening the black bowling bag that she was holding. There was a picture of a skull wearing a Marlon Brando biker hat on the front of the bag and when Frank looked inside he expected to see a bowling ball.

'Bill?' Frank said.

'What?' Beth said.

Laura opened the bag to show Beth and then Jimmy, who was perhaps most surprised of all as he didn't even know the cat was in the country.

'I found him down the street,' Laura said. 'I wasn't sure it was him. I guess it isn't the only stars-and-stripes cat collar in LA. But look at his face.' She opened the bag again and Bill looked up. He made no attempt to escape from the bag.

To be honest, it's good to get out without being tied to a piece of string. What is this place? It smells like a hospital.

The doctor came back and asked to speak to Beth. Laura quickly closed the bag.

'If he tries to escape, call security,' Beth said to Laura before following the doctor into the hall. 'And I'm not talking about Bill.'

Laura sat down with the bag on her lap. She opened it again.

'It must have cost a fortune to fly a cat over from the UK,' Jimmy said. Frank said that Bill had paid for his own fare. He told him that he was one of those fat cats they're always talking about on the television. He asked Jimmy if fat cats were a thing in America and Jimmy said that he thought that they had pretty much invented the term.

Frank looked at Laura. She'd opened the bag as wide as possible on her lap and she was stroking Bill like Donald Pleasance in *You Only Live Twice*. His granddaughter's genius was far from evil but the way she'd been dictating her mother's sights and sounds and even the food that she'd been eating for the past few weeks in the hopes that it would remind her of her estranged husband was certainly a form of genius. And now that the family were at least temporarily back together it seemed as though her master plan might have worked.

Frank didn't know where the Reunion Project began and ended any more. He couldn't distinguish between plan and fate, accident and design. How much of what had happened today had simply been serendipity – which, incidentally, was the title of one of the films that Laura had selected, with its story of a separated couple trying to get back together – and how much had been set up by Laura? Was there another secret itinerary for Laura's eyes only? Frank began to doubt whether coming on holiday had been his idea at all. It seemed just as likely that Laura had hired the landlord or an actor to play the landlord and turn up at the door with a cheque, purely to get Frank over to America with his photo albums and his memories and ultimately to get himself lost. Laura had given Frank her business card and talked about him having his hair cut and she'd pointed out where it was that she worked. Was that all intended to plant in Frank's head the idea of going to the salon? Perhaps Venice Slice wasn't even anywhere near where Laura had pointed and she'd done so just to make sure that Frank would definitely get lost. He was certain that he remembered her playing 'walk' in last night's game of Scrabble: Eleven points, between 'wife' and 'luckiest'. And then there was today's page of the itinerary: *Home Alone 2: Lost in New York.* She'd got the name of the city wrong but, otherwise, who was this black-clothed sorceress? Even the chocolates that Frank had brought over from England for Beth were Matchmakers, of all the chocolates available in the world. Had Laura somehow engineered the Christmas Day phone call to take place after eight o'clock just so that it would lead to Frank bringing some suggestive candy with him? And had Laura's entire master plan, the music, the food, the films, the Scrabble and the chocolates all been leading up to this, her pièce de résistance, getting Jimmy to save Beth's father's life?

Of course not.

But Frank watched her stroking Bill inside the bowling bag and he doubted that he had ever been quite so proud of an evil supervillain in his life.

Beth came back and she said that Frank had been dehydrated and he'd fainted, there was a small bump on his head and his legs felt like jello (Frank's words, he was really fitting in), but otherwise he was fine and would soon be free to go home. Frank asked if she meant home or *home* and when he questioned whether he would still be able to go to Universal Studios or not Beth looked as though she was counting to ten before she said:

'You're not going anywhere, buster. Consider yourself grounded.'

Which was more than ever exactly what he wanted. He wanted to stay on the ground.

Half an hour later, they left the hospital with Frank in a wheelchair. In the car park Jimmy said goodbye. He shook Frank's hand and, when he turned to walk back to his car, Beth stopped him and said, 'You're probably hungry.'

Laura must have felt like throwing the bowling bag with Bill inside high up into the warm Californian evening air.

CHAPTER 25

It had taken longer to get out of the car park than it had to drive back to Euclid Street. If Frank had known how close the hospital was to the house, he would have fainted earlier on in his walk. He could have been ambulanced to the emergency room, been checked out and given the all clear in time to walk back to the house without Beth knowing that he'd even left.

It was after 10 p.m. when they arrived at the house. Frank leaned on Jimmy as they walked from the car to the front door and, once inside, Beth took Frank straight to bed like a child at the end of a long journey. He closed his eyes and drifted in and out of sleep, catching brief sounds of talk and hushed laughter coming from the living room. He wanted to get out of bed just in case he was missing something but he just didn't have the energy.

When Frank pulled the alarm clock that had somehow found its way into the bed and under the pillow out from under his face, he saw that it was 11 a.m. and that he'd been asleep for over twelve hours. He'd woken up with a plan of action that was so clear that he must have been dreaming it. He was going to tell Beth about the landlord and the cheque and how he'd used it to pay for his and Bill's airfares and as a result he only had a couple of weeks left before he would have to vacate his flat. It was so simple and he felt like a fool for not having told her the truth in the first place. Although he did consider how he might put a spin on it all to somehow make it sound just a little more positive. The flat was too large. He didn't need the rooms. He wasn't interested in the garden. The stairs were becoming difficult. If he filled his mouth with cotton wool he could adapt his discontinued Marlon Brando impression and reintroduce it as an impression of the landlord and repeat everything to Beth that the landlord had said to him. He could make it a funny story. He lay in bed rehearsing his script, just as he thought Troy at the planetarium and Robert on the Hollywood mini-bus tour must have done before going public with their presentations. Even the waiter at the Cheesecake Factory had probably practised reading the flavours and the specials in front of his mirror at home before coming to work. If Frank had to break the bad news to Beth he could at least make it entertaining. If only he had some video clips and music prepared.

He climbed out of bed – and not since his accident with the milk float had getting out of bed felt more like climbing – and he began his descent from the mattress to the floor. As soon as he put the weight of his body on the ground, pain ascended through his ankles to his shins, his calves, his knees, his thighs and hips as though it had been stored overnight in the rug, building up intensity the longer that he slept. The blister on his heel had grown. His right foot had gone up a shoe size. There were also blisters on the balls of both feet and when he touched his nose he knew that it was sunburned. There was an indentation on his cheek from where he'd slept for the past half an hour on his alarm clock.

He got dressed. He pulled a T-shirt over his head and noticed that his arms hurt too. He didn't know why his arms hurt. They just seemed to be joining in. He slowly put his trousers on like he was dressing a wound. He picked his wallet up from the dressing table and took out the landlord's cheque and put it in his trouser pocket. After a short glance in the mirror, which he regretted, Frank opened the bedroom door. He opened it with the same uncertainty as his first morning on Euclid Street. He didn't know whom or what would be on the other side. Anger and recrimination or all's-well-that-ends-well smiles and laughter. A round of applause perhaps.

He hadn't heard anyone leave. Jimmy could still be here. All three of them might be sitting in the living room waiting for him to appear. But the living room was empty. He went into the bathroom.

When he came out, Beth was waiting for him. She didn't look angry.

'How are you feeling?' she said.

Frank looked around the living room.

'Where are the stairs I fell down?' He visibly wobbled.

'You'd better sit,' Beth said. She took his arm and led him the few steps across the room to the sofa. He winced with each step.

'I'm all right,' he said.

'Sure. You look great. America's next top model.'

She helped him onto the sofa. He groaned involuntarily as he sat down. He was out of breath just from walking to the bathroom and across the room.

'Are you hungry?' Beth said.

'I'm not sure. Not yet. I am thirsty. Could I have some English Blend?'

Beth went into the kitchen and made him a cup of tea. She pulled a small side table over and put the cup on a saucer on the table. Frank tried to forget about his own condition and assessed Beth's. She was wide awake so he marked her sleep pattern eight out of ten. Her appetite he also gave an eight (she was eating a banana) and he scored her an eight for her energy levels as well. Her outlook seemed good and her mood was almost definitely Sandra Bullock: evidence of Jimmy's recent presence in the house – that and the straightened picture above the living-room desk.

'We're a bit late for the tar pits,' Beth said. She

picked up the itinerary and sat on the sofa next to Frank and read the day's entry out loud:

'*Volcano:* Beth and Frank go to the La Brea Tar Pits. Natural asphalt that's seeped up through the ground over thousands of years and preserved the bones of animals trapped in the tar. Movies filmed at these locations include, and are possibly only: *Volcano* and *Last Action Hero* (although *Last Action Hero* was actually shot in a stunt tar pit elsewhere, so just *Volcano* then). Today's Fact: The La Brea Tar Pits is a tautology and literally means "the the tar tar pits".

Beth said that she hadn't really wanted to go. She'd been once before with Jimmy – which explained why Laura had included it on the itinerary – but she hadn't enjoyed it that much and it was a long drive.

'And Laura has the car,' Beth said. 'Unless you wanted to walk?' She looked at Frank, perhaps expecting him to answer yes, but he said that he never wanted to walk anywhere again. 'And I really don't think we should go tomorrow either,' Beth said. 'A theme park is probably not what the doctor ordered for you at this time.'

Frank had dearly wanted to go to Universal Studios but for the moment at least his aches and pains forced him to agree.

'You should still go, though,' he said, a little too knowingly selfless and heroic. 'You mustn't waste all the tickets because of me. I know they were incredibly expensive.'

'Let's wait and see,' Beth said.

Frank took a large drink from his teacup. He placed it back on the saucer with as much assertiveness as he could muster, to show that he was about to mean business.

'Elizabeth,' he said.

'Yes?'

'Do you know how you said that you were an unhappy number on an unlucky street?'

'Oh don't worry about that, Dad,' Beth waved her hand to emphasize how far she had moved on, 'I was tired and emotional.'

'I know that. It's just that I think I'm more of an unlucky number on a happy street.'

'What do you mean?'

'I've had such a wonderful time here. Really wonderful. The weather's been glorious and so have all the places that I've been to. I couldn't have asked for a better holiday. Even yesterday's walk was enjoyable for a while until I didn't know where I was – and fainting and breaking that man's whiskey and all the rest of it, of course.' From Beth's puzzled expression Frank remembered that he hadn't told her about the homeless man and the smashed bottle but he forged ahead with his confession. 'Apart from you and Laura,' he said, 'and Mum, of course, I've never thought of myself as a particularly lucky man,' he paused. 'I'm not a winner, Elizabeth.' He took another sip of tea. 'I didn't win on the Premium Bonds.'

'What?' Beth said. 'What?'

Frank put his hand in his pocket and took out the cheque. He unfolded it and handed it to Beth and he told her everything, only pausing so that she could ask him to repeat what he'd just said and to check that he wasn't joking, surely he must be joking, he was always joking, it wasn't funny but he must be joking, he couldn't have made himself homeless for the sake of a holiday, where did he expect to live? He said that he hadn't really considered that at the time. He agreed that yes he'd been foolish and he knew now that it had been a ridiculously rash decision and he should have asked her for her advice or opinion at least; at the very worst, she might have been able to haggle with the landlord and get ten grand. Most of all, Beth couldn't accept how, after all Frank's bragging about how he always so expertly and amusingly dealt with the window cleaners and roofers, the insurance and equity-release salesmen and women and all the other hustlers and doorstep flimflammers, the legendary banisher of bunco artists, the scourge of swindlers, the all-great and powerful Frank Derrick would just give his home away on the doorstep.

'He gave you the cheque and you gave him your home? As simple as that?'

Frank nodded.

Beth had to stand up and walk around in circles for a bit to come to terms with it and to assess the damage from his latest bombshell. She couldn't seem to stop shaking her head; every time she thought of another consequence she shook her head again. Bill walked into the living room, disturbed from his elevenses by the pacing. Beth looked at the cat and shook her head again. He would be homeless too, or equally culpable.

'What am I supposed to do now?' she said.

'You don't have to do anything,' Frank said.

'*Really?*' Beth said. 'Jesus, Dad. Why didn't you ask me for the money?'

'I didn't like to. You have one less pay cheque at the moment . . .'

Beth interrupted him, 'Don't try and use me as your excuse and you didn't know about that until I told you this week.'

'You were ill,' Frank said. 'And I'm old and I was worried I might not see you again.' There was an audible lump in his throat.

'What's the time?' Beth said.

Frank looked around for a clock but Beth was asking herself the question. 'What's your landlord's phone number?'

'I don't know,' Frank said. 'It's in my address book.'

'Here or at home?'

'In my overnight bag. Do you want me to get it?'

'Stay there,' Beth said. She held out her open hand in case he didn't understand. She went into Laura's room. Frank regretted his confession. If he hadn't told her she never would have found out and he could have taken his secret back to England and moved into a new home and, as long as he kept the same phone number and went back to his old flat to collect his post twice a year on his birthday and at Christmas, Beth would never have known. She came out of Laura's room holding the address book. There was a strong sense of purpose that had taken her over. It was almost frightening and Frank was afraid to speak.

She picked up the phone. 'What's his name?' she said and opened the address book.

Frank couldn't remember the landlord's name. He wasn't sure that he had ever known it. 'He's in the book as the Godfather.'

Beth was too focussed on whatever it was that she was about to do to question why he was called the Godfather. She turned the pages of the address book and dialled the number.

It was the evening in England. Frank's landlord was eating his dinner when he answered the phone. The serious tone of Beth's voice very likely put him off his pudding. She asked him what he thought he was doing; did he realize that her father was in his eighties? How did he feel about throwing an old man out onto the street? Did he have a father or a grandfather? How would he feel if he was made homeless? She said she wasn't sure that what the landlord had done was even legal. Had he recommended that her father should take legal advice? Were there witnesses to his signature? Why had he given him a cheque when he had no intention of honouring it? Was he trying to bamboozle an old man? Yes, bamboozle. An elderly man living on his own and vulnerable? Her calm assertiveness reminded Frank of Sheila when she was resolving issues and disputes – often financial, usually created by Frank. Beth's voice was obviously more transatlantic than Sheila's and she seemed to exaggerate her Americanness, because to Frank it made her sound more like she meant business and it must have sounded the same to the West Sussex landlord on the other end of the line. She spoke as though she had a billion-dollar team of hard-ass lawyers in the room with her instead of just one single five-thousand-pound dumb-ass. Even when she wasn't talking, Beth was still the one in charge of the telephone conversation. She ended the call with, 'I'll be expecting that today.' She didn't say goodbye. She put the phone back on the desk next to the address book.

'Done,' she said. 'Whatever money you have left after your taxi fares and anything you need to get you home, you're going to give that back to him. I'm going to wire the balance. You can pay me back. He's tearing up the agreement that for some cockamamie reason you signed,' Beth said, knocking Laura's 'I'll pop the trunk' into second place as the most American thing that Frank had ever heard outside of a film.

'Just like that?' Frank said, summoning all his remaining willpower to not do a Tommy Cooper grunt and hands gesture.

'How much of the money is left?' Beth said.

'About half, I think.'

'I'll transfer the full amount from my account and you can pay me back. Soon. Before you spend it on a trip to Paris or a romantic weekend in Las Vegas with Bill.'

'I'll get a job,' Frank said.

'Yes, Dad.' Beth sat down heavily on the sofa like a sigh. She didn't say anything for a full minute and then, 'I told him you'll be dead soon and he can have the flat then for nothing.' She gave one final shake of the head. 'Numpty,' she said and Frank could only agree.

They sat together on the sofa. Frank apologized again and Beth said that he should shut up about it now and although she was angry with him she was far more angry with the landlord and Frank should take advantage of that before she changed her mind.

The room was at last calm and Frank was surprised, considering how little he'd been looking forward to returning to the flat, how relieved he was to know that he could. When he did go home, even if it was covered in snow and his flat was a supermarket, Fullwind-on-Sea was going to seem frightfully dull.

Beth might still have felt more like killing than caring for Frank at the moment but she spent the rest of the day nursing and waiting on him. She put after-sun on his nose and his forehead and she repeatedly rearranged the cushions on the sofa when they became familiar and uncomfortable. She made him breakfast and lunch and cups of tea and rummaged through the medicine cabinet in the bathroom and the cupboards and drawers in the kitchen until she found painkillers that he could swallow – 'the ones that aren't shiny get stuck in my throat'. She tied his hair back in a ponytail and cleaned his glasses because he could still see the thread of a spider's web. She made him open his eyes wide so that she could try and see a loose hair or a speck of dust. She told him to close his eyes again and she blew sharply on his eyelids. With the ghostly spider's web gone Beth put on a TV channel showing old black-and-white movies.

She stood by the sofa and looked at Frank and she thought about how he used to tease her that one day he would become so old and infirm she would need to look after him. She would have to have to wheel him around in a bath chair, bathe him and feed him and change his underwear.

'I thought when I put five and a half thousand miles of land, sea and border control between us I'd managed to escape this,' she said. Frank smiled back at her. Like the *Jurassic Park* dinosaurs, Frank Derrick had found a way.

Between Laurel and Hardy and *The Treasure of the Sierra Madre* films they talked about when Beth was ill and off school and she'd spend the whole day on the sofa like Frank. Sheila would send Frank out to the shops to buy a colouring book and colouring pencils and a bottle of Lucozade wrapped in gold cellophane and then he'd have to go back out again as she started to feel better to buy the banana ice lolly and mandarin oranges that she craved as her appetite gradually returned.

'It's all Gatorade here,' Beth said.

'I don't think I know what that is,' Frank said. 'Is it made from alligators?'

'Yes.'

Frank wished that he'd been there to buy colouring books and unwrap sugary drinks when Beth had been recovering from her cancer. He had no doubt that Laura had been more than adequate in fulfilling that role but he couldn't help feeling guilty for being so far away.

'Will you tell Jimmy now?' he said. 'About Lump?'

Beth was surprised to hear him using Laura's nickname.

'One step at a time,' she said.

There were steps! Frank couldn't wait to tell Laura that there were steps.

'He could always have my Universal Studios ticket,' Frank said.

'Maybe,' Beth said, casually answering so soon that she must already have considered it herself.

Frank had so much to tell Laura.

CHAPTER 26

Psycho: Universal Studios, Hollywood.
Movies filmed at these locations include:
Almost anything you can think of.
Today's Fact: When Jim Carrey was at the studio filming Man on the Moon, *in which he played comedian Andy Kaufman, he dressed up as Norman Bates's mother and leapt out from behind the* Psycho *house with a rubber knife and jumped on board a tram on the studio tour, scaring the passengers.*

Ever since seeing Beth's photographs from when she'd first moved to America, Frank had wanted to go to Universal Studios. It was the one day of his holiday that he'd planned himself. Laura's itinerary was just a reminder. Frank had taken two different brochures home from the travel agents and he'd watched videos on the Internet of strangers enjoying themselves on the rides and in particular on the studio tram tour and he'd imagined that the videos were of him and his family instead. Frank felt that he knew his way around the fake streets of Universal Studios, quite clearly better than he did the real streets of Los Angeles. There were thirteen city blocks and four acres of fake streets with names such as Alfred Hitchcock Lane, Bing Crosby Drive and James Stewart Avenue that he'd looked forward to being on, and a century's worth of former movie sets on the vast studio backlot that he wanted to see in real life and try to guess which films and television shows he recognized them from: Cabot Cove where Jessica Fletcher lived, Courthouse Square from *Back to the Future* and the fake cobble-stones of Little Europe and the Court of Miracles, where *Dracula* and *Frankenstein* had been shot in the 1930s. When the tour tram slowed or stopped for a bridge collapse or an earthquake in a subway station or for King Kong or the *Jaws* shark to jump at him, Frank would have screamed with exaggerated surprise or fright and when the Jurassic dinosaur spat water at the tram or there was a Mexican flash flood, Beth and Laura would have laughed because they'd made sure that Frank was the one sitting in the outside seat of the tram where he was guaranteed to get wet.

When he read the warning signs at the entrance to the rides: *Persons with the following conditions should not ride: Heart Conditions or Abnormal Blood Pressure, Back, Neck or Similar Physical Conditions, Expectant Mothers, Motion Sickness or Dizziness, Medical Sensitivity to Fog Effects, Claustrophobia, Recent Surgery or Other Conditions that may be aggravated by this ride*, Frank would have insisted that none of the warnings applied to him. He would have held his head high and kept his back as straight as he could and on the ride he would have tried not to hold too tightly to the bar across his lap as the promises of high-speed tilting, dropping, stopping, climbing, accelerating, spinning, tilting and jarring were fulfilled. He would have hoped that nobody had noticed that at times he had his eyes shut or that his lips were tightly pursed because he feared that his dentures might fly out, ruining the ride for everyone when a member of staff had to turn all the lights on to look for Frank's false teeth and they all saw that they were just being shaken about in a chair in front of a film screen. Frank had really been looking forward to the trip to Universal Studios. But as he stood on the doorstep watching everyone leave without him he was happy to be taking another one for the team.

When Jimmy had arrived that morning he'd shaken Frank's hand and called him sir and asked how he was feeling today and while Jimmy waited for Beth and Laura to finish getting ready he sat on the sofa next to Frank, the two men like ghosts of a Christmas past. Aside from the grey streaks in Jimmy's beard and the absence of paper hats, neither man had changed greatly in the years since the photograph that had mysteriously found its way into Frank's photo album had been taken. Jimmy lightly joked with Frank, asking him if he had any more walks around town planned. Frank said that Beth had hidden all of his shoes.

When Beth and Laura appeared in the living room they were both impatient to get going, as though it had been they who had been waiting for Jimmy. Before they left, Beth hung back in the doorway and hugged Frank.

'Are you sure you'll be okay?' she asked. 'I feel terrible leaving you. I don't have to go, shall I stay?'

'You have a great time,' Frank said. 'And forget about me. I'll still be here when you get back.'

'Should I get that in writing?'

'Once you've gone I won't even open the door,' Frank said. 'Even if there's a fire.' Seeing the concerned look on Beth's face, he thought that she might actually not go to Universal Studios if he didn't say, 'There *won't* be a fire.'

He stood on the grass in front of the house in his airline socks and he waved until the car was too far away to tell if anyone inside was waving back but he carried on waving just in case. When they were gone he stayed outside for a while and listened to America waking up. To the sounds that were now familiar to him. The perpetual hum of traffic on a distant highway or from the street's air-conditioning units. He might never find out which. There was also the sound of birds that he hadn't yet seen. Who knew, maybe there were no birds at all and the tuneful whistling was being fed through speakers hidden in the well-kept front yards and in the trees that lined the street. There were some other more local traffic noises. Mailmen and milk trucks, Postman Pat and Benny Hill in cooler uniforms and a honk of a fire truck speeding to a towering inferno or a backdraft. Perhaps none of it was real. None of it except for Frank, the only person in the audience, and also the star of the movie, just like Jim Carrey in one of the first films that he'd watched as part of the Reunion Project.

Frank felt Bill down by his feet, rubbing his nose against his leg. Bill's holiday was over too and he made no effort to escape through the open front door. As he nuzzled Frank's shin he pivoted his head to look up, hopeful that Frank had forgotten or not seen that Beth had already fed him once this morning. Frank looked down at the cat. He could never be in a movie, he just didn't have the range of facial expressions.

Our work here is done, Francis. Shall we go back inside and pack?

Frank closed the front door and went into Laura's bedroom and lifted his suitcase up onto the bed. He opened the case and removed anything that he hadn't unpacked yet and he began packing to go home. He folded his trousers and shirts and put them all in the case. He packed his flip-flops with the soles like Liquorice Allsorts and took the four clocks down from the dressing table – New York, London, Paris and Berlin. He removed the batteries and laid them on a towel in the suitcase and folded the towel over the top of them. He didn't want to put them in his hand luggage and have to explain why he was travelling with so many clocks again. He took the socks out of the drawer and the cardigan and the bright shirt out of the wardrobe and put them in the suitcase. When he removed the shirt from the wardrobe it was like switching off a light.

He laid his camouflage pants on the bed and put the cut-off legs back in place below the knees. There were a few inches of material missing as a result of his gradual trimming of the trousers. He put the legs in the wastepaper basket, folded the shorts and put them in the dressing-table drawer and closed it. If he left something behind that meant that he was coming back. He looked through the two photo albums on the bed and, before putting them in the suitcase, he removed the photograph of him and Jimmy asleep on the sofa at Christmas. He took the shorts back out of the drawer, slipped the photo into the back pocket and put the shorts back in the drawer.

He packed any toiletries that he wouldn't need and left his pyjamas out on the chair with his clothes for tomorrow. He was going to wear the sweatshirt with the planets on the front that he'd bought at the Griffith Observatory because he wanted to look like a tourist when he arrived at Heathrow, a visitor in transit who was just passing through. He put Laura's business card that smelled of a spring meadow in the inside pocket of the suitcase along with the piece of paper from the Zoltar machine that told him that his wish had been granted. He hoped that it had. He closed the case and looked at the address label. The suitcase had finally been on holiday and it would be happy about that. Soon the suitcase would be reunited with the smaller case that Frank had so cruelly left behind alone while he took the rest of the family on holiday.

He went into the living room and watched TV. He was still tired but he felt so much better than he had the day before. He had probably recovered enough to have gone to Universal Studios but he'd been happy to exaggerate his limp and feign a bit of extra discomfort and pain for the sake of the greater good and for the future of his family. For love even.

In the afternoon Laura rang. She had to shout above all the excitement going on around her.

'We're having a blast,' she said. 'Mom and Dad are on the *Revenge of the Mummy* ride.'

'Is that one not for you?' Frank said. 'Too tame?'

'No way. It's terrifying. I let them ride it alone.'

Frank said that he was surprised that Laura could be afraid of anything and she said that she wasn't and that *The Mummy* was one of her favourite rides. Frank wasn't the only one taking one for the team.

'I wish I was there,' Frank said. 'But at least the ticket didn't go to waste.'

'One of them still did,' Laura said.

Laura had been confident that Jimmy would be going to Universal Studios all along and so she'd bought four tickets. Frank could have gone after all. His martyrdom had been unnecessary. Laura said something about Scooby Doo walking towards her and then she told Frank that she loved him and the line was cut. After Frank put the phone down he realized that Laura had just called Jimmy 'Dad'. Frank probably wasn't the number one Dad on Euclid Street any more but he didn't mind relinquishing the crown, and until Laura found a boy or a man who wasn't an idiot, at least his Number One Granddad title was still safe.

It was early evening when Frank was woken from a sofa doze by the engine of Jimmy's black sports car. It was followed by the nagging ding-ding-ding that told the driver a door was open or a seat belt was unfastened and then Frank heard the expensive South Korean clunk of the closing car doors and the short beep-beep of the central locking. He sat up straight on the sofa to greet everyone and when Beth came in she couldn't hide her relief at finding him still there. Laura and Jimmy came in behind Beth. Laura was carrying a large Spider-Man toy under her arm.

'I won you something,' she said.

She held the plush superhero out to Frank. It was four feet tall and so overstuffed that the blue legs were straining at the seams. Laura placed the obese superhero on the sofa next to Frank. She couldn't bend the legs and Spider-Man had to stand bow-legged and awkward with his fat arms out at his sides as though he was ready to quick-draw a pair of pistols.

Jimmy helped Beth cook and after dinner everyone showed Frank pictures from the day on their phones but they were too small for him to really appreciate. Beth promised that she would have some printed and she would post them to him to fill the empty pages of his incomplete Laura birthday photo album. Laura didn't ask to see the photo albums and Frank was relieved as he didn't want a day that had clearly been filled with laughter to end in tears. He was still unsure whether Laura hadn't already looked through the photo albums anyway.

Frank was also glad that Beth didn't tell Laura and Jimmy about the landlord or the five thousand pounds. He would tell Laura himself on the phone or by email in the future when it would become an amusing anecdote once he'd had a little time to forget some of the details and add a few new ones. It was so much easier to lie electronically.

After Jimmy had insisted on washing up the dishes and reconfigured the cutlery drawer, he said that he had an idea and he went out to the car and came back with a tablet computer. He transferred the photographs taken on his phone onto the tablet.

'I need to get one of these,' Frank said as he swiped his way through the pictures. Jimmy showed him how to get onto the Internet on the tablet. Frank looked up Fullwind on a map and zoomed in on his street and on his flat, hoping to see himself walking back from the shops or Bill sleeping in the long grass by the shed. He switched to the satellite view of his flat and thought that he could see that there were slates missing from the top of the building and that all the cold-calling roofers that he'd sent away from his doorstep had been right all along.

While Frank and Jimmy were online, Beth and Laura cleaned Bill's plastic pet carrier inside and out. Beth laid a special absorbent pad that she'd bought from the pet store on the floor of the box like a carpet and put two herbal cat treats inside the box to see Bill through the long flight. Laura shadow-paw boxed with Bill and got him to chase a toy mouse around, gradually leading him closer to the opening of the pet carrier until she put the mouse inside the box. Bill was cautious at first but he soon followed the mouse inside. He stayed in the box for a while, sitting on his new carpet and sniffing the herbal treats. If he became acclimatized to the box now, whoever had to put him in there tomorrow might end up with fewer scratches on their hands than Frank had two weeks ago, particularly as they were in a city where nobody owned any gloves.

Frank didn't want his last full LA day to end. He wanted all the shows on TV to be interrupted by a newsflash. He waited in vain for a strike at the airport or an eruption in Iceland.

Jimmy pumped up the air bed for Laura. He inflated it so quickly that if he hadn't been such a genuinely humble man, he might have been accused of showing off. He was, in fact, one of the few people that Frank had met in the past twelve days who wasn't a show-off.

'I've been playing the drums at my brother's,' Jimmy said, barely out of breath. 'This is my kick-drum leg.'

When Jimmy left he said goodbye to Frank and he hoped that he would see him again soon. They shook hands and it wasn't something that he would ordinarily do, but Frank put his other arm around Jimmy's back and patted it. Jimmy hugged Laura and walked to the front door with Beth.

'You could stay,' Beth said, halfway to the door, but Jimmy, ever the gentleman, said:

'I should go.'

Beth nodded. There was an awkward moment where neither of them knew what to do next. Jimmy held out a hand as though he was expecting Beth to shake it and she took his hand and seemed to pull him towards her. Their embrace was awkward at first, as though they'd forgotten the shape of each other's bodies and how well they used to fit together but then they settled.

Laura cupped her hands around her mouth like a loudhailer and whispered to Frank, 'It's so romantic.'

When Frank went to bed he didn't expect to sleep.

CHAPTER 27

Day 13. **Airplane II: Flight to Fullwind.**
Movies filmed at this location include:
Nightmare on Sea Lane *and* Charity Shop
of Horrors.

T hey drove along Euclid Street, stopping
at the first junction to let a jogger cross.
Frank looked at the logo on the jogger's
shirt and thought it might actually be the same
jogger that he'd seen on the computers in Fullwind
library. Being captured on an Internet camera
with a potential viewing audience of the whole
world was no doubt regarded as fame these days.
At the end of the street they turned the corner
onto Santa Monica Boulevard and Frank counted
down the streets, 12th, 11th, 10th and 9th before
they turned onto 8th Street, which, for supersti-
tious reasons or a mathematical error, was called
Lincoln Boulevard.

They were in Beth's car; she was driving and
Laura was in the back with Bill next to her in his
box. Bill hadn't wanted to get into the box but
now he was there he seemed fairly calm and he

wasn't banging around inside or trying to bite his way to freedom any more.

On a short detour along the coast, Frank looked out at the sea one last time. It was bluer than ever. They drove past the old men playing chess, the gymnasts, joggers and cyclists and a t'ai chi class. Before they reached Muscle Beach they turned the corner. It was possible that they went along some of the same streets that Frank had been lost on but nothing looked familiar to him until he saw the sign sticking out from the front of a building with its picture of a pair of scissors cutting through a pizza. It was the same image that had been printed on Laura's business card until Frank had put it through three or four wash-and-spin cycles. Beth pulled over in front of the salon to drop Laura off for work and for one last bonus event that Laura had arranged for Frank.before Beth drove him to the airport. Laura and Frank got out of the car and Beth went to look for a parking space.

Everything in the salon, the walls, the floor, the ceiling, the chairs, the washbasins, the fixtures and fittings and the clothes of the staff, were black. Frank felt like a man who'd gone to a wake mistakenly thinking that it was a fancy dress party.

'This is my grandfather Frank,' Laura said and everyone said hi. 'And these are all the guys who work here,' she said, sweeping her hand in front of her like a bored magician.

There were three members of Venice Slice staff

other than Laura. A man with a beard the same as Zoltar the fortune-teller's was washing combs in a sink, another man named Henry was sitting on a high bar stool chewing a stick of red liquorice and a third man with sideburns in the shape of fish skeletons brought Frank a bottle of mineral water from a glass-fronted fridge, unscrewing the cap with the same hand that he was holding the bottle in. He introduced himself as Oscar.

'Oscar's my boss,' Laura said. 'He'll be your barber today.'

'If you'd like to step this way,' Oscar said.

Frank followed Oscar to a row of barber's chairs in front of basins and mirrors. It was still early and there were no other customers. Oscar stopped by the furthest of the chairs and motioned for Frank to sit down.

'Looks like you caught the sun there,' Oscar said, looking at Frank's face reflected in the mirror.

'Frank tried to walk all the way here from our place,' Laura said, which seemed to get everyone's attention as it sounded no less crazy than if she'd said that he had tried to cartwheel all the way there. 'He was stopped by the police.'

'They don't like walkers,' Henry said.

Frank watched Oscar in the mirror. He was standing behind him with a hot towel in his hands and then everything went dark as Oscar placed the towel over Frank's face. After a few minutes he removed the towel and started to work up a lather with a brush in a large mug of shaving cream. He applied the thick white foam to Frank's chin and neck and his cheeks and under his nose. He swirled the foam into peaks and painted it on like he was icing a cake. He wiped away the excess lather and left it to settle while he took out a leather pouch that he folded open to reveal a row of impressive and incredibly sharp-looking cutthroat razors.

The last time Frank had been to a hairdresser's there were black-and-white photographs on the wall showing the only three haircuts available: numbers one, two and short back and sides. There was a spinning pole outside and it had cost him a pound.

Oscar stretched Frank's skin and held it in place and began shaving.

'Is this your first time in the States, Frank?' Oscar said.

'Yes it is,' Frank said. 'I did nearly go to Canada once when I was evacuated in the war but the ship was torpedoed and we had to turn back.'

'Wow,' Henry said.

'I didn't know that,' Laura said. 'Is that true?'

Frank nodded, almost losing an ear. 'We were put in lifeboats and taken to Scotland in an oil tanker.'

'How old were you?' Zoltar said.

'Eight.'

'*Man.*'

Frank didn't like talking about the war. Not because the memory was painful, he remembered much of it as an adventure: guns and bombs and uniforms and hiding from aeroplanes. It was just that it had happened such a long time ago and it made him sound like he was a stone-age man. But as he was pressed for more of his war story he started to enjoy himself and he began to embellish the tale, describing the weather and the smell of the oil tanker and the colour and width of the stripes of the pyjamas that he was wearing when the torpedo had struck the Dutch cruise liner and he had to abandon ship.

Oscar carefully and expertly shaved around Frank's earlobes and levelled his sideburns so that they were perfectly symmetrical. He had to pause as Frank became particularly animated describing an explosion or a wave. Every 'gosh' or 'wow, man' from the others in the salon encouraged Frank to add more colour and detail to the story, remembering things that he'd forgotten, some of which were now so vivid to him that they might have actually been scenes from *Titanic*.

He didn't notice Beth arrive. She sat on a chair near to the door with Bill on her lap in his travel box. She'd heard Frank's war story before but never told with quite so much relish or passion. Frank had been inspired by Troy at the planetarium and Robert on the minibus tour and everyone else whom he'd met this past fortnight to give his childhood adventure a Hollywood remake.

When Oscar had finished the shave he rinsed Frank's face with a cold towel and smoothed after-shave balm onto his skin. He refused to accept any money from Frank. He said that the story was the payment.

For the twenty minutes that Frank was in the salon everyone fussed over him like he was a sick child at a pop band's meet and greet. They laughed heartily at jokes that deserved far less, angled a fan in his direction when he said that he was hot, and offered him drinks and food, pointing to a glass partition on the far side of the salon through which Frank could see a chef spinning a flattened-out lump of dough like a circus plate. When it was time to leave, Beth went away to get the car and Frank shook hands with Oscar and Henry and when Zoltar – whose name was Greg – held his fist out, Frank gently punched it, amazing his granddaughter one last time. When they heard Beth honk the car horn outside, Laura told Oscar that she wouldn't be long and she stepped outside to say goodbye to her grandfather.

They hugged on the sidewalk by the open door of the car and Laura put her hand on Frank's hair.

'If you ever need a haircut,' she said, 'we're open seven days a week.'

'I've got your card.' Frank patted his chest even though there was no pocket on the sweatshirt and the card was in the suitcase in the trunk of the car, the words long since rinsed down a Euclid Street drain.

Laura moved her hand from his hair to his cleanly shaved cheek to feel how smooth it was. She stepped away from the hug. Frank touched his cheek. 'It feels like somebody else's face,' he said.

Beth had got out of the car to help Frank in and, not wanting to be left out, she leaned over and touched Frank's face too. Passers-by must have wondered if he was some sort of shaman or lucky totem.

'I'll email you,' Laura said.

'Not if I email you first,' Frank said.

A young man cycled along the sidewalk towards them and they had to step aside. As the cyclist passed by he rang the bell on his handlebars. Frank looked up to the heavens. 'Attaboy, Clarence,' he said.

It wasn't Frank's greatest-ever Jimmy Stewart impression but it was good enough for Laura to recognize and she almost cried, her David Bowie eyes visibly wet. She said goodbye quickly to stop herself from crying and went back inside the salon.

Beth and Frank drove through the back streets of Venice until they were on Lincoln Boulevard again, which took them almost all the way to the airport. Frank was now blasé about the boulevards, the highways and freeways. He hardly noticed the liquor stores, the gun shops, the drive-thrus or the huge roadside billboards when they passed them by. The cop cars and yellow school buses were just cars and buses.

Beth parked outside the cargo building and they took Bill inside and handed him over to Joan or Jackie Collins behind the high counter. They exchanged paperwork and the heavily made-up woman took the pet carrier through the door behind her. Beth waved to Bill but the cat didn't wave back. Frank bought a Milky Way from the vending machine knowing that it was actually a Mars bar. He would never be that surprised by biting into a bar of chocolate again. They drove to the airport, Beth parked the car and they sat outside the building for a while because they were too early to check Frank's suitcase in.

'What time is it in England?' Frank said.

Beth counted on her fingers. 'It's ten after eight,' she said.

Frank nodded.

They sat in silence for quite a while, looking at the other passengers being dropped off from taxis and stretch limousines.

'I could never eat ten After Eights,' Frank said.

'Oh I think I could,' Beth said. 'I think I have.'

When they went into the airport building the airport announcements and in particular the deep and dramatic movie-trailer voice warning of the destruction of unattended items was one last piece of Hollywood showboating before Frank left.

'Has your name ever been called out over a tannoy system?' Frank said.

'I don't think so. Has yours?'

'I can't remember it ever happening. But when I hear an announcement, I always expect to hear my name being called out and I get an awful feeling of dread.'

They checked his suitcase in and walked together to the security hand-luggage scanning area. When they'd gone as far as Beth was allowed without a ticket, they stopped.

'Make sure you call me as soon as you get home,' Beth said. 'Even if it's late.'

'Of course,' Frank said.

Beth put her arms around Frank and she didn't release him for such a long time that they were like a new sculpture on the airport concourse.

Almost 604,000 flights on 70 airlines, serving 87 domestic and 69 international destinations, take off from and land at LAX airport every year. Over sixty million passengers pass through the airport, all watched from hundreds of different angles by over three thousand CCTV cameras, relayed to a vast wall of monitors in a security-camera control room, where, as usual, there was nothing worth watching, just another passenger in a souvenir sweatshirt saying goodbye to his daughter and about to have his bag and his shoes X-rayed, hopefully without his trousers falling down. Today he was travelling under his Native American name, Old Man Going Home.

CHAPTER 28

Frank sat in the waiting area at the departure gate psychologically profiling the other passengers and speculating who he might be sitting next to: 'Teenage Boy With Loud Video Game' or 'Sniffy Woman'. Perhaps he would meet Dustin Hoffman in *Rain Man* again. He wouldn't mind that.

A woman in an airline uniform walked over.

'Excuse me, sir,' she said quietly with a smile to let him know that he wasn't in any trouble. 'Are you travelling alone?'

Frank thought for a moment, wondering whether to include Bill in his sums or not.

'Yes,' he said.

'We're a bit empty today. We'd be happy to offer you an upgrade.' She asked him for his passport and his ticket. 'Would you like to come with me, Mr Derrick, and we can get you on board.'

Frank stood up and he followed the woman to the gate.

'Have you been on holiday?' she said.

'Yes. I came to visit my daughter and my grand-daughter.'

'Oh that's nice. Did you have fun?'

'I did,' Frank said.

The woman made a note and scanned his ticket and Frank walked through the enclosed walkway, once again denying him his Beatles moment, and onto the plane.

Frank sat in a seat that was more comfortable than the one waiting for him in his living room at home. He had a complimentary glass of wine in his hand and an English newspaper on his lap so that he could catch up on anything important that he'd missed while he was away. He would just browse the headlines, look at the pictures and guess the rest. The seat was soft and wide, with a leg rest and legroom. He didn't need women's tights to prevent deep-vein thrombosis in this part of the plane. His meal would be served to him on a tablecloth with stainless-steel cutlery and his complimentary items would come in a faux-velvet wallet.

He wondered where Bill was on the plane in relation to him. If he got down on the carpet and called to him in a voice like Beth's or Laura's, would he hear Bill reply in four-letter meows from the hold beneath him? Frank didn't even know whereabouts on the plane the hold was.

He relaxed. He folded the newspaper into the seat pocket in front of him and browsed the inflight entertainment guide. There was a new Scandinavian crime show that he hadn't seen yet and a film that Laura had recommended. He looked out of the window. The sky might never be this blue again. There was music playing and every now and then it was interrupted by an announcement. Nobody paid any attention except Frank. He didn't feel as anxious as he'd felt on the outward flight though. He was a frequent flyer now. Soon they were up in the clouds and then they were above them. He was suddenly very tired. He closed his eyes and he thought now, now would be a good time to go, while everything was just perfect; he could take his final bow and quit while he was ahead and still at his best, like *Fawlty Towers* or Buddy Holly.

What was actually keeping him alive? Apart from the pilot, the co-pilot and the autopilot there was the air outside the plane and the system of regulating valves, heat exchangers and mixing chambers that brought the air into the cabin and if all of that failed, there were the masks that would drop from the ceiling. There was an inflatable slide that would fall from the emergency exit if the plane landed on water and there was a life jacket under his seat with the whistle and the light. There were the highly trained cabin crew and all the search-and-rescue teams that would come from all over the world in helicopters and Naval cruisers to find him if the plane went down. There was so much keeping him alive right now. Most of all, he'd promised to Beth that he'd phone her when he got home. In his suitcase there was the tablet computer that Jimmy had given him before he'd left after inflating Laura's bed with his kick-drum leg. Jimmy had shown Frank where the built-in camera was and he'd set up a webcam chat account so that Frank could talk to his family whenever he wanted to. He'd had nothing to give to Jimmy in return and had asked Laura if she minded if he gave Jimmy the Spider-Man that she'd won by throwing a ball through a hoop at Universal Studios. It was too large to fit in Frank's suitcase and Laura said yes, of course. Jimmy thanked Frank and acted far more delighted with his gift than he could possibly have been, seeing as how the over-stuffed toy looked so little like Spider-Man and wasn't in a sealed box.

Frank looked at the tiny plane on the seat-back screen as it began its return journey to Heathrow. He wondered if anything would have changed while he'd been away or if the whole world really did stop without him there.

He hoped the estate agent had removed the FOR SALE sign and that none of his neighbours saw him when he arrived back at the flat. There'd be too much for him to explain, with the sign and the suitcase and the sunburn on his nose that had already begun to peel. He would spend some of the flight time working on his story and try to make it as entertaining and informative and as Hollywood as he possibly could. He was practically looking forward to it now. If there was no one outside the flat to greet him, he would signal his arrival by pressing his cockamamie doorbell.

It was a twelve-hour flight to Heathrow and

allowing for a couple of hours in customs and passport control and waiting by the baggage carousel, plus the three or four more hours in a taxi from Heathrow to Fullwind and a while longer trying to remember how Jimmy's tablet computer worked, Frank expected to be seeing Beth again just after lunchtime. He wondered what time it would be in Los Angeles.

EPILOGUE

F rank was lost in LA again. Somewhere in the back streets of Venice, he suddenly had no idea where he was or in which direction he was headed. Then he was in a strange parking lot and in the middle of a college campus and then he was up in the sky. He clicked out of the online map and started again. He was back on Euclid Street now, a road that he recognized. He tapped the glass of Jimmy's tablet computer with his fingertip until the arrow at the centre of the road moved him forward ten yards at a time. He made his way past the jogger and the police car until he was outside the small house with the tree beside it. He was almost expecting to see Beth standing outside the open front door waiting for him, barefoot and wearing a baggy grey sweatshirt and matching trousers. Or maybe she would be sitting on a striped garden chair on the communal lawn, drinking tea or stroking Bill who sunbathed next to her with a length of string attached to his stars-and-stripes collar.

Frank looked over at the cat who was fast asleep in front of the gas fire, possibly dreaming of the time that he'd spent in America and thinking about Beth or Laura stroking and tickling him. After they'd returned from their holiday, Frank had tried to be more hands-on with Bill but even with his illegible face Frank knew that Bill found the uncharacteristically tactile show of affection just as uncomfortable and awkward as Frank did. When Frank had tried talking to him in a high-pitched voice, Bill had simply looked up at him as though he was insane.

Frank was waiting for his weekend video call from America. Every Saturday or Sunday he'd chat online with Beth, Laura or Jimmy and sometimes all three of them squashed together on the sofa and they would talk about their day, Frank's that was almost over and Beth's, Laura's and Jimmy's day that was just beginning. Occasionally the screen of the tablet would freeze and Frank would need to reset it in the way that Jimmy had shown him so that they could reconnect and pick up with their chat where they left off. But sometimes Frank would wait for a moment, holding the still image of Beth, Laura and Jimmy in his hands like a framed photograph. He thought about clearing a space on the mantelpiece and putting it there, next to the picture of him and Sheila taken in a Portuguese hotel bar on their last holiday together, the whole family reunited again on the mantelpiece amongst all the giraffes.